The Seven Royals:
All Good Things

Jacob Airey

Abuzz Press

ISBN: 978-1-64438-483-1

Published by Abuzz Press, St. Petersburg, Florida.

The characters and events in this book are fictitious. Any similarity to real persons, living or dead, is coincidental and not intended by the author.

Library of Congress Cataloging in Publication Data
Airey, Jacob
The Seven Royals: All Good Things by Jacob Airey
FICTION / Action & Adventure | FICTION / Fantasy / Action & Adventure| FICTION / Fantasy / Epic
Library of Congress Control Number: 2018914381

Printed on acid-free paper.

Abuzz Press
2019

First Edition

Acknowledgements

I would like to acknowledge my grandmother Beth Ann Smith whom I affectionally called Nana. She always encouraged my writing and I miss her very much.

To my wife Rachel along with my parents and sister, who all cheered me on while I wrote. My friends Tim and Christina who helped me tremendously.
Finally, I'd like to thank my mentor Theresa who saw so much potential in me, but also nurtured it.

Thank you.

Chapter 1

Cold. That was what he felt.

Skin, nails, bones, hair, teeth, all of him, his whole body, it felt cold. The scar across his left eye, that felt the coldest.

"I feel that I am waking from a sleep, a very deep sleep," he thought. *"Opening my eyes, I only see blackness, as if I'm gazing into a blindfold. My eyes see nothing, and it is nauseating. My stomach is in knots, all of it knots! Why? Why am I in this dark place? Why am I trapped in the cold?"*

He could barely move. He rubbed the side of the enclosure with his elbow. He felt steel or iron, damp to the touch. *"I am in something made of metal, and it is so cold. Is this a metal coffin? Have I been buried alive?"* His breathing became labored as he began to wonder how he had been put in this situation.

"I want to go home, but, how can I?"

He banged against the metal but came to a realization. *"I cannot remember home. I have forgotten things, important things. I am wanting to fight, but I am too weak, and the nausea. Every time I move, even the slightest, I feel as if I will swell."*

"Cold," he thought as goose bumps covered his whole body. *"So cold."*

He swallowed hard and forced his body to relax as he lay there. He slowed his breathing and began to count.

"I must focus. I must remember. I must push past the nausea, the darkness, and the cold. I must see it. One word, just remember one thing to my past or identity."

He reached into the deep recesses of his mind. He tried to grab onto something, anything. He needed something to give him a clue as to his identity. There had to be something he could recall.

"Yes," he thought. *"I can recall one word. It is one saving word: Jasher. My name, my name is... Jasher. That's it! Jasher Kenan, I am wielder of the Blue Blade. The Blue Blade, yes, it is my sword. Jasher, yes. That is my name."*

The memories, they began to slowly trickle back. He began to recall things about his childhood. They were more like facts than actual memories, but he was remembering, and that was important to him.

"I know who I am. I am from the continent known as Craih. It has the seven kingdoms of the great creatures. I am the eldest of the Seven Royals, Crown Prince of the nation of Teysha, the dragon kingdom, and heir to the throne.

"The other royals, they are children, while I, yes, that is it. I just came from a party. It was my eighteenth birthday party, but something happened. Something terrible has happened.

That is why I am here. It's not a coffin, but a ship. It is a ship small enough for me and my armor. The nausea, it is from a very long sleep. He, the High Priest, he put me under, using science, not magic. Yes, magic would not have worked on me. I am immune to it."

He began to feel joy as more faces, names, places, and experiences began to come into his mind. It was enough to bring a smile to his face.

"I still feel cold, but it is slowly fading. I taste salt in the air. I must be by the sea. The nausea, it's almost completely gone now. The darkness fades as well. The sun is peaking through from above. It is a window, but covered in all kinds of grime, but the sun peeks through, chasing away the darkness.

"And the blade, is it here? Yes, I am clutching it. I must have been clutching it as long as I have been asleep. My hands cannot release it. They are sore and refuse to budge.

"I am remembering now. I can remember all that has transpired. Though I am in a weakened state, my memories are returning to me now. I remember being a squire, a detective's apprentice, and everything, even seeing battle, though just a teenager."

Jasher swallowed, his throat was dry, making him cough. He needed water for he felt dehydrated, but that was not on his mind. He focused on the memories he began to recall, everything.

He saw his home continent of Craih. He saw the roving hills, forests, and rivers that raced through. All led to the capital Grandfire City, a place built of white marble with massive columns and at the city's gate, a giant marble statue of the dragon that embodied his family.

He had grown up in the beautiful column decorated palace with its great halls and straightforward, practical designs.

"I can see it all in my mind's eye. Now, I wish these memories would flee from me. Because I remember what happened on that fateful eighteenth birthday. If the prophecy is true, ten years ago..."

Chapter 2

How do these stories begin? Oh, yes, once upon a time...

There once was a weakling of a prince named Jasher, a Crown Royal from the nation of Teysha. He was the son of the beloved monarchs, King Gideon and Queen Deborah who ruled their nation from Grandfire City.

Their oldest child Jasher was thin as a twig and as weak as an insect. He barely had a patch of black hair on his head, making him seem to be little more than a skeleton wearing skin. He was frail and sickly, especially when compared to his younger brother Aikin. Though Aikin was not particularly handsome, he stood straight and tall and could at least wield a weapon.

Even Jasher's sister, the beautiful Abigail, his only true friend, was superior in strength compared to him.

This put a desperate longing inside Jasher. Every night when he looked up into the darkened sky, he would wish upon the brightest star to be a great warrior like the heroic knights from the old fairy tales.

However, because Jasher was so weak, many of his parents' friends, advisors, and relatives came to them suggesting they should revoke Jasher's inheritance and birthright and place his brother Aikin in as the Crown Royal, since he was healthy, strong, and very cunning.

One evening, Jasher could bear this disgrace no longer. He ran into the only place that gave him any comfort: the Bluetree Forest. It was a woodland with a river running through it that was just west of the palace that had long been rumored to be mystical.

Jasher would wander into these enchanted woods sometimes with Abigail. They would seek glimpses of wisps or fairies. Jasher had named almost every tree and would talk to them like ordinary people. Though they did not reply, their silence and listening skills were far more welcoming and friendlier than the humiliation he received within his own palace.

That same evening not long after his twelfth birthday, a falling star crossed the sky in the Bluetree Forest. Jasher chanced to wish once more. He wished to be a great warrior, as he did every night, but this time he said it with such fervent conviction, he felt as if the trees and the river whisper back to him.

To his surprise, the falling star crashed to the ground about ten yards away from him. He went and found a large glowing space rock, lit with a pale blue light. The night was very cold, and he had no wish to return home, so he lay beside the warm space rock and rested.

The next morning, Jasher was awoken by birds singing in the forest. The stone no longer glowed, but it retained its pale blue color. He looked at it with a deep curiosity. He touched it and realized its warmth was gone.

The young prince stood and stretch and made an astounding discovery. He was taller, able to reach a high branch from above. That was not possible before.

Jasher also realized that his clothes seemed tighter. He ran to a nearby stream and this made him realize he was running at a faster pace than he had before.

When Jasher got to the stream, he looked at himself and realized he was completely different. His hair had turned brown and grew long. His eyes were a deep piercing blue. He was larger than before, making his clothes rip. He finally tore the shirt off his chest, seeing himself now, even at twelve, with a muscular build.

He fell to his knees and splashed his face with water to make sure that he was not dreaming.

It was then he realized he was not just physically changed, but everything, his eyesight, hearing, and even sense of smell was heightened.

Jasher waited no longer to test this out. He ran through the woods, catching fish with his bare hands, lifting fallen branches, and even heavier stones.

He ran through the Bluetree Forest and jumped high in the air filled with joy.

After several minutes, he did not break a single sweat. He ran to the stream and jumped in. He just had to confirm once more that this was not a dream.

When he did not wake up, he gave a shout for joy to the Creator for the falling star had come down to earth and granted his wish.

He hid the mystic space stone deep in the woods, saving it for an appropriate time.

After that Jasher went and showed his strength to his family. At first, they did not believe it was him, especially Aikin. He recited memories to them to prove it was him. Abigail was the one who noticed the final proof. The scar above his eye remained.

They celebrated with him on this day. He was no longer an embarrassment, but a someone, even at the age of twelve, that could be a strong and mighty leader.

He began to test out his limits and went on to apprentice with the best knights, detectives, soldiers, archers, Martial Artists, and anyone who would train him in the ways of the warrior. He even helped defeat pirates and rebels with his masters, the youngest warrior that they had in eons.

Though he longed to be a knight, he made a vow to himself. He vowed that when he became the King of Teysha, he would be a noble one. He would be a wise ruler who would bring peace, justice, and prosperity to his people.

Chapter 3

"And that is my story..." Jasher concluded this tale. He had reiterated over a thousand times, it never got old for him.

He stood in the ballroom before those attending his birthday party. He was six-foot-tall, lean, and muscular with slightly broad, square shoulders. He had long legs and long arms, and big feet, yet his hands were average and rough from these years of training and service. His thick brown hair cut short and was lighter these days. The blue eyes he had spoken of in his story were in fact very piercing. It was not a dark blue like the ocean or a bright blue like the sky, but an almost icy deep blue that appeared to see right through whomever he was speaking to. Over his left eye, there was a scar that went from the bottom of his forehead to the tip of his cheekbone. It was a single distracting feature that most had to force themselves not to stare at.

The party was being held at the limestone castle of Grandfire City. It was a circular city built in the Gold Valley at the foot of one of the Seven Patriarchs, a mountain range in the center of the continent. Each mountain represented one of the seven kingdoms of Craih.

To the kings and queens attending Jasher's birthday party, they felt safe behind the mountain range and they clapped at his story, though not as much as their children.

Jasher smiled at his fellow Royals before him. Though he had just transitioned into his eighteenth year, the children before him were not even ten. He was the oldest of them and they looked up to him. It was a role he relished and one that he held close to his heart.

The first was the red-haired Connor, Crown Prince of Seayarn, son of Felim and Edna. He was a scruffy, tanned, and rough handed boy, who loved the sea. His family ruled the Southern tip where and several nearby islands.

The second was the long-haired Rapunzel, Crown Princess of Osterburg, daughter of Detlef and Ida. Always dressed in pink and purple, she had brown eyes to match her long, beautiful, flowing blonde hair. She was short, thin, and had alabaster skin. She loved listening to streams gurgle and rivers flow, but her true heart was with the animals she met there.

The third was Belle, Crowned Princess of Kalataya daughter of Emyr and Siani. She was the oldest, save Jasher, with short dark brown that was always tied in a bun. She was tallest of the princesses and had rough hands and rougher feet from being barefoot. She had almond colored eyes that glowed in the light. She wore a dark green dress, but only because her parents made her. She preferred clothes she could move about in, for she wished to not be a princess, but a warrior.

The fourth was Philip, Crowned Prince of the Northwest kingdom of Sheyer. He was the son of Bartel and Lea. A boy dark blonde and a freckled faced with a pale complexion and green eyes. He was very bright and talented, excelling at everything like a true savant. He was dressed in a thick brown sweater with black trousers and boots. He was full of honesty and integrity, even at a young age.

The fifth was James, Crown Prince of Monokilin son of Graham and Sybil. James' body had a farmer's tan and his head was decorated with thick, curly black hair. He was the tallest of the boys, but also the skinniest. He was quiet in demeanor and suspicious by nature, but no one doubted the loyalty that burned in his violet eyes. He was dressed in chain-mail armor with a dark yellow blouse over it. It was difficult to move in, but he cared not. He, like Jasher, desired to be a warrior.

The last was Crown Princess Talia of Hemorford daughter of Hamon and Diot. She was the quintessential princess. Besides being the smallest and youngest of the group, and distant cousin to Connor, she was the social butterfly of the group. She had long, auburn hair, ivory skin, and was very beautiful. She was smart, artistic, and already seemed to be becoming a mystic. She loved music, especially from birds. She listened to their songs every morning before school. She was dressed in the finest silk blue dress with a diamond necklace around her neck. Though she was the youngest, her parents were the oldest of the monarchs.

These children were Jasher's first duty and he felt a closeness to them that he could not explain.

He been to each of their birthday parties and enjoyed watching them as they grew older as he did.

Like these six younglings would grow up to be crowned king or queen of their kingdom and he felt a strong sense of purpose in helping them rise up to become Royals.

Chapter 4

Jasher's father King Gideon stood up. He was the splitting image of his son, except for a large beard. He said, "Thank you, son, for indulging your fellow Royals. Now..."

James shouted, "Wait, how did you learn to fight?"

Jasher replied, "When I was thirteen, I lied about my age and joined the military. My parents thought I was off at a boarding school or apprenticing. I was, sort of. I fought rebels, pirates, and even some magical creatures. It was two years before anyone discovered my true identity. Yet, I was allowed to continue my training."

He paused for a moment. "Don't do that to your parents. It is very unwise, and I wish I had been more open with them about my decisions."

"Can you shoot a bow?" Belle asked.

"I can, but I prefer the sword," Jasher acknowledged.

Philip asked, "Have you ever saved anyone?"

"Well, not me by myself. I have been a part of some rescues."

"Have you ever sailed?" Connor demanded to know.

"Um, once or twice, but I'm not very good at it."

"Have you ever met a dragon?" Talia squealed,

Jasher paused for a moment. "Yes, yes I have."

Rapunzel seemed to shake. "Was it, was it scary?"

Jasher bent down to their level. "No, my young friends. Remember, the dragons brought Craih together. Long ago, the seven kingdoms fought each other, until we were invaded by the Sorcerer's Society. They enslaved us for two hundred years. After hearing our prayers to the Creator, the dragons came from the mountain sky and helped us fight them back. They united us and ushered in our golden age before returning to the air. That is why each kingdom has a dragon on its banner and a golden dragon over the flag of a united Craih. They are our friends. Never fear a dragon."

The children stared at him in wonder.

One final question was shouted, "Come on, have you really seen a dragon?"

This last question, spoken in a mocking tone, came from the back. She was the daughter of one his father's friend, someone Jasher had known for a time. She was not one of the seven Craih Royals, but a special guest from another land.

Jasher folded his arms. "Of course, I saw a dragon."

King Gideon cut in. "Yes, yes, very good son, enough questions children, it is time for a very special surprise."

Jasher felt himself overcome with anticipation.

His father approached the front of the room with his mother. His mother, the queen, approached as well. She was short, somewhat curvy woman with puffy lips and strawberry blonde hair.

His father spoke, "I am King Gideon Kenan of Teysha."

His mother spoke next, "And I am Queen Deborah Kenan of Teysha."

King Gideon turned to his guests. "Today is a very special day. My eldest son Jasher has turned eighteen. Many once doubted him, but he stands today having proved them all wrong. He has, on occasion, gone against his mother and my wishes, been involved in adventures as he told you earlier."

"That is conventional wisdom, but my son is not a conventional boy," Queen Deborah added.

There was an applause from the other monarchs and their entourage.

King Gideon continued, "As is tradition, when a Crown Royal has come to the age where he or she can rule, he or she is given a special sword. We asked Jasher what type of sword he would like to be forged to honor him. He told us the stone from his space rock, and so, we have granted that requested."

His sister, Abigail approached from the back. To all, she was the most beautiful person in the room. She wore a blue dress and had brown hair that was crowned with a silver tiara. She had high cheeks and a wide smile, with soft pale skin.

She smiled at her brother and gave a bow to him as she placed the box in Queen Deborah's hand. She opened it, revealing a sheathed sword.

Both she and King Gideon turned around and set it into Jasher's hands. The wooden sheath was impressive. It had an embroidered dragon whose tail started from the bottom, to its head that went to the top. The handle was simple, only about ten inches long, wrapped in blue leather that was comfortable to hold.

Jasher excitedly unsheathed it, revealing a blue blade.

It was one-of-a-kind. The blue blade was two foot long, single edged. The sharp end went straight to the top, and then curved to a point. It was a serrated on the back side a few inches from the top and about half down to the bottom. It was perfectly balanced.

As Jasher held it in his hand, he had a feeling of completion. It was a unique weapon and he knew it. He had seen steel, bronze, silver, gold, and even black metal blades, but never a blue one. He could not shake the feeling that the blue blade belonged with him. Not simply as ownership, but as a part of his soul. He had never felt that before when handling any other swords. It was a connection he could not fathom, but he felt down to his very bones.

Before he could thank his parents, and aging man dressed in purple robes approached the makeshift throne. Everyone stared on as the man approached.

Jasher bowed. "High Priest Tyroane, you honor me with your presence."

High Priest Tyroane seemed to be ancient. He was the head of the Church of Craih, a humble and peaceful man. He had a long beard that went past his chest. No one knew his real name, for once you entered into the priesthood, you receive a holy name which becomes your true identity for the rest of your life.

The High Priest was the highest of the religious ranks. Little was known about Tyroane other than he was an expert in the mystic arts and a great healer. Everyone loved him for the loving kindness that he shared for all creatures. Though he lived in a monastery not far from Grandfire City like his predecessors, he often traveled to speak with everyone in the kingdom.

High Priest Tyroane smiled and said, "Jasher, my prince, give me your sword." The Dragon Prince humbly obeyed.

High Priest Tyroane took the sword and addressed the crowd. "Every eighteenth year, we honor the Crown Royal with a rite of passage ceremony. It is a sign that they are ready to lead."

He turned to the young prince. "Jasher, you are the first in this generation of royals. I believe our God the Creator will shine on you for you are a young man filled with honor and inner strength. I proudly proclaim you the Crown Prince of Teysha and by the authority given to me in our seven kingdoms, I knight you Sir Jasher, knight of Grandfire City. May the Creator always guide you."

Everyone in the room let out a thunderous applause as Jasher rose. It was rare for someone so young to be knighted, even a prince, but as Jasher looked out over his friends, and saw their applause. The Crown Royals were all yelling joyous cries as they applauded their hero. Their parents were nodding approvingly at the young man.

His parents and his sister never looked so proud in their lifetimes. They approached him, each placing a hand on him. None of them, including Jasher himself, ever thought that this moment in his life would come. He allowed himself just the smallest amount of pride to surface for the accomplishment that he had achieved on this day.

High Priest Tyroane spoke over the applause. His voice seemed to boom over it. He grabbed Jasher's left hand, and placed the blue blade in his right hand, saying, "Behold, Crown Prince Jasher, now knight and someday the future king of the great nation of Teysha!"

The guest erupted into a thunderous applause that was so loud it made Jasher blush.

It seemed to be a very joyous occasion and one that seemed like it would never end. At least, it started to feel that way for Jasher. He was truly enjoying his eighteenth birthday.

High Priest Tyroane declared, "Let us truly begin to celebrate!"

Soon after this jubilant declaration, the royalty in the hall began to do just that. As minstrels played, the kings and queens to the high paced celebratory music that was coming from the musicians.

Chapter 5

"May I have this dance?"

Jasher turned around to see a close friend of his standing in a beautiful white silk dress, decorated with golden tassels. She was young, only about sixteen years of age, with flowing black hair, alabaster-like skin, and a tall, slim body. The one thing Jasher noticed, more than anything, were her eyes. They were bright, white irises that he found incredibly beautiful.

"Princess Ezri Snow of Maxia," he said, giving her a bow. "You honor me with your presence."

Snow blushed and waved her arm, brushing this aside. "Oh, Prince Jasher, drop the pomp and circumstance. I know we haven't seen each other in a year, but I enjoyed your letters."

Now it was Jasher's turn to blush. "Um, yes, well, I enjoyed reading yours as well."

He looked around. "I don't see your dad. It would be good to see him since he did so much to help my training when I visited your kingdom."

Snow hung her head. "My dad is very sick. My mom brought us here through a rabbithole. Normally, that would be dangerous, but my mother has gotten quite good at opening them."

That's when she realized, "Hey, you owe me a dance."

"Well, I..."

"All hail the king!" The voice came from the back of the room. It interrupted the music and the dancing.

Jasher let out a sigh when he heard the voice. He knew who it was right away. He turned around and faced the interloper, leaving Snow standing there with her arms crossed in aggravation.

"No, seriously," the voice continued. "Why do you stop the merrymaking? Don't you know, my older brother will be king one day? And all because of a lucky space rock!"

Coming out of the crowd, a well-built teen with greasy black hair, and athletic build emerged. He walked into the center of the room, right up to Jasher, who had to step back from the smell of alcohol on his breath.

"Aikin, this is not the time," Jasher whispered to him.

His younger brother appeared not to hear him as he wrapped a hand around Jasher's shoulder and leaned hard against him.

"Come now, brother! You didn't tell the best part of the story," Aikin said. "You didn't tell them how you were almost forced to abdicate to me, but a space rock change all that."

King Gideon stormed up to him as he thundered "Aikin, are you drunk? How dare you behave this way in front of our friends!?"

Aikin's expression changed as he shoved a finger in his father's face. "You dare! I was to be king! I was..."

Jasher shoved his hand down, moving in between his brother and their father.

Aikin's face twisted from anger to humor. "Ha! You think you can beat me! I was training to fight when I was merely a child. I was strong, powerful, long before you! You get a space rock and some military experience and think you are a challenge? I don't hide from the moon like you do!"

Aikin shoved Jasher. "Take your shot!"

Jasher turned around to walk away.

"You dare turn your back to me, coward!"

Jasher stopped and approached him. "I'm no coward. Not anymore."

Aikin said, "Ooh, are you going to go crying to our mother, like you did the night I gave you that hideous scar?"

Jasher removed his belt and sheath handing it to Snow, who almost dropped it from its weight, but managed to hold it in both hands.

Queen Deborah approached them. "Boys," she pleaded. "Please, don't do this."

Jasher held up his hand. "Mom, stay out of this."

King Gideon grabbed his wife's shoulders and pulled her away. The party-goers formed a circle around the brothers.

Aikin lifted up his hands in a boxing position. "Finally, you're fighting your own battles."

Jasher's eyes narrowed. "A man has got to settle his own accounts."

Aikin threw a punch. Jasher dodged and countered with an upper cut, but missed, allowing the younger brother to land a punch in the gut.

"Is that all you got," the younger brother gloated.

Jasher grimaced briefly and then smiled. "Aikin, your punches couldn't hurt a fly."

Aikin's surprised turned quickly as he threw a wild haymaker, but Jasher blocked it and punched his brother right in the nose.

Aikin felt blood and reached to wipe it. When he saw his own blood on his hand, he looked down in disbelief and then his face completely twisted in rage. He lifted up his hand and yelled as a fireball shot from his fist.

The crowd gasped as the fire headed right for Jasher, who did not move. When it hit him, it did not nothing, but seemed to absorb into his skin.

"Fool," Prince Jasher said. "You forgot I'm immune to magic. Any direct attacks against me, just disappear. If you think you can be a king, at least know your enemy."

Aikin started to march toward Jasher, who did the same, but before they could come to blows again, a wall of ice appeared between them.

"Enough of this!" Abigail yelled, her hands were blue from the magic she used to create the cold barrier.

Aikin turned to his parents. "Satisfied, are you? A son of fire, a daughter of ice," He looked at Jasher through the icy haze. "And an heir who got his power through luck."

Queen Deborah yelled, "Get out!"

Aikin opened his mouth to answer, but his father more forcibly repeated, "Get out!"

The younger son got the message and left the ballroom, leaving an awkward silence around them. The ice began to melt quickly.

King Gideon waved at the minstrels and the music began playing. "Cake," he shouted trying to salvage the party.

Snow approached him with his blue blade. She uttered something, but Jasher did not hear her. He simply said, "Thank you," as he headed toward the cake.

As he reached for a plate, the young prince had the uneasy feeling he was being watched. Of course, the people in attendance were watching him, but this was different. It was as if a presence was disembodied, spying on him, his friends, and family. He quickly looked around, making sure his brother was not gone. He breathed a sigh of relief but remained ill-at-ease.

Chapter 6

Off the coast of Craih, sat an island barely in view from the beaches.

This was Gorasyium. From the distance, it was beautiful. Limestone architecture rose gardens all across the way, but in fact, it was a kingdom in disarray.

There King Midas had not left his castle in ten years. The people, not seeing their king, had fallen into a stupor and went about their days in monotony.

Now he saw it in royal chambers, looking old and haggard with a long gray beard and golden robes. He sat in front of his magic mirror scowling as he watched Jasher's birthday party.

His butler Porlem entered. He was a small, hunchback of man with a grim face and oily hair. He was the only one allowed to enter Midas' presence without an announcement.

Porlem said, "My Lord..."

"Why is it?" Midas thundered as he watched Jasher cut the first slice of cake.

"Sir?"

"Those seven monarchs have everything! Yet, I have nothing, yet, I can give my people anything." He rubbed his temples. "Everything."

He took off his gloves and then grabbed a hairbrush. It turned to gold.

"I wanted my people to no longer be in poverty! So, I made a deal with that quivering imp to spare his life! He gave me the golden touch and these magic gloves. Now, I can't touch anything without it turning to gold."

He turned to a golden statue in the corner of the room. It was of a beautiful. She stood as if she was reaching out.

"Why? Why? Why did you reach out to touch me, Aeolia? This is all your fault!" This was the first time he realized that he had shifted the blame from himself to his beloved queen.

It was at this time he realized Porlem was still standing there. He quickly regained his composure.

"I'm sorry, Porlem. Did you need something?"

Porlem hesitated a moment, and then swallowed hard. "My king, you have a visitor. He said you have invited him."

King Midas replied, "Tell him to enter." The king need not ask who it was. Only one visitor had been invited to his palace since his wife had been turned to gold.

Porlem called out, "You may enter." He announced, "My King Midas, may I present, the Grand Mage of the Sorcerers Society, Fabius Thorne!"

Fabius, dressed in a black silk cloak, entered the room, bringing with him an atmosphere that seemed foul, yet also pleasant. Though he was very old, he looked very young. He had an abnormal pale tint about his skin. His eyes were red and glowed unnaturally. He had long, thin hands with long well-manicured fingernails. His hair was black, curly, and long, but it had a shine to it. He could be charming, but it was also whispered that he very devious and shrewd. It was said that he became the Grand Mage after destroying a whole village with one spell. The village was home to his predecessor who was never seen again.

King Midas turned to welcome him. "Ah, my friend. I have searched for you for many years. I apologize for interrupting your travels abroad, but I must consult with you."

Though the Sorcerer's Society was known to harbor the most wicked of Paraina, all sorts of people with evil intentions, many, like King Midas, saw them as allies who could help them with the powers of dark magic. He saw no evil in Thorne, only someone with the ability to help him.

Fabius bowed gracefully. "No, my king, I apologize for not getting here sooner. I know I am a difficult man to find, such is my ways. However, you are good to sorcerers, and I should've made myself easier for you to contact me, whether by magic mirror or some other means." His voice was smooth and seductive, almost musical.

Grand Mage, there is no need for apologies. I just need your help."

Fabius stood tall. "I am your most humble servant."

"Have you heard of my condition?" King Midas asked.

Fabius nodded. "Yes, my king. On my journeys, I have been studying. Imp magic is very hard to break, I am afraid.

Imps, elves, dwarves, and even vampires are more attuned to magic than us mere humans."

King Midas said, "You cannot cure my beloved wife? What if I gave my own life? I would gladly give it up for her."

Fabius shook his head. "She has been turned to gold, of which there is no known cure, but I can cure you, oh, my king, but it will take some time. I will continue to study in order to find a way to break the imp magic. It is hard, even for someone such as myself. I have sent out my own imps to find him, but that has proven futile thus far."

King Midas sighed and looked out the window. "Grand Mage, you have been good to my family for generations. If I had known what I was wishing for, I would've stopped. I look at my neighbors to both the east and west, and their happiness drives me mad. I would gladly do anything to take their happiness and make it mine. Are we not all allowed a happy ending? I know it sounds selfish..."

"Forgive the interruption, my king," said the Grand Mage. "But I must say that selfishness is not evil. It is what pulls us together. If this be your wish, I shall grant it."

"But you said it would take time to undo the condition of the golden touch."

The Grand Mage nodded. "Indeed. I did, and I meant what I said, but you can have that which you desire." He motioned to the magic mirror as it showed Prince Jasher's birthday party. "You desire family and love. You desire joy. You desire a happy ending."

King Midas agreed, "Yes, Grand Mage, it is as you say."

Fabius told him. "A happy ending is not something that can just come to you. You must take it by force from those who would keep it from you!"

"Will I not appear as a villain?"

Fabius let out a laugh. "My King, there is no heroism or villainy. There is only the strong and the weak. I can make you strong. I can give you what you seek, but you must be willing to do whatever it is to take it. Say the word, and I can summon armies that pay homage to the Sorcerer's Society and we will march on Craih. We did it once and they forced us back. Together, we will march again!"

King Midas walked to the mirror, tore off his glove, and pressed his hand upon the looking glass. The magic of the golden touch overwhelmed the enchantments of the mirror. In an instant, it turned to solid gold.

Seeing this, King Midas' face turned to anger, and he cried out, so loud, that it loosened dust from the castle.

Servants, soldiers, noblemen, and peasants all shook when they heard the outburst. They had not heard anything from their king in a decade and it made them shiver with fear. For these past years, there had been silence, and now they had heard a cry that was as a wounded animal.

"Show me how to do this, Fabius," the king demanded. "I want the Happy Ending that was taken from me. If I cannot be made free of this curse, then I shall be happy by force!"

Fabius nodded with approval. "I ask for a few things in return."

"Anything. Name it."

"Make me your chief adviser and your viceroy, second only to you. I shall be your eyes, ears, and mouth, and muscle. As such, you will allow the servants of the Sorcerer's Society asylum wherever your kingdom spreads and they shall be bound to you and to me. Likewise, your army and people will be bound to me as well."

King Midas ordered, "Porlem, take a notice!"

Porlem came limping in with a scroll. "I am here, my king."

"Henceforth, the Grand Mage Fabius Thorne of the Sorcerer's Society is my viceroy. He is second only to me and his commands shall be mine. His people will be mine and my people his. To speak against him, is to speak against me and shall be punishable by death. I will seal this with my signet ring."

Porlem ran to the courtesans to deliver the message.

King Midas turned to Fabius. "Well, my Viceroy, I am eager to hear your advice."

His new viceroy smiled. "If it pleases the king, as I said before if what you desire is beyond the sea, then we must go there and take it for yourself. I can help and call upon allies from all those who dwell in the night."

King Midas asked, "Can you not weave a spell that can change this?"

Fabius shook his head. "No one has ever been able to bend a thing so powerful as the mystic force on Paraina to do something so impossible, but I will tell you that my forces will overwhelm the seven monarchs. In my possession is a smoke machine which will cover the sun. Normally, it would take months to cover this range, but I have weaved a rare enchantment that will enhance the smoke's speed in covering Craih. With it, the armies of darkness will have no weakness of sunlight and they shall march on and be able to conquer the seven kingdoms faster than they can route their armies."

King Midas gave his first smile since his beloved had turned to gold. "Viceroy Thorne, it shall be done."

Chapter 7

Jasher loved the library at the palace in Grandfire City. It was said to be the greatest on the continent with books on every topic imaginable. It was a wide room and had ten levels with the grandest oak shelves that required ladders to get to the highest books. There were lanterns to help the readers at night. It was decorated with the finest items from all seven kingdoms from pottery, to candlesticks, to desks, to shelves, and so much more. A large window on the eastern wall allowed the best light in during the day and often the moon at the night. It was decorated with large curtains in case of a cloudy night.

Jasher loved to read and he had a strange ability to retain the information he gathered.

He was trying to distract himself from the embarrassment his brother caused at his birthday party. It had started on a high note, but Aikin's drunken interference angered him.

He tried studying Paraina's sister planet Quaraina. A planet visible in the northern sky at night. For a long time, others thought it was just another star, but through telescopes, people could now see that it was a planet. The descriptions varied, but the only agreed upon fact was that it had less of an ocean than Paraina and as many three large moons. Of course, most of what he read was speculation.

The passage he read said this:

During the Fall and Autumn seasons, Quaraina's largest moon can be seen in the night's sky. It illuminates so brightly early astronomers thought it was a moon of Paraina that remained hidden until that part of the year.

Jasher shuttered when he read that line. Moonlight had no appeal to him. He could not stand to be in the open when the moon was out. He hated it, in fact. During the autumn season, he took great pains to not be exposed to the dual moonlight. In ten years, he had not stepped foot in the moonlight.

He looked out the window. and noticed that the moon would be coming soon. He quickly headed for the curtains and just before he closed them, he noticed a particularly strong cloud that seemed to be entering the sky. He shrugged this off as inconsequential and closed the curtains.

He lit the lanterns and sat on one of the many couches on the first level. This time, he picked up a book that covered mysticism, a form of light magic and sorcery, a form of dark magic. For each, there were four unbreakable rules version had to follow:

1. *Nothing that has died can come back to life. Something can be made undead, but not once its spirit passes into the spirit world.*
2. *You cannot change time. It is permanent.*
3. *Sentient beings can become more skilled in magic with practice and training.*
4. *Magic always comes with a price.*

Jasher curled up with his book, but felt the words blur. He sat up when he heard someone come into the library.

Abigail walked in, still wearing her blue dress from the party. She smiled. "I couldn't sleep, and I was not about to let you hog the library with your own dreaming."

Jasher smiled back. "Oh, I had not yet entered the dreaming world."

He sat up and moved over so she could have a spot next to him there was an uncomfortable silence between them.

Abigail finally broke the silence. "That's quite a sword you received," she said. "I've never seen a blue blade before. I have no doubt it will be the grandest in our kingdom. I bet you are looking forward to naming it after the first battle."

Jasher picked it up. It was still in its sheath, leaning against the couch. He unsheathed it and said, "Yes, that is a tradition of Craih that I will proudly oblige."

He turned to her. "This is not what you wanted to talk about is it?"

Abigail shook her head. "Listen, the past is behind us. Let us move on from it. There is no need for any animosity between the two of you. You and Aikin can be friendly. Just reach out."

Jasher chuckled. "I have tried and tried. He still believes that he should be a Royal. When truly, you should be."

Abigail became angry at her other brother's words. "Do not mock me!"

"I am not mocking you, sis. You would make a better ruler than Aikin and I combined."

Abigail said, "Don't change the subject. He will not amend things, you must. You are the leader."

Jasher shook his head. "I extend a hand and he slaps it away. The ball is in his court, as it stands. When I become king, I will offer it once more and no more."

Another awkward silence fell between them.

"How goes your training?" Jasher finally asked.

Abigail sighed. "Brother, magic is a strange thing. You know mysticism partners with faith in your skill and gifts. It produces good, and with the proper training, you can do anything within the laws of magic. However, I was born with the gift of ice. I don't know why. I could practice other arts, but ice is where I'm a prodigy."

She paused for a moment. "The priests training me have told that the sky is the limit. Yet they warn that sorcery is taking advantage of that. It is more seductive, but not more powerful. Sorcerers are soothsayers and monsters who manipulate, not partner, but even they are not all powerful. No one, not even the most powerful of practitioners, mystic or sorcerer can break the laws of magic."

She looked at her older brother. "Have you thought about magic?"

Jasher folded his arms. "My path is the warrior path."

"What do you mean? I've seen you use magic."

Jasher was taken aback. "What? What're you talking about? I'm immune to magic. Everything that's thrown at me is dissipates around me."

Abigail laughed, oblivious to her brother's growing unease with the conversation.

"I know how you tweedle in the night. I've observed you," she said. "When no one is looking, and the moon comes out, you glow."

Jasher stood up suddenly. "I, uh, I don't know of what you say you've seen from your spying, but it is not what you think! I have no such power."

Abigail stood up and assured, "So you say, but I do not believe you for one moment. Some of us are more naturally inclined to magic. Though our parents are not, it appears that we are. It's nothing to be ashamed of."

Jasher looked away. "I don't wish to discuss this anymore."

Abigail was taken aback. "Excuse me? You are not king yet! Are you ashamed of your brother and sister who have magic! Is that what is it?"

Jasher scooted back. "No! Please stop this!"

Abigail continued, "That what's this is really about, isn't it? You're ashamed!"

"I am, but for a different reason. The moon..."

"How dare you! Is that what this rivalry with Aikin is? It's not about who should be king, but about this!"

She waved her hands and the curtains pulled back by her magical tug. The moonlight came in, and suddenly, Jasher's the scar over his left eye began to illuminate, but not just that scar, every scar on his chest, back, torso, arms, and on his right hand lit up with a light blue glow.

Jasher started to breath heavily as panic began to set upon his heart. Though most of the scars were faded, the light of the moon illuminated them, some so bright, they shined through his clothes.

Abigail suddenly realized what she had done. "Oh, Jasher. It's scarring. The moon shows your scars."

"My failures!"

Abigail quickly released the curtains and let them fall back into place. When the moon disappeared, Jasher returned to normal.

Jasher's panic seemed to float away, and he looked up at Abigail. "Every one of those scars was before I became what I am. The new ones disappear over time, but those, the moon reminds me of every night I'm not hiding from it."

Abigail pleaded with tears in her eyes, "Jasher, I'm so sorry, I..."

Jasher said, "Each of those scars were ones Aikin or some other bully gave me. It reminds me of how weak I once was and that makes me ashamed."

Jasher and reached for Abigail and said, "Sister, please, understand," but she pulled away and ran from of the library crying, embarrassed at what she had just done to her brother.

Without another word, she dashed from the library and burst into her room, falling on the floor. Her tears decorated the ground beneath her. She heard a sound. She looked down and saw that her tears had begun to freeze the carpet.

"I'm sorry, brother," she whispered.

Jasher stood alone in the library. He starred at the empty hallway. A feeling of loneliness crept in around him as he heard nothing, but the silence.

He shouted in rage and ran to the window and pulled open the curtains defiantly only for his scars to glow blue again. He looked at the moon and saw a strange cloud begin to cover it.

Tears of rage fell down his cheeks and as he turned away, laying back on the couch, trying to understand what had just happened. As he wrestled with his thoughts, fatigue soon overtook him, and he fell into a deep sleep full of nightmares.

Chapter 8

Jasher awoke the next morning, feeling less awake than when he fell asleep. He stretched his arms and yawned. As his senses came to him, he realized that he heard people shouting outside. At first, in his morning grogginess, he thought it was the day beginning in Grandfire City. However, he soon realized that these were cries of terror and fear.

"What's going on," he asked as he ran to the library window and braced himself for the morning light, yet none came as he pulled back the huge curtains. Instead, there was a huge cloud that blocked the sun. There was still light coming through, but it was hazy and unimpressive.

He could see from the window out into a nearby courtyard that people from the city were gazing upon the cloud and pointing as if wondering what could have caused such a thing.

Jasher rushed from the library, desperate to find anyone who give him any details on what was going on in Craih.

It was in the hallway where he almost bumped into High Priest Tyroane.

"My Prince," he said. "I've been looking for you everywhere! You must come with me!"

Jasher demanded to know, "What is it, sir? What is happening?"

Tyroane did not reply, but instead led the prince to a room with an oak table surrounded by fourteen occupied chairs.

Jasher knew this place immediately. This was the war room. Except for a banner with dragon on each wall, it had no decorations nor windows to provide any distractions, for this is where the kings and queens of Craih gathered to discuss only one thing, and that was war.

Here today, all of the kings and queens of Craih were there in the war room waiting for him it would seem.

His father grabbed him, pulling him into a table. "My son," he said. "You must listen to me."

Prince Jasher demanded, "What is going on?"

King Gideon had tears in his eyes as he began to speak. "Craih has been invaded!"

Jasher grabbed the hilt of his sword. "Have the rebels returned?"

King Gideon shook his head. "No, it is King Midas from Gorasyum. He engaged in a sneak attack against us deep into last night. His forces have overwhelmed our armies."

Jasher was stunned. "What? How is this possible? His forces are not that powerful."

"They are allied with the Sorcerer's Society and their Grand Mage Fabius Thorne," King Gideon replied.

Jasher's face curled in anger. "What? He allies with our enemies? Why? We've never been to war with Gorasyum."

"We don't know why, but he has," said King Gideon. "He brings with him a dark army of orcs, vampires, werewolves, witches, and wizards for which he caught us unprepared. We're trying to stop them, but their onslaught is too great. It's almost as if they know all of our major fortress locations. They have blocked out the sun! The dark armies are marching through our shorelines as we speak. Yet, they do not stop there. They are forming ranks, we believe, to take Grandfire City."

Jasher felt his knees go weak. He could not believe he was hearing this. "How, the sun? How is it blocked out?"

None gave him an answer. All had their faces down, as if avoiding a direct look in his eyes.

Now his mother, Queen Deborah, approached him. "Oh, my son," she cried as she tried to hug him.

Jasher avoided an embrace. "Mother, there's no time! I must join the fighting! I am immune to magic and I can overcome those that might get in my way. If King Midas has brought the Sorcerer's Society's dark army, so be it! I am a knight and I must protect our land."

As he turned to leave, a hand grabbed his shoulder.

"No, you mustn't. It is too late," the voice was High Priest Tyroane. "The dark armies of Midas are already overwhelming us and killing our armies."

Jasher spoke defiantly. "Then I shall gladly perish with honor alongside my fellow knights of Craih."

Tyroane said, "My Crown Prince, no one is doubting your courage. It is the plan that we have."

"What plan?" The prince inquired.

Tyroane replied, "If Midas takes this land, and then captures the monarchs of the seven kingdoms, the people will lose all hope. I have foreseen this. I see he wants to take the Seven Royals out of nothing more than envy."

"We are wasting time," the Dragon Prince said. "What does all this mean? What is the plan?"

Tyroane lifted a hand. "I have foreseen how we will hide you and your fellow royals. We can only hope that we can somehow fight them off or at least hold them until we get you and the other Royals to safety. The priests of the Church of Craih are sending them out across the continent and even into Icester. We will hide them until such a time, when they can rise up and lead a rebellion. You must go with them. I have foreseen it; you and the other six Crown Royals will return to us one day."

"But..." the Dragon Prince started.

Queen Deborah interrupted him, "Oh, Jasher, I would give anything to keep you with us, but alas, fate will not allow us. You say you are a knight, then go forth to bring them back. Do you accept this duty?"

Jasher did not want to leave. The idea of taking a stand was far better to him than hiding until 'the right time' to rise up and call forth his brothers. However, a sense of duty overwhelmed him. He pulled his blue blade from its sheath.

"By my blue blade, I swear that I shall return with my fellow royals, and we shall retake this land."

King Gideon said, "Then by the authority vested in me as King, I give you a field commission as a Captain."

The kings and queens of Craih applauded him. His mother and father embraced him one last time, and all three had tears in their eyes.

Jasher knew his duty was to obey his orders, but for a brief moment, he did want to. As his parents held him tight, he could not shake the feeling that he may not see them again. His parents seemed to be holding them as if it was their last time as well. He could not be sure, but he felt his mother's tears hit his armor as she held on.

Before he had a chance to say anything else, Tyroane grabbed him and said, "We must move quickly. Midas' armies are fast approaching."

King Gideon nodded. "Yes, of course. Go with him now, Dragon Prince Jasher."

Queen Deborah stroked her son's cheeks. "Goodbye, my son. I love you."

As they approached the exit to the palace, Abigail and Aikin ran to catch up with him.

"My brother," his sister said. "I could not leave without giving you a parting gift! This is my birthday present for you. I wanted to give it to you last night until we had our little, well, never mind. Here it is."

She handed him a dagger in a sheath. He pulled it out and it was indeed a grand knife. The blade was two-feet-long and five inches wide. It was a clip-point type blade with a black handle six inches long.

She explained, "I know it is not as grand as the blue blade, but I pray it keeps you safe."

Jasher kissed her on the cheek. "It is grander," he told her.

Aikin said, "Brother, I'm...sorry for last night. I let my jealous overwhelm me and that was unfair to you. Now it all seems so trivial. Where do you head now?"

Before Jasher could answer, Tyroane replied, "He's being sent for. I'm taking him to where he needs to go."

"Secrecy? No doubt to route any traitors who aided Midas. All traitors deserve to die. I must leave now, for duty calls. Farewell, Jasher."

He held out his hand and Jasher shook it. His anger at Aikin had dissipated. Like his younger said, it was trivial. This parting gift was more than he could ask for.

Aikin departed as Abigail turned to Jasher. "I'm sorry about last night. I hope the dagger makes up for it."

He rolled up his right sleeve, revealing a leather bracelet with a dragon on it. He said, "I know it is a man's bracelet. I got it during my first battle. My sergeant gave it to me to commemorate my courage, though I was scared silly. He explained that courage is being scared but saddling up anyway."

He looked into his sister's eyes and then pulled her into a hug. "You are brave, Abigail. I love you."

"I love you, brother." As she released him, she bowed, and a guard called for her to come with him.

"Goodbye, Jasher."

"Goodbye, Abigail."

High Priest Tyroane said, "Hurry, my prince! We must leave now."

Jasher nodded and they departed the castle. They exited through the courtyard. Jasher took one last look where he realized that while Abigail was still waving at him, Aikin was gone.

Chapter 9

High Priest Tyroane had obtained a unicorn to fly them to the coast of Hemorford. Jasher dared not look at the ground as they flew. He knew if he saw the fighting and the battles that it would cause him to want to go down and join the battle, forsaking his oath.

They soon landed on a beach, from there Tyroane brought Jasher to a large wooden building in a cave. It was a monastery on the coast facing the western ocean. They could see vessels approaching, but they were farther away. Again, Jasher was faced with this temptation to flee, not out of cowardice, but to run toward the battle.

Jasher fought this urge, for he desired to accomplish this mission, whatever it was. He paused for a moment and looked back. He could hear the sounds of clashing metal and breaking wood. He gripped the edges of the doorway so hard it began to crack.

Tyroane grabbed his shoulder and then motioned him forward.

As they entered the monastery, the high priest spoke, "Do not despair, Prince Jasher, knight of Grandfire City. I assure you, the Church of Craih has taken every precaution. You must come with me quickly."

Jasher nodded and followed him inside.

Tyroane led Jasher past the glorious hall entrance where the priests silently prayed and into his study. Before Jasher could say anything, the high priest pulled a candlestick and the bookcase moved, revealing a hidden staircase. They traveled deeper and deeper. At last, they came upon an underground cave.

Jasher asked, "Where are we?"

Tyroane explained, "Before the kingdoms united, pirates hid their gold here. There was enough loot to buy the whole continent. After Craih became united, the gold was divided among the kingdoms to help begin anew. The Church of Craih later built a monastery over it."

Jasher was not interested in a history lesson. He had other thoughts to preoccupy his mind. "What happened to the dragons here on Craih? Why are they not rescuing us as in the days of old?"

Tyroane replied, "If I know those mighty beasts, they will and can take care of themselves and us. They always have and always will. The only reason they do not come down is because they can't. At this moment, I have a feeling the Grand Mage has taken precautions to ensure they do not interfere with his plans."

At the end of the staircase, they came to the edge of the cave with a body of water. Jasher could see that it led to the ocean. However, it was the metallic tubular container that was about his size that caught his attention.

Jasher asked, "What is this?"

"Magic will not work on you, so we will have to use science." The high priest explained to him.

"What do you mean?" The prince was getting impatient. He already did not want to be here.

Tyroane walked to the machine and pulled a lever. "I call it arctic sleep. I saw it in a vision once and built it. It's a device that will put you in a hibernation of sorts for a time, similar to bears in the winter time. It will preserve you."

"And, you've tested this?" Jasher asked, unsure of what to make of all that was happening.

"I will be honest, my prince, I have tested it, but not for as long. Your body will be preserved, though you might lose some strength. The only other option is to hide you, but Thorne's dark army will be searching everywhere for you. They cross the swamp and the peninsula to get into Icester to find you. The others are so young, they are easy to hide among the populace. You, you are special and will be easy to find. This is the only way. Do you trust me?"

"With my life, High Priest."

"Good," Tyroane said smiling.

"When you awake, Prince Jasher, find the other seven royals."

"Find them?"

"Do you know why I knighted you?"

Jasher shook his head.

"You are not just better physically, you are wiser, more mature. It was not because of that space rock, Jasher, it was your experience. You could have chosen to do evil with your power, but even at a young age, you sought to learn how to be noble and faithful. You even disguised yourself, so you could learn from our greatest warriors. You even saw battle and emerged from it more mature."

"High Priest, I am flattered, but I still don't understand what you are telling me." Jasher clapped his hands silently, growing impatient.

"My prince, you are the eldest, and I trust you. Now, will you do your duty or not?" Tyroane asked emphatically.

Jasher looked at the device. After a moment, he sighed. "Where will the other royals be?"

Tyroane pointed out to the sea. "My priests have divided them up among the people of Craih. They are so young, they will be impossible to find even with all of Midas' resources."

"You separated children from their parents!" Jasher's accusatory tone did not intimidate the high priest.

"I did not have a choice, my prince," he said. "I sent them by way of land and sea, so they will be harder to track. They will grow up, some fighting in the resistance that is already forming. Others will get experience and will come to your aid when you find them."

Jasher could not fathom how these young children would feel being separated from their parents, but in the end, he knew Tyroane was right. They would be hurt by Thorne if they remained, or worse.

"How will they know me and how will I find them," he asked.

Tyroane had a wooden box sitting there. He opened it, revealing a bracelet with a small rock. "Use these. They are made out of the same material as your space rock. Fragments exist in the most bizarre places."

"What does this..."

Tyroane interrupted, "If you are able, go to the Kingdom of Maxia, all will be explained."

"How long will I be, uh, hibernating?"

39

Tyroane looked at the ship. "For ten years."

Jasher exclaimed, "What? Ten? Why?"

Tyroane looked up at the cloudy sky. "While in prayer, I asked, and the number that was given was ten." He put a hand on Jasher. "You will still be young but will have to grow up some. As for the others, you will lead them. Be patient with them, guide them, help them. Do for them, what all of your mentors did for you. You all will return home and lead your people to freedom."

Jasher looked up at the sky. "How do we do this?"

"Look to the Creator. He will guide you. No one is promised a perfect life, but it's how we handle the imperfection that determines our character. Right now, sorcery, evil magic, has replaced the mystic ways, but you can stop it along with your fellow Royals."

Jasher asked, "What about our parents?"

Tyroane shed a tear. "They are leading the war effort. Even now, it goes ill for the forces of Craih as the dark army marches through almost without any quarter. Quickly now, slip into the clothes I laid out."

Jasher found a plain white tunic and put it on before drawing his blade. "What if this goes missing?"

Tyroane laughed. "That blue blade is forever drawn to you. It is bound by the same mystical energy that granted your wish. When you are in need, call upon it, and it will come. It may even help you find the others."

Tyroane gave him something to drink. "This will relax you."

Jasher drank it and then climbed into the strange machine.

"It runs on a magical energy, Prince Jasher. While magic won't affect you, it will power this engine. When ten years is up, you will awaken, possibly on the Spyne or the coast of Icester. Make your way first to Maxia and then back to Craih find the others. From there, you will lead our people to freedom. My prayers will be with you, always."

"I feel cold, High Priest."

Tyroane laughed. "I do not have time to get into the mechanics of it, but I promise, it is normal. Now, go, my prince. You are our last hope."

Jasher weighed everything in his head. He was about to leave the only world he had ever known. When he woke up, he had no idea what to expect. He wanted to tell the High Priest but had no way of expressing it.

Finally, he said, "Is this the end?"

Tyroane shook his head. "No, Jasher. This is the beginning of all good things."

Jasher suddenly felt very sleepy. His eyes closed, and he fell into a listless dreamless sleep. The tube closed around him and the arctic sleep machine drifted into the ocean.

High Priest Tyroane watched as the ship's engine carried the crown prince into the sea. He said a silent prayer and then looked into the cloud riddled sky before returning to the church.

Chapter 10

High Priest Tyroane entered the church's sanctuary where he found Aikin waiting for him.

"My prince, what are you doing here?"

"Where is my brother? We need him for the war goes ill." Akin's eyes became narrow.

Tyroane saw something suspicious about the young prince. "He just departed. You barely missed him."

Aikin eyed the high priest. "Where is he?"

Tyroane suddenly came to realization. "Aikin, what have you done?"

Aikin looked around the church, observing all of the religious carvings and decorations. "Tell me where my brother is. It would be ashamed if this beautiful place burned to the ground."

Tyroane swallowed hard. "I'll tell you nothing. You are not a military person. I owe you no such explanation."

Aikin's hands suddenly filled up with fire. "Have it your way."

Tyroane felt the room get hotter.

Chapter 11

King Midas' soldiers led him and Fabius Thorne into the courtyard of Grandfire City riding a grand chariot, dragged by four horses. It was painted white with gold trim. On the front was a golden hand.

All of the warriors were chanting a victory song as they led their king through the city gates and along the lonely road leading through Grandfire City and up to the castle.

At last, they came to the palace where, at the edge of the steps, the fourteen monarchs were lined up, all on their knees. They all tried to stand, but King Midas' men forced them to bow.

"Midas, why? We've always been allies. Why do you throw in with the lot of the Sorcerer's Society?" King Gideon asked as he looked at his former ally.

King Midas laughed. "Because I wanted it. Now, Craih is mine!"

Gideon said, "Your touch turns things into gold. Why must you take our nations captive?"

Midas motioned to Grandfire City. "You hid this great marble city on this island, away from everyone, even your own people. Such selfishness. I wanted it, so I took it."

Gideon growled as he said, "You call me selfish, yet you steal what does not belong to you. You are no conqueror, you are just a common thief."

Before Midas could say more, Fabius demanded, "Where are the children?"

King Gideon spit. "I don't answer to you, Grand Mage!"

Fabius slapped him. "Don't you speak to me like that, worm!"

King Midas laughed. "Tell him where the children are."

King Gideon had a bloody lip. "They are gone. We sent them away."

Fabius growled in anger.

King Midas shook his finger. "It matters not. I have Craih and all its riches, don't I?"

Fabius said, "I fear rebellion, my king."

"They scattered the children, no doubt. They are not of age. So, I fear not."

Fabius nodded. "As you say, my liege." Though he said it, Thorne did not mean it. He grimaced and gave a loud huff. *"I shall deal with this later,"* he thought.

King Gideon broke the silence. "This will not make you happy, Midas. Our kingdoms and our glory will not replace all you have lost. Whatever this soothsayer is telling you, it is all lies."

King Midas slapped him with his gloved hand. "How dare you! Your children would've been raised as my own and to rule the kingdoms again one day, but so be it! You chose to send them away like cowards. You think them safe, perhaps, but Craih is mine now."

King Midas looked at the monarchs before him. For brief moment, he paused and begin to wonder if he had done the right thing. He looked into their eyes and saw concern for their people, same as him. He saw the love and fear they had for their children and for one brief moment, Midas froze.

Then he looked around and saw the Grandfire City, built within the Gold Valley, against the mountain. He saw that it was his and realized if they lived, they could take it from him.

He removed his gloves and without another word began touching kings and queens before him one at a time. Soon all fourteen monarchs of Craih had been turned to gold.

Fabius laughed with joy. "Yes, now the people will despair. They will bow to none other than Emperor Midas!"

Midas smiled when he heard that. "Emperor?"

"Yes! You now rule seven kingdoms and the fabled Gold Valley! You are an Emperor! The greatest emperor who has ever lived!"

Midas had not considered the prestige of that title. "Then as my first decree as emperor, this valley is not to be called the Gold Valley, from henceforth, it shall be Aeolia Valley after my beautiful wife."

"A precious and worthy name, my Emperor."

Midas smiled. "I think this will be my new home. I shall rule Gorasyum and Craih from here. We will build another army to go out and conquer, for this world shall be mine."

Fabius' smile grew even bigger. "Yes, O mighty, Emperor Midas!"

Midas looked at the statues of the Craih monarchs. "Melt them down." While the Orcs cheered, his men said nothing. They just looked on silently. All of them questioning what they had done.

With Grandfire City secure, the armies of Midas and the Sorcerer's Society began a conquest that was almost as over as soon as it began.

While the dark armies, looted and plundered to celebrate their victory, the soldiers of Gorasyum looked on, unimpressed at the mindless carnage. Though they served their emperor, they took no pleasure in harming the men and women of Craih.

Fabius Thorne was not interested in the ongoing party. He was too busy breaking into the library. He pushed the doors open with magical energy. He walked in and found the book on the lunar cycles. "Hmm, someone has impressive taste. I remember when this book was written."

He waved his hands forward and two Orcs carried in a giant mirror that they set on the ground.

"If I'm going to find those children, then I'm going to need some help. No doubt, they are scattered every which way on Icester. It does not matter, I know what to do."

The Orcs nodded in agreement with him and then made themselves scarce.

He gazed deep into the looking glass as he pulled out his wand. "Mirror, mirror, on the wall," his enchantment began. "Contact my Inner Circle, one and all."

Thorne watched as silver liquid poured down from the mirror and from them formed several mirrors that scattered to different parts of the room.

Though the images were darkened, he could see vampires, wizard, witches, fairies, and one man whose resembled a scarecrow. His raggedy clothes covered wooden skin looked wood, almost like a scarecrow. He was the second-in-command of the dark armies. This was the Inner Circle, the leaders of the Sorcerer's Society.

Thorne began with no acknowledgement or greeting. "I have seized Craih. It is ours. Now send your armies, for soon we will conquer the entire region. We will then march onto the peninsula, take the border fortress of Revenant, and soon spread our forces onto the neighboring continent of Icester."

The Wicker Man asked, "And the children, what of them?"

Thorne sighed dramatically. "They have been scattered all throughout the kingdoms. They will be difficult to find, though a prophecy that they will return in ten years has surfaced. I give it no mind. For now, Craih is ours and it is a haven for the Sorcerer's Society."

No one replied to him. They all stood silently and staring at him.

"Don't worry about the dragons, I have sent our troll army into the mountains to keep them back until I can figure something else out."

Now the silence was getting agitating. They did not cheer or acknowledge the Grand Mage's achievement in taking the seven kingdoms.

"Why are you silent?" He demanded, "Don't you get it? We've won! I have succeeded where my predecessors have failed. Craih is ours! This time, the dragons will not unite them. The clouds I have created with the smoke factory will keep the vampires and orcs out in the day. Our armor is broad and our weapons sharp, and we have Midas' navy to command the seas. A minor prophecy and seven lost brats will not stop us."

He continued, "Long have we been forced to live in the shadows as the world ignores our cries for comradeship. We are the chosen who must lead this world of Paraina and from Craih, we will begin our march into the world and spread our will!"

At this, the Inner Circle began to applaud. Thorne smiled and took a bow, though when he looked up, he realized the Wicker Man was not joining in the cheer.

Thorne said nothing, however, for the Wicker Man was the one person that he knew could challenge his power.

After the images faded away and the mirror came together.

He aimed his wand again. "Mirror, mirror grant my request, show me the seven royals so I may rid the world of these pests."

The mirror answered back, "I'm sorry, my Grand Mage, I cannot find them. They are simply gone."

Thorne for a moment stretched out his wand to blast the mirror, but he stopped when he remembered that magic mirrors are hard to create.

"Very well," he said. "Now we wait ten years."

Chapter 12

The Kurve is what the locals called a string of Archipelago islands that followed along the Southern coast of the continent of Icester.

The Kurve islands formed an almost spinal shape that followed the Southern edge of Icester, and that was how they got their names. It was home to many island kingdoms. A few here and there allied together with coastal and maritime kingdoms, but most were independent. The people of the Kurve were great fishermen, sailors, and shepherds, but the islanders to the west were also great warriors. Legends of the great warriors of the Kurve warriors all over Icester and beyond. There were pirates who patrolled and looted the area looking for weak ships to plunder, but very few dared when they saw the colors of a Kurve war vessel. Though pirates value treasure, what they valued most was their lives.

Unbeknownst to Jasher, this is where he had awoken, a decade later. This is where he rested and tasted the salty sea from inside his metal capsule. He had made it out alive. As he lay inside, he wondered if he could get out, but as he tried to move, another wave of exhaustion washed over him, and he collapsed back down.

He wondered, *"Will I ever make it out of here?"*

Chapter 13

The atmosphere in the darkened room was ripe with the same humidity that permeated the swamps. It was just enough to make a person sweat, but not so much that one could not breath.

The octagon shaped room had the perfect amount of darkness that, even though it was hot, it still sent a shiver down your spine and goose bumps down your skin.

The floor was painted black, but vines came from the center of the room and into the corners and up to the ceiling. The vines formed a cluttered chandelier that drooped in the middle of the room. Hanging in the center from a thick vine was a glowing crystal ball.

To all who entered the room, it gave them a shudder and most avoided coming in here all together.

However, to its current occupant, this was home away from home.

This room belonged to Fabius Thorne, Grand Mage of the Sorcerer's Society and Viceroy to Emperor Midas.

Though a decade had gone by, he had barely aged. His eyes glowed with an unnatural red. His fingernails had grown shaper his blackened hair had grown longer.

He was wrapped in a black silk cloak with the golden hand of Midas smeared onto his chest area.

Fabius approached the crystal ball. He pulled out his wand from inside his silk robe and pointed it at the orb. A pulse of energy came from the wand and turned the crystal ball into a body-sized mirror.

He said, "Mirror, mirror on the wall, contact my allies on Craih, one and all."

Suddenly, he was surrounded by several mirrors, each taking a spot on the corners of the hexagon with him staring into the middle one.

The images of his most trusted advisers appeared, only ten years ago.

He greeted his inner circle, "Hello, my comrades. This is to give you an update on the war situation."

He explained, "The two of us have built a second smoke factory to create a layer of cloud so thick that it blocked out the sun. As you know, the first allowed us to take Craih.

As you know, Emperor Midas, and I are headed to Gorasyum for our annual trip. Our Emperor still insists we do this even though it means nothing. The people there are lethargic and have no desire to please me or our emperor. However, Emperor Midas especially wanted to do this since our second smoke factory has moved to Revenant and it is the tenth-year anniversary of our victory. I am trying to rebuild the spell that sped up the growth that overtook Craih, so it can spread faster on Icester. The spell will take time as many of the ingredients I need our extremely rare."

Thorne paused, looking for a reaction. "Some of you have suggested that I am spreading our ranks too thin, but we are still marching toward victory."

He looked at the dark silhouettes, but no one seemed to move.

"No sign of the Seven Royals," he said. "We have not found a trace of them, but we have reached the ten-year mark. I know many of you our frustrated with the growing resistance on Craih. They seem to be gaining more courage as they feel the Royals will return. We will ensure they do not end."

He observed a few nods, but again, no reaction.

"Now, to the war effort."

Chapter 14

On the islands the farthest west in Icester, three muscular, ebony skinned fishermen, with their long black hair and long black beards were pulling in their catch of the day.

At first, the fishing seemed to be going well. They were pulling up a catch that they could easily trade at the local markets or to feed their families.

Zuberi threw his net in, but when he tried to pull it up, he realized it had latched itself onto some foreign object.

"Father," he called out. "My net is caught on something. It is a heavy object."

His father Jengo was a retired sailor and captain whose long hair was slow graying. In his later years, he was trying to enjoy the quiet life with his family. His sons were Zuberi and Imamu. They were twins who looked like younger versions of their father. Zuberi, the eldest twin, wore his hair in a ponytail while Imamu wore his in dreadlocks. All three were mighty men of valor. They were honest and fair to all who were fair to them, but they dealt fiercely with those who would try to harm their families and friends.

Jengo walked over to watch as Zuberi tried to pull whatever was down there. "It is stuck on something good and tight. Imamu, climb down and see what it is."

His son nodded. "Yes, father." He climbed down on the rocks and he saw what appeared to be a metal capsule. He looked it over but could not determine its origin or its design. He had never seen such a foreign vessel anywhere, not even in his studies.

"Father, you must see this!"

Jengo and Zuberi both climbed down. They too were shocked when they saw the tubular shape. All three had never seen anything like it before in their lives. For a moment, they stood gaping at the vessel, unsure of what it is.

Zuberi finally asked what was on all of their minds, "What could this be?"

Jengo walked over to it and said, "If I didn't know better, I'd say it was a vessel, designed to go under the water. I've heard rumors that a few were experimenting with that sort of invention, but none have ever been developed as far as I know."

Jengo looked it over. "It looks like it was designed in Craih. All of their designs are made from optimization with very little imagination like most of their sea vessels."

Imamu exclaimed, "Incredible." He dared to approach it closer and saw a window. He wiped off some gunk on it and called out, "Father, there's someone inside!"

Jengo and Zuberi walked over to it. They both gasped when they saw his face.

The father told his sons, "We must get him out of there immediately! Help me try to find a way to open this giant metal tube."

Imamu said thoughtfully, "We don't know anything about this, Father. What if we kill him when we bring him out?"

Jengo weighed his son's words, but ultimately shook his head. "This is something that was clearly designed for escape. It was meant to go underwater yet has no weapons. We must take the chance and awaken him, whoever he may be."

The sons obeyed their father and the three of them began looking for a way to pry it open. Jengo found the top of the capsule where a lever was located. He pulled it, and a hissing sound emitted from the capsule. It opened up and a frosty air burst forth from it. It made all three of them shiver.

Jengo leaned in, suddenly, the person woke up and grabbed his collar, gasping, "Help me. I must find them." With those words, he collapsed, quivering and shaking.

He ordered, "Let's get him out of here! He's cold to the touch. We have to warm him, or he could get frost bite."

Imamu observed, "Father, there's the symbol of a dragon where he was laying. He's is definitely from Craih."

They lifted the young man out of the capsule as he clutched onto his sword, but he was weak, and the blade fell to the ground. His sword fell from its sheath and unleashed a bright blue light that made them cover their eyes. It went straight up to the sky and as quickly as it happened, it went out. The young man tried to stand again, but this time, he lost consciousness.

Jengo's jaw dropped. "I know who this is! Get him out of here! We must hurry!"

"Yes, father," the twin sons said in unison.

Jengo folded his hands together as he realized the legends were true. A young warrior from Craih was coming to collect his brethren to retake their homeland. Jengo was honored and proud to be the one to help bring this young prince out of his metallic case.

Chapter 15

On the other side of the world, the continent of Craih had not seen the sun for ten years. A giant cloud blocked out its light and the dreary darkness made the people of Craih dreary as they were forced into servitude. Though there was a revolution that had formed against the dark forces of Emperor Midas and his Viceroy Fabius Thorne, their reach seemed unstoppable.

In the occupied kingdom of Teysha, the capital Grandfire City, the once glorious palace of the kingdom was beginning to decay. It was made in a circle, with four main entrances to represent a compass. While it sat near a mountain, it did not build onto it, but rested in its shade. The decorative alabaster stone had become covered in black scum and the vines that had once grown out-of-control on the columns were now rotten. The stench of the rot traveled all through the halls and rooms of the decrepit palace.

The people of Craih had long since gotten use to the rotting stench, for it mattered not to the kingdom. Teysha was an echo of all of the seven kingdoms on the continent.

Deep inside the Grandfire City palace, there was a man, or at least, the people thought him to be. He was King Midas' adopted son Omri.

Omri was seven feet tall and very muscular. The size of a gladiator. His skin was a pale-white sickly color and always seemed clammy. He was always wearing black and a blue rock around his neck. His head was bald and tattooed over his blackened eyes were red diamonds. Though his talents in the skills of violence were legendary, what was also for certain was he was a sorcerer, trained personally by Viceroy Fabius Thorne.

Soon after Teysha had fallen under the occupiers, Omri had been chosen to rule over the palace. It was rumored that he had been a Teysha soldier but had defected and possibly spied for King Midas' army. The truth of the matter is that no one knew much about him. It was all conjecture and speculation. Though many legends existed about his origin, he remained suspiciously quiet about the matter.

Omri was at the entrance of the royal bedroom. It had once been home to the king and queen. Now, it was his to do with as he pleased. He maintained minimal servants and kept the place darkened, for he preferred it that way. The dark was inspiring to his thoughts, making grow fond of it.

There in the once royal bedroom a young girl waited for him, a virgin from a nearby village.

He opened the door and saw she was dressed in a white dress, looking scared. He smiled. He liked that.

It was said that no amount of woman's company could slay his lust. His harem was great in numbers, though many of the women did not last long under his harsh care.

He looked upon the innocent girl before him and licked his maroon lips with a blackened tongue before smiling to show his yellow teeth. He wanted her flesh so bad he could almost taste it.

"Perhaps I will," he thought.

He said slyly, "Don't be afraid. No harm will come to you." A cruel smile began to form on his lips. He almost laughed at his own lie. There would be harm to her like so many others, as he was Overlord over the Teysha kingdom.

He took a step toward her and she flinched, but she did not run as others had tried before her. Things were worse if they tried to run. If she had tried to run past her, he would torture her. This one seemed brave, but that would prove to be futile.

He took a step ahead, but the rock around his neck unexpectedly shined a blue color, then shattered. It happened so quickly that Omri was caught completely off guard as a strange energy shot through his body.

The girl placed a pillow around her face to shield her eyes from the bizarre glow.

The effect was even worse for Omri. He visibly gagged and tried to keep from throwing up. He failed, spilling his guts all over the floor.

After he wiped his mouth, he whispered in horror, "It cannot be."

He looked at the young girl. She was even more shaken by his display. She thought that maybe he would reject her. She could not bear the thought of that. It was said, if he rejected a girl, he sacrificed her to the dark spirits. However, his lust was gone. He looked at the girl for a brief moment and turned away, saying nothing to her.

He stormed out of a room where a sniveling human servant was waiting for his orders.

"Sir," the man said.

"Are father and the Viceroy back?" Omri demanded to know.

The servant rapidly shook his head. "No, my lord. When I glanced into the magic mirror, the speech had not even started yet."

Omri smashed a nearby vase. He dare not interrupt his adopted father's trip.

"I need to speak to them as soon as they get back!"

Jengo began to give mouth to mouth to the young warrior before him. They had managed to get him and capsule to their island when they realized the prince's breathing had become shallow.

"Come on, Prince! Wake up," the father shouted

His sons were pouring dirt on him in an attempt to warm him up.

Finally, the prince sat up and started gasping for air, at first, they were relieved, but then his breathing became labored and he began to shake uncontrollably as his face turned purple.

"He's having a panic attack," said Jengo. "He could hyper ventilate."

Imamu replied, "What do we do?"

Jengo suddenly punched the prince right between the eyes. Jasher fell back onto the sand, unconscious, but his breathing returned to normal.

"What did you do that for?" Zuberi demanded to know.

Jengo said, "It was the only way to snap him out of it. Whatever device that was, it kept the prince in a state that his body was not use to. It could be days before he recovers, but he may not have that much time."

"Why not?"

"You saw the light, Imamu. Someone else may have. Someone who is hostile."

He ordered, "Zuberi, go to the village and get something to carry him back to our village."

After his brother was gone, Imamu asked, "Father, who is this man? And why do you call him a prince."

"This is Jasher, Knight of Grandfire City, Dragon Prince of Teysha, and Captain of the Seven Royals."

Imamu swallowed hard. "The story is true?"

Jengo nodded. "I had my doubts too. Yet, he found his way to our islands here on the Kurve. For ten years, he's been sleeping and now he comes to us. We must help him recover. It is our duty to help him, so he can free his people."

Imamu reached for the hilt on his belt, but his father stopped him.

"No, my son."

"But I want to see the Blue Blade."

Jengo shook his head. "He should be the first to draw his sword."

Chapter 16

To the East of Craih, was the continent of Icester. The two lands were connected by a peninsula and a small mountain range littered with swamps.

While Craih had a somewhat round shape and housed mainly humans and dragons, Icester was three times as large and five times as long. As such, it was home to humans, Elves, Dwarves, Vampires, Orcs, and Fairies alike. Some lived in the mountains, others in the forests, some in the coasts, but many lived in the beautiful valleys that swerved their way all through the beautiful land.

It had kingdoms great and small all around the rich land. It had independent serfdoms and villages that held no allegiance to any one monarch. It had tall, majestic mountains and deep, dark forests to the north, and green, sunny forests to the south, enriched with canyons, plains, and green hillsides.

On the Western side of Icester, an all-girls academy of mysticism was situated on a mountainside. All the girls were wearing the white dresses of a student.

Two teachers, one with black hair and the other with white, were dressed in the traditional black dress, were rushing through the halls.

The white-haired teacher asked, "What has that girl done now?"

The black haired one replied, "Headmistress, she is a prodigy with the mystic arts. It is good for the school to have such a powerful student. She did save her friends from that ghoul, but sometimes it is bad for us. Remember when she changed the entire red bricks to that bizarre green color? It took hours to repair it."

"Remember what she put an enchantment on the food and it started to sing and dance? Most of our staff fasted for a month."

"What is this time?"

"Her healing technique teacher said that everything was fine. Suddenly, the girl's bracelet started to glow, and she won't stop dancing."

The headmistress stopped dead in her tracks, alerting the other to do the same.

The black haired one asked, "What is it, ma'am?"

"Get the girl. Tell her to pack immediately."

"What? Why? We can't banish her for dancing."

"No, this is something bigger. I must get her mystic staff."

"But..."

"Go now! There's no time to waste!"

The white-haired teacher sped off.

The black haired one kept going until she could hear the cries of joy from the girl from all the way down the hall.

When she came to classroom door, she could see a strange blue light.

At a knight encampment, outside a dense forest on Craih, a group of warriors were enjoying some leisure time. They were jousting, singing, and eating around campfires.

The sergeant-at-arms was a gruff man with a scarred face and a thick brown beard. He was in silver armor was seated at his desk penning a letter to his daughter.

The corporal, a young tan fellow, walked in and said, "Sergeant, permission to enter."

"Granted."

"Sir, have you seen Philip?"

"I believe he's visiting the graveyard, paying respects to his friend."

"We must fetch him, sir."

"Why?"

The corporal held a black leather wristband with a glowing blue rock. "One of his brothers saw this in his tent."

The Sergeant jumped up. "Don't just stand there! Get him! I'll alert the captain."

Corporal saluted. "Aye, sir!"

Deep inside that same forest, a giant rat was on the hunt. A thick mist had permeated the forest, but it did not stop the rat. His master had made sure he could see through it. The rat was sent to find the one person who could stop his master's plans. Though he had some intelligence, he would still obey.

At last, he caught a scent and he begin to follow it until it came to a tree with a carved out hollow.

This was it, the home of the nuisance. He began to sneak and bear his teeth, ready to strike.

Suddenly, a quiet, calm voice spoke, "Oh, my."

A bright blue light shot from the hollow, sending the rat scurrying back into the woods out of fear of the light.

On board a sea vessel hugging the coast of Icester, a sailor aboard a small buccaneer vessel approached the helmsman who was navigating the calm Paraina ocean.

The sailor said, "Alter course. We are to head to Denoka."

The helmsman shouted, "Why would we head to that bloody place?"

"It's time."

"Wait, we're losing our shipmates? Has it really been ten years?"

"I'm afraid so."

The helmsman began to adjust course. He waved signals to the crew on the deck, prompting them to adjust the sails.

The helmsman asked, "Why can't they all just come aboard, and we can keep attacking Midas' fleet?" The sailor shook his head. "That won't save our homeland, my friend. They need to be together to rally us all together. They've been good mates, but you know that they are destined for royalty."

Chapter 17

Emperor Midas was walking through the garden in Gorasyum. He smelled the air of his homeland with a small sense of pride. "The air gets more and more stale every time we come here."

Fabius Thorne nodded. "Yes. It does have a uniqueness to it."

He asked, "Emperor, why do we do this? Every year we come here, and it is always the same. Let's leave these people to their squalor."

"It is important, Viceroy," said the Emperor. "You cannot forget where you came from or you may lose sight of where you are going."

Midas looked out over the land. The sky was clear unlike the cloud-covered Craih. He said, "I have not seen the sun, not truly, in a long time."

Thorne replied, "I do not like the sun. Its brightness aggravates me. The Orcs and the vampires cannot march in its light. If you'd like, I can order the construction of another smoke factory."

Midas waved this off. "Trying to take Icester so soon could be a mistake. Let's focus on stabilizing Craih for a time."

Thorne asked, "What if the rumors of Icester kingdoms striking back here are true? How will we hold Gorasyum?"

Emperor Midas said, "I've already transferred many of Gorasyum's navy here to fortify."

Thorne exclaimed, "What! My lord, I was not informed of this decision!"

Emperor Midas turned and pointed his finger at him. "I do not require permission from you! You are my viceroy and I am your emperor!"

Fabius bowed his head in a hurry. "Forgive me, my emperor. It is just that, Gorasyum was the only navy we had to protect our ports. The Continental Army could seize this opportunity."

"Viceroy, I have already ordered the formation of a navy from Werewolves who were former naval officers. They will protect our ports. Now come, it is time to give my speech." He continued to walk forward followed by his entourage.

Thorne stood still for a moment. He had to work to hide his anger and his rage. *"Soon,"* he thought. *"Once I am rid of the Seven Royals, I will have no more use for you. Then I will kill you and take your place."* He looked around the port. *"Then, I will unleash my vampires here on Gorasyum and let them devour every single person on this forsaken place."*

Emperor Midas stood on a castle balcony that overlooked a growing crowd of the people of Gorasyum gathering in the royal courtyard. His butler, Porlem, was in the shadows ready if Midas needed anything and Thorne stood behind him.

Midas spoke of the future and how the empire had expanded. He spoke of good times and though the war in Icester had been lost for now, Craih was still under control with the help of Sorcerer's Society, the empire's great allies.

He emphasized every detail and put a completely positive spin on it. There was nothing in his speech that did not praise Gorasyum, but he grew increasingly aggravated.

Though the crowd was growing, he could see Thorne had the palace guards bribe, intimidate, blackmail, or threaten them into coming. That was not what was bothering him. It was the expression on their faces.

It was the same look they had on their faces when he invaded Craih ten years ago. It was a look of complete ambivalence. The people had no pride, no joy, no sadness, no interest, not even an acknowledgment that they were following him.

"So," he continued his speech. "With this in mind, we must remember that our greatest days are ahead of us. Citizens of Gorasyum come together. Unite behind your emperor, for there are only good days ahead. We shall have a happy ending!"

That was the end of the speech. He had nothing left.

The crowd had no reaction. They just stood, staring straight up at him. The faces were as blank as they had been.

Thorne made a motion with his hand. The palace guards started to applaud. The crowd joined in, but their expressions never once changed.

Midas clenched his gloved fists together and stormed passed Thorne. Porlem wisely got out of the way as the king rushed past.

Midas charged into his old throne room. They had brought the golden statue of Aeolia and had placed it beside his throne where it had been before. He yelled out in pain, not physical pain. The anger, the hatred, the grief, all swarmed inside him.

Thorne walked in alone. "My emperor," he said. "It was a fine speech. To celebrate, I have a surprise for you. We are throwing a party." It was true, though Fabius had made sure that he could access the emperor when he needed it.

"Do not flatter me," ordered Midas. "What do they want from me? I know that in the years after I turned my wife into gold, I deserved to be shunned by them. I was not a good king then, but I have more than doubled their empire. Yet, they stare at me as if I am a stranger. It's as if they do not recognize me. It makes me angry!"

Thorne decided on a half-truth. "It's true that they do not recognize you, my emperor. They see you above them now and you are."

Midas began his habit of pacing. Its annoyed Thorne. It was true the Grand Mage did his share, but Midas seemed to need it to breath.

"Do you remember why we did this, Thorne?" Midas asked as he stopped walking.

"Yes, my emperor. It was so you could take what you rightfully deserved. You saw others had the happiness you wanted, and you took it. Like any good leader, you taxed those who had abundance, so you could have it."

"Yet here I stand, my Viceroy. I have moments of pleasure, but happiness, it still eludes me."

Thorne just looked on as he let his disappointment in Midas wash over him. He kept it to himself for now. He was angry he still needed this broken shell of a monarch, but he did. Right now, Midas' army and navy would only follow his orders. They would not listen to the officers of the Sorcerer's Society no matter how much they were threatened.

To force their loyalty, Thorne had secretly ordered some of the Midas officers bitten by vampires, but they all chose to die instead of drinking the vampire's blood.

Midas interrupted his thoughts. "Are we villains, Thorne?"

"Excuse me?" The question shocked Fabius Thorne. In all of the people he had taken advantage of and manipulated, none had asked such a question. "What do you mean by, uh, villains?"

"Well, in all of those old stories, there was always a hero and he had an antithesis, the villain. He could be a kidnapper, a dark warrior, a bad parent, it mattered not. They stood in the way of the hero, whether man or woman, and they were always defeated. Villains never got a happy ending."

Fabius chuckled and that turned into a laugh. "Forgive me, my emperor, but the world is not so simple. There is no good or evil. There is only power. You either have it or you don't and if you don't, you try to take it, steal it, or force those that have it to give it to you. Those old stories provide parents with a false sense of morality to make their children behave. That's all there is to that. In those stories, the heroes are all the same and the villains are composites of those people fear. No one is completely heroic, and no one is completely a villain. There's too much gray here on Paraina."

Midas seemed to take stock of what he had just heard. He looked down and saw a dust bunny beside his throne. Normally, this would make him infuriated, but he picked it up, removed one of his gloves and touched it, turning the dust bunny into a solid sphere of gold.

He sighed heavily and said, "One of the problems with gray is it's like fog. No one can see through it."

Before Fabius could respond, a servant walked in and whispered, "Forgive the interruption, but we found him."

"Jasher? What of the others?"

"Not Jasher, my Viceroy. We found HIM."

Fabius realized what his servant was trying to say. He gave an evil smile and said, "Emperor Midas, why don't you get some rest before the ball tonight. I'll be sure Porlem sends you some fresh blankets."

Midas nodded in agreement and headed for the door.

Fabius turned to servant. "Make sure he is at the ball tonight. I want to make a big show of this."

As the servant moved away, Thorne could not help but smile. Soon, Midas would mean nothing. For now, he needed him to keep control of the Gorasyum army, but soon, that would no longer be an issue.

With this new prisoner and the inevitable capture of the Seven Royals, his rule would be solidified, and Midas would no longer be needed. Human resistance would not be a factor.

When that time came, he would kill Midas and establish the Sorcerer's Society for all of eternity.

"I will no longer be a viceroy, but the High King of Craih," he allowed himself a satisfied chuckle.

Chapter 18

Jengo's wife Zuri worked on Jasher. She was the doctor on the island and was very striking in her dreadlocks and animal skin dress.

She was warming Jasher in the medical tent by covering him in blankets and placing a hot towel on his forehead.

Jengo asked, "How is he, my darling?"

Zuri said, "He's still shivering. Whatever he was in, it was cold. Very cold. I'm trying to treat him for hypothermia, but I'm not sure what this was. I'm not sure if he'll wake up."

Suddenly, Jasher's eyes opened and he sat up in bed. "Where am I?" He breathed heavily and gasped for air.

Jengo whispered, "I guess we know now."

Zuri ignored him and said, "Jasher, Dragon Prince, you're on the Haven Isle in the Kurve."

Jasher was panicking and shaking. "Haven? How did I get here? What happened? Where's my mom, dad, siblings?"

"Should I knock him out again?" Jengo whispered to his wife.

Zuri pushed her husband away. She grabbed Jasher's shoulders and shouted, "Prince Jasher! You are safe! Everything is fine! No harm will come to you!"

Tears streamed down his cheeks. "They're dead, aren't they? My family is dead." He started to shake and cough as the realization came to him that everything he knew was gone.

Zuri pulled him to her and let him cry on her shoulder. Jengo got behind him and placed a hand on his back.

He said, "I'm sorry, Prince Jasher."

Connor stood on the desk of the ship. He had curly red hair, a thin mustache, and a tanned athletic body. His rapier hung on his side, loose. Women would swoon as he passed them in his white sailor suit, black trousers, and strapped boots. Though he would look at them with a wink and a smile of shiny teeth, he did not care for their attention. His thoughts rested on one special lady.

He smelled in the salty air and let out a satisfied sighed.

"You told them to change course." The voice was forceful, yet feminine.

"Belle," he said as he turned around. "He's out there. We have confirmation."

She was strongly built and well endowed. She had wild brown hair, naturally curly. She wore a green blouse and beige trousers. Her brown cloak blew in the wind. Though she was beautiful, her face was intense and fierce.

"How do we know he really is?"

Connor nodded. "He is. I can feel it. Therefore, we must head to the nearest port."

"Denoka?"

"Yes, Denoka. He can find us there."

Belle stood next to him. "Wherever he has been, he hasn't been fighting them like we have."

Connor raised an eyebrow. "It may have been out of his control. Wherever he is or has been, we have been called. We must save our people."

She turned to him. "What if..." She paused.

"What?"

"Nothing."

He turned to her and gazed into her eyes.

"Whatever happens, we will be beside one another."

He leaned in and kissed her passionately. She returned the kiss and pulled him in deeper.

After it ended, they held each other in an embrace.

She stilled. "The others can't know about us."

Connor pulled away. "Why not?"

Belle looked out over the sea. "We are all strangers at the moment. For all we know, only you and have found one another. We can't let our relationship be a distraction. We fight Thorne and then we can be together. Agreed?"

"No."

"Connor, this will make me happy. Promise me."

He huffed and tapped his hand to his forehead, but at last decided to do as she asked. "So be it, but under protest."

Belle winked at him and grabbed his hand. "That's never stopped me, except when it really counted."

The feeling of their skin touching sent shockwaves through both of their bodies.

She gripped it tighter. "I never thought I'd love again, but you have taught me how. I'll never forget that."

Connor gave her a childish grin. "You love me?"

Belle shoved him. "Of course, I do."

Connor looked out at sea. "I love you too."

Chapter 19

Emperor Midas was holding a fantastic ball for all of the nobility in the kingdom of Gorasyum. However, the ball was going about as well as the speech Midas made. Most of the noblemen and noblewomen just stood without saying a word. They ate and drank, but otherwise, there was no discussion or merrymaking.

All of them just stood as if in a dream, not showing any interest in the hired entertainment or the music playing.

Porlem brought a goblet of wine to his Emperor who tapped it impatiently as he stared at his party guests.

"This is infuriating! I'm throwing a huge party for them and all they do is, well, nothing." Midas roared at his butler.

His eunuch looked down at his feet. "I'm sorry you feel that way, my Emperor." He then shuffled away.

Fabius Thorne brushed into the room and said, "How goes the party?"

Emperor Midas grunted and said, "It seems that they are feeling the effects of boredom."

"Not for long. Your viceroy has some entertainment that will remind everyone of who you are and the power that you wield."

Thorne lifted his hands in the air and clapped three times. He used his magic to enhance the sound. That was the signal that the musicians and minstrels needed. In a few moments, all who remained were the guests.

The Grand Mage took the center of the ballroom to make his announcement. "Ladies and gentlemen, Emperor Midas has long ruled this fine nation and now Craih. He is known as a man who fair, but also firm. He is a man of judgment. Why? Because he must punish all of those who stand in his way. Today, there is one who has caused our emperor a great deal of pain."

Midas straightened when he heard that.

Thorne turned to him. "Today, my emperor, you will have revenge."

A cloud of black smoke swirled in the center of the room. After it cleared, Omri stood there with a golden chain. At the end, there what seemed to be person chained by the neck. However, it became obvious it was not a man, but an imp. He had pointed ears, not quite as defined as an elf. He had bright skin and shiny white teeth. He was dressed like a jester and wore red boots with a bell at the end.

Thorne pointed to him and said, "Behold, Emperor Midas, it is the imp that gave you the accursed Golden Touch. It is him. Sometimes he is a satyr named Silenus, but you know him as Puck!"

Emperor Midas felt himself go red. He clenched his gloved fists until he bruised the inside of his hands.

Midas approached him with a face twisted with rage.

Puck looked up and chuckled when he saw Midas. "So, this is what this is all about. That's why I gave you my gloves. They cancel out the magic while you are wearing them

He looked up at Thorne. "I have to give you credit, Thorne, the Sorcerer's Society has upped its game. These chains have canceled out my magic totally. It's a shame they only work on imps. They could have helped your emperor here."

Midas shouted, "Don't look at him! Look at me! I am the man you ruined!"

Puck rolled his eyes. "You're kidding me, right?"

Midas bent down to his level. "Be careful what you say, imp."

"I warned you to be careful what you asked for, but you made that wish."

Midas grabbed the chain around the neck and pulled it forward. "My wife was turned into gold trying to embrace me!"

Puck shook off Midas' grip and then stood up. "You're blaming me? You were going to put me to death for falling asleep in your garden. I offered you a wish to save my life. You could have wished for your crops to have a good season. You could have wished for your all your sick people to be healed. You could have wished for anything to help your kingdom. Instead, you wished for the Golden Touch. Everything you touch turns to gold. You should be showered in wealth, but I can see from the faces here, that is not the case."

Thorne ordered, "Don't talk to him that way."

Midas lifted his hand to silence him, keeping his eyes on the imp. "I take it back! I take the wish back!"

Puck laughed. "I'm not a genie. I cannot take the wish back. You have to live with the choices you make. The only cure is to bathe in a mystical river. You know how rare those are."

"You're lying! Take it back or you die!"

Puck shook his head. "I cannot! Stop blaming me for your poor decisions."

Midas roared in rage. Without a second thought, he removed his glove and before Puck could say anything else, the emperor touched his right index finger to the middle of the imp's forehead.

As Puck turned to gold, he smiled. "I saw that coming. Humans, so predictable."

When he turned completely gold, Midas grabbed a flower from a vase, but it too turned to gold.

Midas screamed with rage and threw the flower at the golden Puck. It struck him, causing it to bizarrely crack into pieces. A light came from the pieces and flew into the sky.

Midas put his gloves back on. "It didn't work! It didn't work!"

Thorne said solemnly, "I'm sorry, my liege. I wish that it had."

Midas raised his fists in the air and roared.

Turning to Thorne, Midas said, "You're the only person who has ever truly helped me."

Thorne said, "My emperor, I live to serve. I'm sorry that it did not provide the cure that you wanted."

"Is it true? Are mystic rivers truly hard to find?"

"I'm afraid so, my lord."

"Are there any on Craih?"

"I do not know, but I shall find out."

Midas swallowed hard and collapsed into a nearby chair. "Revenge does not taste as sweet as I thought it would."

Thorne replied, "It is only the disappointment of him refusing to cure you. I know from experience."

Midas looked up at Thorne. "You are sure we are doing the right thing here, my viceroy?"

Thorne nodded. "I have absolutely no doubt, my lord."

Midas stood up. "Take me back to Grandfire City! I don't want to wait for a ship. Use your wand and open a rabbithole. I cannot stay in this place another minute!"

"As you wish, my Emperor."

Rapunzel sat staring at the bracelet with the glowing rock. She was a tiny, short young woman with long flowing blonde hair that went down to her lower back.

She sat in a cave that was decorated with drawing of animals from all across the forest. She looked outside and saw a heavy fog outside.

There was a bright glow, but it did not startle Rapunzel.

She stood up smiling. "It is good to see you."

A purple colored fairy formed from the glow. At first, she was small, but then she grew into the size of an adult woman. The Purple Fairy said, "Oh little princess, it is good to see you too."

"Did you find the source of the bizarre fog?" Rapunzel asked in her small voice.

The purple fairy shook her head. "No and the rats continue to grow in numbers."

She paused for a moment. "You know that is not why I'm here. Your bracelet glows. He is coming for you. The prophecy is coming true."

"I know and I'm excited to see them." She paused and asked, "But what can I do?"

The purple fairy says, "You are gifted in magic arts and animal whispering."

The princess shook her head. "But I am weak. I have no weapon to help retake my kingdom."

The purple fairy waved her hand and a staff appeared. It was as tall as Rapunzel, colored purple, and formed into a heart at the top.

"As I recall, you were quite good with the staff when we were training you," the fairy said. "This will serve you well."

Rapunzel picked it out of the air and said, "Oh my..."

"We will miss you, little princess," the fairy said. "When we found you alone in the woods, your hair glowing, we thought you were a lost child, until we found the letter on your dress after that knight died saving you from an Orc. At once, we knew you were meant to do great things. We raised you well and it seems our magic has affected you physically."

"That's a rarity for humans," she added with a smile.

Rapunzel looked at her long glowing hair. "What do you think it means?"

"It means you are special, little princess. Never forget that."

Chapter 20

Emperor Midas and Fabius Thorne exited the rabbithole portal at the foot of the entry to the palace courtyard.

They created by the many of the pillars and statues of golden people. The dark army had taken down the statues of the dragons that represented the seven kingdoms, leaving a golden brick road into the now called Aeolia Valley that was aligned with enemies he had turned to gold. It was a message to anyone who dared cross him that he would not tolerate any dissent.

Midas and Thorne entered the palace as their minions, guards, and human servants bowed. They entered the throne room where only the Emperor, Viceroy, and the Inner Circle were allowed to visit. Gone were the images of dragons, now it was a blank golden slate.

Omri was informed of their arrival and dashed into the halls before arriving at the hall to the throne room where he greeted by his adopted father's butler.

Porlem spoke up, "Overlord Omri, how may I…"

"I must see father and the Grand Mage. It is a matter of most urgency."

Porlem started to speak, but Omri pushed past him before he could utter another word.

Porlem called out, "Please, they just got back from…"

Omri glared at him, "I gave you an order, servant boy. Take me to them!"

As Porlem led Omri, Emperor Midas and his viceroy Fabius were talking in the throne room. They were speaking over a stand at the head of the table were two maps. The first was of Craih. Each incident of rebellious occurrences from citizens were marked. The second map was of Icester, where they had begun their invasion.

Thorne hurried to explain, "The smoke factory had great success here in Craih. Its unnatural clouds have made it possible for vampires and orcs to march across the land and hold it despite resistance. It has poisoned the air, not to any humanoid life, but to dragons. There will be no rescue this time. We have moved that smoke factory here in palace, in the unused front tower."

"I thought we gave the tower to Blue Beard."

"No, sir. We gave him the West Tower. There is a somewhat hidden one right behind that was used as a secret lookout. We hollowed it out for the smoke," he continued. "We built a second smoke factory at Gorasyum for taking Icester. With its help, we have taken the fortress known as Revenant and are now moving it there to move forward deeper into the continent."

"This is perfect for distracting me from Gorasyum, but I must ask, is it rushing it to move the factory right after the victory?"

Fabius cringed at the questioning. He hated it when Midas poked too deeply into strategy. "I believe so, my Emperor. The kingdoms of Icester are scattered and divided. My allies on Gorasyum are keeping a close eye out with the magic mirror I gave them for any insurgency that might cause us a problem."

Porlem knocked on the door and then came straight in. "Forgive me, my emperor and viceroy, but Overlord Omri is here and says it is a matter of great importance."

Omri pushed passed Porlem. "Father, master, forgive me! It is very urgent!" Both men could see that the overlord was in great distress. That was very unusual for him.

Emperor Midas waved him in. "My son, there's no need for forgiveness. What is it that has you looking so distraught?"

Viceroy Fabius nodded. "Yes, please tell us."

Omri held up his broken necklace. "The rock broke upon my neck. The Dragon Prince Jasher has returned. It is the only explanation."

Emperor Midas furrowed his brow. "No, it's not possible. He's been gone for ten years. We searched all of Craih and sent bounty hunters in every direction on Icester looking for him just to be safe."

Fabius walked up and grabbed the necklace. He held it in his hand. There was one small piece of rock, no bigger than a pebble, attached to the string. He began to chant over it and then it too shattered, sending him staggering backwards.

The viceroy sighed. "No, your adopted son is correct, Emperor Midas. Only the sword, which now has the highest concentration of that space rock could cause that reaction. It was contained for so long, but someone just released whatever mystical energy it has. Curious, since Prince Jasher is immune to magic, both curses and blessings. Whatever mystical properties is contained in this space rock, it is truly powerful."

Omri added, "If he is out there, he will try to find the others. He has returned after ten years as the prophecy has foretold. The revolutionaries will have hope. It will spur their campaign to dethrone us."

Emperor Midas stroked his beard. "Several of our bounty hunters are still out there looking for him. Is there a way to inform them of his return?"

Fabius nodded. "It shall be done, my emperor."

Omri asked, "What about the other six? If all seven unite, they could take command and lead a rebellion against us!"

Emperor Midas laughed. "They are all still children, my son. If this gives the revolutionaries, what do they call themselves, the Continental Army? If this gives them hope, it is a false hope."

"But, father, it is known that they have grown in numbers. Some members of the Gorasyium army have already begun to defect into the rebellion."

Emperor Midas let out another hearty laugh. "You worry too much, my son. They cling to prophecies, but the truth is, they are just myths and legends. All who oppose us are swiftly dealt with and traitors are discouraged." He looked at his hand to further emphasize the point.

Fabius thought about this for a moment. "We should still be cautious. Legends and myths weigh heavy in the mind of these people. Those who do not practice magic cling to the stories of heroes who are greater than they in the belief that their mediocrity means something. We must do something about this, for even if Jasher is dead and someone simply found the blue blade, then we must squash this. We cannot allow this to bring what we've built to a halt."

Emperor Midas sighed from exhaustion. "So be it. Send out our mercenaries to kill this prince. The two of us must keep our focus on the invasion of Icester. I will send word to General Bloont to move the smoke factory as you advised, my viceroy."

Omri stepped forward, "Father, I know how this prince thinks. If it is him, as you say. I know his strengths and weaknesses. Put me in charge of finding him. I will not let you down. I will make sure he does not stop our plans."

Emperor Midas looked over at Viceroy Fabius who nodded to show his approval.

"Very well," said Midas. "Then you shall be placed in charge. All mercenaries and bounty hunters will report to you. Triple the reward, in fact. Bring me Prince Jasher and the other Royals, dead or alive, but I want that blue blade!"

Overlord Omri smiled, his yellow teeth glistened. "It shall be done."

He bowed to his master and adopted father. He left the palace and paused for a moment. *"So, Prince Jasher,"* he thought. *"You return to plague us now."*

Omri walked to a temple that had once been used by the Church of Craih. It had been a typical parish with pews, a stage, a pulpit for speaking, and a single office for the priest. It had been decorated in oak and pine, with blue pews and a what some would call a simplistic, but happy atmosphere.

However, Fabius had desecrated it, removing all mentions of the Creator. Mystic ways had been replaced by the Sorcerer's Society's propaganda. Where the statues of dragons of Craih once stood, now there was the symbols of the pentagram. The pews had been removed and replaced with mats. There were black candles lit everywhere, releasing an almost toxic and nauseating smell.

All who entered felt a shiver down their spine and all noticed a dark shadow come into the room. They all looked on and saw Omri walk past the lobby and walk past them. Every one of them backed away when they saw him. In the short span of ten years, Omri had already amassed a reputation as a vicious sorcerer.

He approached a crystal ball that was set on a pedestal where the pulpit had once been. He placed a hand on it and began chanting to it and all across the world of Paraina, he began calling out to the werewolves, the orcs, and the vampires.

Across the plains in Icester, he could feel them connect to him through their own sorcerer totems.

Omri began issuing orders, "Be on the lookout for Prince Jasher and his now legendary blue blade. The reward is now triple for whoever finds him. Bring him in alive or dead, but his head must be cut and ready for display. If you killed all seven, the reward will be even greater. I will be arriving on Icester soon to take charge of the search. Now go, find him!"

When Omri finished, he sensed all of them had heard his message. He said the final incantation to end the connection. He debated inside his mind on what he should do with this situation.

"He will find me if I don't find him first," he thought. He secretly hoped that Prince Jasher did return with the other royals in tow. Omri wanted to kill them all personally.

A thought crossed his mind. *"What if this person is a fake as my father suggested? What if Jasher is dead and someone just found his sword? I need to find him myself to prove that he is still alive..."* Omri shuddered at that last thought.

He turned around and headed out of the desecrated place of worship, determined to find out if Jasher had indeed returned.

He mounted a black steed and raced out of Grandfire City. The speed of the horse was unnatural, as he used his power to give the horse more energy.

Omri, however, eventually began to tire. Though he was powerful in the sorcerer's ways, even he had his limits.

James kicked a bucket as he emerged from the thick fog of the forest. He did not need to offer any explanation to the villagers as they watch him head for the tavern.

He was tall, extremely well-built with muscles protruding through his clothes. His black hair had been cut down to a short style. He was known to all as a man of might.

He wore a light metal armor covered in black leather and black trousers, it was the armor of a peasant.

He burst into the empty tavern and sat at a table. He gave a frustrated yell and then pounded the table.

A handsome, yet rough man, he could have any maiden in the village and normally they would bat their eyes to try and get his attention. Today was different. His frustration told everyone to avoid him as the sword on his side wobbled and the shield his back shook

The woman he knew as a sister walked up to him and sat down, passing a glass of water to him. She was a tiny woman with a plain face and long curly black hair like him, dressed in a plain green dress.

"Maris, I'm sorry," he said.

"It happened again. You could not find my daughter," she said in a mousy voice.

He nodded and took a sip.

"You have other things to worry about." She pointed to the glowing rock on his bracelet.

"No. I'm not leaving till I find Red."

She reached out and grabbed his hand. "This is your destiny. We understand. The whole village has known."

James shook his head. "Not until I find her."

"Maybe they can help."

James tapped the table. "They better because this has been my home for over a decade. I'm prepared to go back and avenge my parents in Craih, but I've got to find the Pied Piper and stop him before he does something terrible to the children."

Maris clasped his hand. "You've been my brother and I will be sad to see you go, but I know this is your destiny."

His giant hand clasped hers. "I will never forget you. That much is true."

Chapter 21

Abigail was crying for help. "Please, someone!" The screech echoed through the halls of his family palace.

Jasher ran toward the sound calling out, "I'm coming," but he could never seem to find the source of her cries.

He ran into the library, throwing open the doors and it was there he saw Fabius Thorne.

The prince had never met the Grand Mage before, but he knew of his exploits of terror across the lands of Paraina and now Thorne was holding Abigail hostage and laughing.

"Let her go!" The Dragon Prince demanded.

The Grand Mage just kept laughing at him. Jasher drew the blue blade, but before he could do anything, Thorne stretched out his hand and pulled the sword to himself.

Before Jasher could react, Thorne stabbed her, laughing all the way.

Jasher screamed his sister's name, but she slowly turned to ice saying, "Why didn't you save me, brother?"

The prince looked up with rage at Fabius Thorne, but Aikin stood in his place.

Jasher woke and sat up in the small bed. He was wearing only a shirt and trousers. He stood up and looked at his surroundings, remembering that he was in a wooden hut made by the hospitable islanders on the Kurve.

He stood up, gathering his balance. His sword had been leaned against the wood.

Jasher put it on his belt quickly and walked outside in the hot sun. The village was oddly quiet with no one in sight.

The prince found Jengo talking to someone on the beach. He came up beside him and said, "Listen, I..."

Jengo turned around. "Stranger, return to your hut! Outsiders are not welcome on our sacred beach!"

Jasher was confused by this display of hostility. He had received nothing, but kindness from these islanders.

"Well, what do we have here?"

The voice came from behind the islander and it was then that Jasher realized it was a werewolf.

Not just any, but an Alpha. It stood taller than the large Jengo with long, sharp claws. He was dressed in a red robe, covering his blackened fur.

"This fisherman was telling me no strangers had washed up on their shores," the beast said. "Turns out, a young man is right in front of me. You look too young to be the prince, but in fact, that scar is a dead giveaway. I saw you once in battle, when I was a member of the rebels on Craih. You helped slaughter my friends. That's why I gave myself to the Sorcerer's Society."

Jasher placed a hand on the hilt of his sword. "It seems like you're doing alright for yourself."

Jengo whispered to him, "Jasher, you're not at full strength...."

"Really?" The werewolf licked his lips. "The rewards says I get double bringing you in alive, but I'll settle for the dead rate." Her claws grew a few inches longer.

"Are you going to talk?" Jasher asked. "Or are you going to get that reward?"

Jengo made one last attempt at pleading. "Prince, allow me..."

"I'll deal with this myself." Jasher interrupted, drawing his sword.

The Alpha pulled off his dark robe, revealing a furry, yet muscular body. "The blue blade. The legends are true."

Jasher pointed the sword at him. "You're still talking. Heel, boy."

The werewolf snarled and lunged at Jasher, who dodged and kicked the Alpha in the back.

"You're good, prince, but I'm better."

The werewolf got on all fours and then jumped at Jasher slashing, but his claws scratched the surface of the blade, not even making a scratch.

The Alpha looked at him with a stunned impression. "It's true. The sword is..."

"Stronger, yet lighter than black metal," he said as he smirked.

The werewolf threw a punch aiming Jasher's throat, but the prince used his momentum against him, grabbing the Alpha's wrist and kneeing his gut.

The werewolf raised his other arm and struck wildly, but Jasher raised his sword, cutting off his right arm.

The Alpha howled in pain as his blood splatter on the ground.

Jasher aimed his sword at the brute. "Surrender."

The werewolf growled, showing his teeth. He lunged at Jasher, who swung his sword again, this time, stabbing the Alpha through the chest. The beast fell back, howling in pain again.

Jasher fell to his knees, exhausted and breathing heavily.

The Alpha clutched his chest with his left hand as he laid on the ground. He said, "My pack is still out there. They will come and kill you. They will kill you all." He closed his eyes and breathed his last.

Jengo ran to the prince. "Are you alright?"

Jasher was breathing heavily. "I must find them. I must find the others. More wolves will be out there. I wish I knew where to start."

Jengo grabbed his shoulder and helped him stand. "I might be able to help, my prince. A message came after I sent word after I found you. You are summoned to the nation of Maxia's capital. The queen is requesting your presence. She sent messengers to fetch you for she would like to help with the beginning of your quest."

"Queen?" Jasher asked as he took a breath.

"Ah, yes, the memory gap. The king passed away and his wife took the throne."

"Then I shall go to her immediately."

The Dragon Prince turned as the villagers began coming out of their tents.

"I thank you, your sons, and your wife for saving me. I'm sorry I brought this wolf upon you."

Jengo waved this off. "We are warriors of the Kurve. Our men and women have been battling worse for many generations."

Jasher grabbed his right shoulders. "Your village took care of me, nursed me back to health. How can I repay you?"

Jengo grabbed his shoulder. "Go, save your people. We were honored to serve the Dragon Prince of Teysha, knight of Grandfire City, and Captain of the Seven Royals."

Jasher smiled and nodded. He picked up the blue blade and wiped it off. "As is tradition, I shall name this sword after its first battle. It shall be Alilth the Blue Blade." He placed it in its sheath.

Jengo asked, "What was it like?"

Jasher look tapped the hilt. "Like I've been using it my whole life."

Philip sat at the grave stone which read 'Gretal, Sister-In-Arms.'

He stood up, struggling briefly under his chain-mail armor. It was black, with purple trim, its blouse was marked with the blue silhouette of a hound's head.

Though he was thin, he had an athletic build with a blonde buzz cut, goatee, and piercing green eyes. His freckles were diminished, but they still somewhat permeated his body.

A voice spoke from behind, "I thought I'd find you here."

Philip turned around and then stood at attention. "Captain Makeda." His voice was smooth, like a singer, though he did not sing or play an instrument.

She said, "As you were."

She was an incredibly tall woman, with a pixie-style haircut, and matching armor to Philip. She was beautiful, with glowing ebony skin and deep brown eyes.

Philip sighed. "I'm sorry for the trouble I've caused."

Captain Makeda waved this off. "No, we all have duties we are trained to do, but hesitate."

Philip touched the grave. "I feel like I'm abandoning my duty to her, to you."

"Philip Hansel, she would want this for you. She was your sister-in-arms for a long time, more like siblings than patrol partners. Though it would've saddened her, she would want you to go and save your people. That is your destiny."

Philip turned to face the captain. "I've been in the Order of Blue Lacies for my entire life."

Makeda nodded and drew her sword. "Yes, and you always will be."

"Captain, what're you doing?"

"Kneel," she ordered.

He did as he was told.

"Philip Hansel, I knight you in the Order of Blue Lacies, and commence you to the rank of nomad lieutenant, so you can roam freely. Now, rise."

Philip rose wiping tears from his eyes. "Even if I become a king, I will never remove this coat-of-arms," he said as he patted his chest.

Makeda placed a hand on his shoulder. "You're an honorable man. Serve the Prince Jasher with the same honor."

Chapter 22

On the Western side of Icester, the city of Revenant had been captured by the dark armies of Midas. It had once been a beautiful university town of music and trade in between the kingdoms of Craih and Icester, but now, it was reduced to a smoking ruin thanks to the dark armies that now marched through it.

It was here that Omri emerged from a rabbithole portal, smiling as he walked into the town-square. The golden hand of Midas waved into the cloudy sky from black flags that been placed on the torn and burning buildings.

As he approached a city of tents, a short, bald, long-nosed, and lanky vampire general greeted him. "My lord, Omri, you honor us with your presence." He was dressed in dark clothes under black painted armor. The golden hand of Midas was imprinted on his chest plate. Though the stench of raw meat that surrounded him disgusted many, it pleased the Overlord of Teysha.

General Bloont was the vampire soldier's name. He had lived for five hundred years and had seen many wars throughout the history of the world. He was well known in his military prowess on land and on sea. Until the Sorcerer's Society allied with Midas, he had been a mercenary giving his expertise to anyone who was the highest bidder. He, of course, came to the call when Fabius Thorne had summoned him.

Omri licked his lips. "Your flattery does you credit, General, but that is not why I am here. I am here on a matter of great importance to my father and the viceroy."

General Bloont bowed his head to Omri, "Of course, Overlord. Perhaps we could discuss things in the command tent."

Omri nodded and General Bloont led him to a large tent constructed from very heavy canvas material. Tables had been put throughout the tent, they were littered with maps and timetables. Though it housed a plethora of seating space, the tent laid completely full.

General Bloont explained, "The war goes well, Overlord. When I heard you were coming, I feared this was an inspection. I had my subordinates running around making sure this command area was clean."

Omri laughed at this. He believed himself beneath such tasks, but he relished the thought of having such a fear tingle in the spines of even the greatest of evil warriors.

General Bloont poured him a glass of brandy. "I have to admit, Overlord, I am hesitant to move the second smoke factory all the way to Revenant. I fear it is too close to enemy lines. Although we grow in number, thanks to our toxic bites and the hobgoblins that are coming from the mountains, I worry that we will spread ourselves too thin if we continue at this pace. They are saying our forces are depleting in the fighting with Craih. This is giving the so-called Continental Army an edge."

Omri chuckled quietly to himself. "Viceroy Thorne is seeing to that personally. I would not worry yourself with matters such as Craih. You mind this front."

General Bloont poured himself a glass of what appeared to be blood. He took a sip as he handed Omri the brandy. "I have asked Viceroy Thorne to allow us to fortify Revenant before we continue our campaign. He has deferred to my judgment, which I am grateful for."

Omri nodded. "Both my father and the viceroy trust their commanders." He tasted the brandy. It was strong and burned as it went down his throat. The sting would cause a normal man to choke, but not Overlord Omri.

"Permission to speak freely, Overlord." Bloont requested hesitantly.

"*Wise, Vampire. Asking for permission. I'm sure you remember what happened to your predecessor when he spoke out of turn.*" Omri's thoughts appeared on his face, and General Bloont flinched.

"Permission granted."

General Bloont sighed with relief. "I worry about Midas' men. They seem very, shall we say, discontent. I worry there could be trouble. They especially can't stand the Orcs. I would turn them all into vampires and werewolves, but I know the emperor would not stand for that. Perhaps they should be sent back to Gorasyum or Craih. It could help the numbers there and we could transfer more Orcs to Icester."

Omri shrugged. "You would have to get permission from my father or his war council. I have no feeling about that whatsoever. I'm sure your judgment is sound. Besides, that is not why I am here. As I stated, I am here on a matter of great urgency."

General Bloont nodded. "Of course, Overlord. How may I assist you?"

"There's a rumor spreading that Prince Jasher has returned," Omri said as he cracked his knuckles.

Bloont laughed. "He hasn't been seen for ten years, my lord."

Omri grimaced, silencing the vampire. "Nonetheless, general, I must make absolute certain."

"Perhaps it is just someone who has a blue sword," said Bloont. "You know, they can do amazing things with paint these days."

Omri was starting to lose his patience with the vampire. "Perhaps, but none the less, I want to confirm. If this rumor spreads any more, it'll only fuel the flames of the rebellion on Craih. I need your assistance to deal with this... rumor."

Bloont nodded. "Is there anything special you would like about the warriors you seek?"

Omri thought for a moment. "I need those who are bloodthirsty and have no conscience. Can this be done?"

"It shall be done, my lord." The vampire took another swig of his blood. "I know you don't mind a little dirt, so I might have something."

Omri did not bother to say anything as he exited the tent. Why should he? He was an overlord of Craih.

He looked to the east. *"Where are you, Jasher? Is this really you? Are you the one that is hiding on the islands of Icester? Are you an impostor? It matters not, I will return with your head on a pike for Emperor Midas and Viceroy Thorne."*

Chapter 23

Jasher had been to Maxia long ago when his father traveled there to negotiate a trade deal. Though it had been over a decade, to Jasher it felt as if it had only a short time ago.

"I don't remember it being so cold," he thought as he wrapped his cloak tighter.

As he rode on the back of large into the capital city of Abena, the magnificence of the metropolis was not lost on him. The buildings were made with white stone and black bricks. The face of a sabre tooth tiger, the symbol of the kingdom, could be found decorating most of the buildings in the cool atmosphere.

Maxia had long been defined as a nation of warriors, but also of culture, art, and literature. They were the founders of the Creator religion and the first to make peace with the dragons.

Jasher recalled his three-month trip to Abena. He had trained with some of their best warriors, learning new Martial Arts styles and studying even more about the moon. He also forged great friendships here.

His caravan approached the palace where he was instructed to get off the camel and follow a pair of guards dressed in bronze armor up the giant steps at the entrance. He could see kingdom officials coming and going from the massive building.

The palace was just as Jasher remembered it. It was dome shaped with the face of the sabre tooth tiger carved above the entrance. As he passed through, he could not help but notice a feeling. It was if he could feel something homing in on him. It was familiar, not threatening, similar in presence to his sword. It felt almost as if he was sensing the space rock that had fallen in the sky all those years ago. That was not possible, though. There were only pieces of the space rock left after they had forged the blue blade. They were extremely rare, and he had made sure they were hard to find.

It opened to a great hall where brick pillars went up through the ceiling. The floor was decorated with paintings of flowers and trees. He came to a hallway lined with statues of kings and queens of old. This passage led to the throne room.

Jasher followed his escort to the doors. They stood at attention and motioned him through. The young prince breathed slightly. He recited the procedure and decorum that he was taught about approaching the monarch of Maxia in his head.

If the new queen would help him get started on his journey, he wanted to show her the utmost respect and honor.

He pushed open the door and began walking toward her. The throne room was aligned with statues of the sabretooth with a guard in between them. These guards wore the bronze armor, but they were decorated with a blue sash, indicating their rank as the queen's personal guards.

He got to the edge of a small stairwell that led up to a podium where the throne chair was placed.

The queen was adorned with a golden dress and a crown made of a tapestry instead of metal and jewels.

Jasher remembered the decorum. He drew his sword and placed it on the last step in front of him. He did the same with his helmet before bowing.

"My queen," he began. "It is I, Prince Jasher of Teysha. I came as soon as I received your message. I thank you for your offer for assistance to my quest. I accept it humbly and graciously. Our kingdoms have long been friends and allies. I am honored that the tradition has been continued under your guidance."

He did not know exactly what to expect, but it was not the queen's reaction. She began laughing. It was a joyous, comedic laugh that caught Jasher off guard.

He looked up at her as she looked down upon him. "Oh, dragon prince, I am sorry, but I remember a young royal who once declared that he bowed to no one. Also, I'm not the queen, though I am her daughter, the Princess Ezri Snow."

Jasher looked up and realized that it was not the queen he recognized before him. She was a beautiful sight to behold. Her face was like that of an angel and her skin glowed with a radiance. She was tall with an athletic build with long black hair, dressed in silver and black armor.

It was her eyes that he remembered. Her irises were not blue, brown, green, or violet. They were white. A beautiful white color.

"Snow White," he said with surprise.

The guard to his right stepped forward. "How dare you address the princess in that casual manner!"

Princess Snow stood from her throne and waved off the guard. "No offense was intended. The dragon prince is an old friend of mine from long ago, though he might remember me as a troublesome kid."

The prince smiled as she descended the steps down to him. When she reached him, she said, "Stand!"

Jasher did as he was told. He remember her as a young girl who was always following him around when he and his father visited for the trade deal. He was sixteen and she was fourteen. She had engaged him in many sparring matches, and though he beat her every time, she came back, stronger and stronger.

Then he saw a different memory. She had been at his birthday party. He had handed her his sword when his brother had caused trouble. She had said something to him after he took the Blue Blade from his hand.

Now as he looked at her, he saw she was not a child, but a beautiful young woman.

As she approached him, he tried to speak, but he kept stammering.

"Oh, Jasher, I've never seen you flustered. Ever. It reminds me of our days when my father trained you. I seem to recall that I could systematically beat you at chess."

Jasher finally shook off his shock and smiled. "Yes, but I always bested you with a sword."

"Maybe, but now that I'm older, I'd like to see you beat me in a duel with a dagger or spear," Snow said, "It is good to see you, Prince and good to see you at the same height. Come with me. The sun is setting. It is time to eat."

When he did not move, she grabbed his arm and wrapped their elbows together. "Come!"

"But, I..."

"Shush," she said with a smile. "To my private dining hall, we go."

They walked down the narrow hallway.

"At your party, my mother got uncomfortable after your brother appeared," she told him. "She opened a rabbithole and forced back home almost immediately. I didn't hear about the attack until days later. I sometimes wish..."

Jasher released from her grip. "No. You were a kid. It was not your responsibility."

She struck a pose. "And now, I'm all grown up."

Jasher swallowed hard. Though he said nothing, he thought, *"Trust me. I see it."*

He followed her to a room on the right. It was a private dining room where a table was already prepared with the best meats, fruits, and soups.

She told her guards. "Leave us. The prince and I have much to discuss."

Her guards hesitated, but then moved to the hallway.

The princess suddenly grabbed the prince and pulled him close. He could feel hot tears on his shoulders.

"Jasher, my friend. I feared that you might be dead. I'm so happy that is not the case."

At first, the hug felt awkward, but then he pulled her close. "For me, it feels like I woke up from a dream."

They released each other. She sat at the head of the table and motioned for him to sit on the right side.

She asked, "Are you up to date with what has gone on the last ten years?"

Jasher nodded. "The islanders informed me of everything, or at least, everything that they could."

Snow began fixing a plate for herself, but she noticed that Jasher was not moving. He just seemed to stare at the plate.

"Good ahead, Prince," she said. "Fix your plate."

"No."

"For goodness sake, why not?"

"I don't deserve it."

The princess looked upon her friend. "What're you talking about?"

Jasher looked at her and declared "I've been in many battles, but the one to save my home I could not participate in. Now I sit here, while the other royals are scattered, and my people are suffering. Where was I? I was sleeping. Now it has been ten years. Here I sit in the company of a great friend with the finest cuisine. They haven't even seen the sun or the moon! I don't deserve to even eat a stale piece of bread!"

Jasher grabbed his plate and heaved it, causing it to crash and shatter against the wall. He looked at the cake before him and with a roar he smashed both hands against it, getting icing and crumbs all over hands.

He clenched his fists so hard that hands began to hurt. "I don't deserve anything! My people must be freed before I dare eat anything of such delight!"

Without warning, Snow reached across the table and grabbed his chin, forcing him to look her in the eyes.

"Listen here, Dragon Prince, the road ahead is plagued with hardship, pain, and hurt. The time will soon come when there is only roots from the ground to eat. For now, your people need you at your best. Eat, for tomorrow when you begin your journey, you will need to be at full strength."

She kissed him on the cheek and then handed him her own plate. "Eat."

Jasher smiled at her as he picked up a fork and looked at her with gratitude. "Thank you."

The woman he knew as Snow reached over and grabbed his hand. "If mother allows it, I will come with you."

Jasher started to say something, but he saw that the sun was almost gone from a window. He got up to it and closed the curtains before the moonlight appeared, fortunately, lamps kept the room lit.

"You and your fear of the moon," she said. "You would think being put to sleep for ten years would make you use to it."

Chapter 24

As they sat eating, a door on the other side of the room burst open with someone saying, "Darling, I heard you brought a boy to the palace for dinner. You know the rules." The women stopped when she saw Jasher, who got up and bowed.

"Queen Rhodesia," he said.

"Prince Jasher, why you haven't aged a day."

Queen Rhodesia was a tall woman, well endowed, with long blonde hair, blue eyes, and sand colored skin. She wore a black dress with a single black feather on each shoulder and had a dark crown upon on her head. Her lipstick was thick and her black eye lashes long. The symbol of an apple was sewn on the belt around her waist.

"Mother, Jasher is still bowing," said Snow.

The queen swallowed. "You may rise, Jasher."

She snapped her fingers and a man in in a feather hat, green armor, and a sword on his shoulder came in. He had a full-grown black beard and short hair. His green eyes were piercing and Jasher felt intimidated by him instantly.

"My Huntsman," said the queen. "Did we receive a message that the Dragon Prince was coming?"

Snow said, "No, Mother, I'm sorry. I intercepted the message and was so excited, I forgot to tell you."

Queen Rhodesia was frustrated with her daughter, but she could not show at this time. She sat down. "Uh, Prince Jasher, welcome."

Jasher nodded. "Thank you, my queen. I was sorry to hear of your husband's passing."

Snow looked to the floor at the sadness of remembering her father.

Queen Rhodesia started to say something but stopped. "Yes, well, that was a long time ago," she finally said. "How are you? Where have you been?"

Jasher sighed. "It's a long story."

The matriarch leaned in. "I'd love to hear it."

Snow interrupted. "Uh, Mother, this is unnecessary. Besides, I have a surprise for him."

"A surprise?" This question of concern came from the Huntsman.

He felt the honing signal again, but this time it was stronger almost a human presence. The sensation was both elusive and strange.

Snow held up her hand. "Do not fear that, Jasher. Tell me something, did you have a strange sensation when you arrive?"

She seemed to know the answer before she asked the question. That surprised him.

"Well, Snow," he replied. "I had the most peculiar feeling that a small part of the space rock that provided the metal for my blue blade was nearby. In fact, I feel it now. When I was a child, I had a gift to be able to home in on it, so to speak. I don't see how that is possible now, though. Since my birthday only tiny fragments of it exist."

A voice cried out from behind, "Oh Heavens! It is you!"

Jasher turned around and saw a beautiful girl. She was short and rather petite, almost like a life-sized doll. She had long, flowing blonde hair and wore a pink dress with blue birds sewn on the skirt. Her eyes glowed with a beautiful blue color. The voice she had spoken with was quiet, but very graceful. She moved toward him, even more gracefully, almost as if she was dancing.

"Talia Rosebriar, Princess of Hemorford. You are all grown up."

Talia wasted no time. She ran up and jumped onto Jasher giving him a huge bear hug. "Oh Heavens, Jasher, I missed you so very much! I am so happy to see that you are alive and well! We must throw a party! Oh, yes, I can make us some party hats and cake! Lots of cake!"

She squeezed tighter with each word, and Jasher had to smile at her. He did not bother to correct her assumptions about a party, knowing it was the excitement talking.

She finally released him, and he beheld her. She still had the same girlish smile and the young-looking face. She could not be more than sixteen. He could tell she had kept her sweet spirit all of these years.

Snow was smiling as the two were reunited, but her mother looked on with a suspicious glance. No one seemed to notice, except for the Huntsman, who stood directly behind her.

Jasher said, "I don't understand. How could this be?"

"The priest who rescued me brought me here," Talia replied. I was put in an all-girls school where I was raised for the rest of my childhood. I was treated very well, but it was not home. I've been on many adventures and have been trained in combat as well as mysticism. Also, I made this!"

She pulled out a mini-staff from behind her cloak. It was black with a silver moon on one end and a sun on the other. She split it apart, revealing two blades. "I call them, Sun and Moon," she said before putting them back together.

Jasher said, "It does my heart good to see you, Talia. How did you find me?"

Snow suggested, "Talia, show him your bracelet."

Talia held up her hand, showing a leather bracelet with a blue stone attached to it. "Each of us were given an identical bracelet when we were sent off. They said it would help you find us. I have guarded it for a life time."

Snow explained, "The remaining pieces of your space rock were scattered, but six pieces were given to all of the royals. You have a strong connection to the materials in the stone. Though you absorbed its power it also gave you a beacon of some kind. This is how you will find the rest of the Seven Royals."

"How do you know all of this," asked Queen Rhodesia.

Snow held out a scroll. "High Priest Tyroane sent this to father. When he passed away, it was sent urgently to the school."

Queen Rhodesia stood up. "How dare you keep this from me!"

Snow was shocked by the outburst. "Mother, I was not made aware until just before Talia arrived."

Rhodesia waved at the Huntsman and marched out of the room with him in tow.

Snow shook this off. "My father, he died after eating an apple. Some sort of virus."

"I remember him. He was a wise man," Jasher said. "He seemed prepared for whatever outcome."

Snow smiled. "Yes, but enough of this. What do we do next?"

Talia replied, "If it helps, I might know where Connor is. As you know, he is my cousin, so it was easy to hear and recognize different types of, uh, gallivanting behavior that he so indulges himself in."

Jasher turned to face her. "Where do you think he is?"

The young princess was eager to explain. "I believe he is on a ship, not surprising. There's a port town called Denoka. It a little northwest from here. It is a pirate town and thus holds no allegiance to any kingdom. Many buccaneers dock there. I've heard stories of a pirate ship that has a young lieutenant who is an excellent sailor and swordsman. There are rumors that his crew are from Craih as part of a navy resistance to the golden hand of Midas."

Snow added, "Craih vessels are now under the control of Emperor Midas, the false monarch."

Jasher remembered the port town. "I have heard of that place called Denoka. Not even the men I apprenticed with would go there. It is a seedy place of deplorable crimes. There is law in name only and very little order in that city. That will not stop me. I shall go there alone and find Connor."

Talia laughed at him. "I don't think so, Prince Jasher."

He started to rebut, but she interrupted him saying, "Oh Heavens! We're wasting time here arguing. We are in this quest to save our land and our nations together are we not? I shall go, and I shall be your squire on this venture to Denoka."

Jasher knew if he brought her, she would be in grave danger. He could not draw the blue blade there lest the whole port descend on them after the reward that was on their head.

He started to protest once more but realized he would not convince her to stay when he saw the look in her eyes. She would go. Despite being so young, she had a courage inside her that even Jasher envied.

He acquiesced on one condition. "If we go, Talia, do not leave my side. You must swear to me, if you to truly be my squire, you shall not depart from me and you must follow my orders."

Talia gave a courtesy bow. "You have my word."

"It is decided then," Snow said. "When do you leave?"

Jasher looked to her, "Right after breakfast tomorrow morning."

Chapter 25

Jasher escorted Talia through the hallways.

She said, "Captain, it is so good to have some alone time with you."

"You can address me as Jasher, Talia," he said with a smile.

The princess chuckled. "Oh Heavens, thank you, Captain, uh Jasher. I look forward to our journey going forward. I haven't been to Craih since..." She got gravely quiet.

Jasher cleared his throat. He wanted to break the tension. "So, you basically grew up here in Maxia."

"Oh yes, as I said, growing up at an all-girls school, being sent on adventures to learn new skills, but I never lost sight of home." She asked, "How about you? Where have you been? I know I was young when I last saw you, but I seem to remember it was your eighteenth birthday. You haven't aged a day."

Jasher sighed. "I was in a stasis of some kind. It was scientific, not based on magic. It took me a few days to... adjust."

Talia said, "Oh dear, you remember everything as if..."

"It happened yesterday." He looked to the floor, hiding his pain.

Talia stopped him and then hugged him. "Oh, Jasher, I'm so sorry."

He patted her on the shoulders. "It's okay. It's alright."

After they released, Talia motioned to the door next to him. "These are my quarters. Thank you for escorting me."

Jasher said, "Of course," as she slipped inside.

Before she closed the door, she said, "Jasher, I swear, you have my loyalty. We will save our homeland together."

Jasher gave her a reassuring smile, but inside, he felt a twinge of doubt as she closed the door.

He looked at the palace guard who was at the end of the hall. The sentry was trying desperately to resist the urge to eavesdrop.

"Hey," he called out.

The palace guard looked his way.
"Is there a training room somewhere?"

Chapter 26

The Huntsman was headed down the hall when he bumped into Snow, who was rounding the corner with a jug of water, which promptly spilled all over the floor.

He said, "So, so sorry, your highness."

"No, it's fine," Snow replied. "I just wanted to take a quick bath before bed. Jasher and Talia are leaving after breakfast."

The Huntsman saw a gleam in her eye when she mentioned the Dragon Prince. "So, you, uh admire Jasher?"

Snow flushed. "Why, I suppose I do. Ever since I was young, I, um, oh listen to me babble. Huntsman, can I ask you a question?"

The Huntsman nodded.

"You knew Jasher when you were my father's bodyguard. I was still a teenager, so I'm curious, what do you think of him?"

The Huntsman remembered Jasher from all of those years ago. He had watched Snow's father train him and saw his dedication. He took a moment, considering his answer. "He's a fine young man."

He looked into her white irises and saw an expression he had seen in many a young person a longing to know more about this young man.

"Jasher," he began as he bent down to wipe up the water. "Well, he's as an unbreakable as a stone, solid as a pine tree, strong as iron, a survivor like a bluebonnet, and as fierce and courageous as a dragon." He stood up, handing the towel back to Snow.

Snow smiled. "You are correct. He sounds like a fine young man."

The Huntsman smiled as he moved past her. "Forgive me, your Princess, but the Queen has summoned me." He paused for a moment. "If you're looking for Jasher, you'll find him in the gymnasium."

Jasher was pounding away at a punching bag. He had taking off his armor down to his shirt and trousers with his sword and armor leaning against the wall of the gym. He was bare-knuckled and though his fist were developing bruises as he punched, he did not seem to feel the pain.

He heard a voice, from behind.

"What did that bag do to you?"

Jasher turned around to find Ezri standing there with two rods and a sack.

He smiled. "It's not the bag, though I'm surprised I haven't torn it yet. I went through at least five a day back in my training days." After pausing, he added, "What're you doing here?"

She tossed him a rod. "Those bags are made with a special material we traded from the elves. You would need a sword to slice it."

He grabbed the rod in the center and began striking the punching bag. For a brief moment, he saw Fabius Thorne's face. Though he had never met him, he knew him from his studies of the Sorcerer's Society.

At once, he felt a hot, white rage inside himself. Jasher's face contorted with anger and he began to beat the bag. He struck faster and faster as an enemy he had never met but had costed everything eluded him. He pounded faster and faster.

Snow watched, sensing the pain coming from him. After a few moments, she could bare it no longer. "Jasher, stop! Please stop!"

Jasher hit the bag so hard, that the rod snapped in two. He started breathing heavily and set down on one knee.

Snow walked up to him and sat cross-legged in front of him with a concerned look on her face.

He looked up at her. "Sorry. I'm sorry. I hope this wasn't a special rod."

Snow chuckled. "No. It was a practice stick." She pulled a small, metal rod from her bag. "This is special. My father gave it to me before he died." She handed it to him. "Carefully."

Jasher held it in his hand and it extended from each side, with a spear point on one end. "Your father was a good man. He raised his daughter well. And he knew how to design a weapon."

He retracted it before handing it back to Snow.

Jasher had a memory of when he last saw her. "After my brother awkwardly interrupted my party, you said something to me, but I honestly wasn't listening."

Snow smiled sheepishly. "Yes. I figured as much."

"What did you say?" Jasher asked as he wiped off his sweat.

"You owe me a dance." She said so quietly he barely heard her.

"What?"

"That's what I said. 'You owe me a dance.' Aikin had interrupted us before we had a chance to dance at your party," she explained.

Prince Jasher said, "Well, it's a shame I can't make that up to you."

"Actually..."

She said it so emphatically that it made Jasher nervous.

Snow opened up the doors to a small ballroom and pulled Jasher inside.

"This was my dad's private dance room," she explained. "He and my mom would have private dinners in here for themselves and close friends. Sometimes, they would let me have tea parties in here."

Jasher looked at the stage in the ballroom. It was empty except for a single grand piano sitting in the center.

"How do we dance if there's no music?"

Snow held up her hand to inform him to wait. She jumped up on the stage and pressed three keys. She walked to the rear and started spinning a lever. She began spinning it and after a few rotations, released it, and it began playing a song Jasher knew well. It was light, medium speed, but a simple tune.

"'The Dragons of Craih,' It's my favorite song," Jasher noted. "It plays Craih music?"

Snow nodded and walked up to him. "Yes. You can record music and then play it back by touching the first three notes of the song."

She grabbed him and pulled him close. "Dance with me, Jasher."

He took her and lead her in a great waltz. They danced to the music, one step at a time. As the music entered the crescendo, they pulled closer, and as the climax of the song played, they stopped, both smiling.

The second entered its second chorus and the dance began again. The two of them smiled and laughed as the song ended.

For a brief moment, Jasher realized the pain he felt was gone. He remembered every moment with Ezri. He saw them training, playing chess, enjoying meals together, and writing each other letters. He knew then that he had fallen for her.

Jasher stroked her chin. "I love you."

A single tear traveled down her chin, she hugged him closer. "I've waited forever to hear you say that."

He began stroking her hair. "Hair like the night. Lips as red of the apples. Skin like alabaster. Eyes like snow. My Snow White."

Ezri stroked his cheek. "Don't leave. Stay here. With me."

Jasher shook his head. "If you love me, you would not ask that. If I don't stop the enemy, they will come here to Maxia. I've heard of the attack at Revenant. They're preparing to march here."

Ezri leaned into his chest. "I do understand, and I do love you. I just wish it could be different."

Jasher pulled her out so he could look into her eyes. "Thank you. Thank you so much. Coming here was a respite for the long road ahead. You saved me, Snow. I'll come back to you. I promise."

Ezri looked up at him. "If you don't, I'll find you."

He reached for her cheek and then the back of her head. He pulled her into a kiss. They both leaned into it, the magic of the moment flowing from each of them.

When they pulled back, each of them blushed, but then held onto each other tighter than they had before.

Chapter 27

Queen Rhodesia sat in her royal chambers starring into her vanity mirror. The frame was golden, decorated with apples. She had curled her hair in what could be perfection. She had done her make-up in the finest way with expensive lipstick and eye-lashes curled with exquisite tools. Her black dress and red corset was made from the finest silk. Her crown was shined to the point of showing reflections. The ruby apple in the center was polished so much it reflected light when she moved.

She sighed and picked up her black wand. It too had an apple, this time at the end of the handle.

"Mirror, mirror, on the wall," she began. "Who's the fairest of them all?"

A silhouette of a face appeared in the mirror. "Your daughter, Ezri Snow is the fairest in the land."

The queen howled in anger, taking her arm and sliding everything off the vanity.

"How?" She screamed. "How does that little brat continue to outdo me? I've done everything. Everything!"

She looked back into the mirror. "Show me the girl! Now!"

The mirror showed Jasher and Snow dancing in the ballroom before finally kissing.

Queen Rhodesia pulled out her knife and stabbed the mirror, it cried out in pain before its spirit disappeared from the image.

"My Queen," shouted the Huntsman as he entered her chambers. "What have you done?"

Queen Rhodesia pointed at it. "It shows her! Her! Her! Her! My own daughter has surpassed me no matter what I do! It's his fault! My late husband! All he did was dote on her, now she... she..."

The Huntsman ran to her. "She is just a girl. You worry about this too much. She may have come of age, but her heart is pure. You and your husband raised a darling girl. Do not be jealous of her, train her."

Queen Rhodesia shook her head. "It doesn't matter. We'll see how her heart is once I turn over her love over to the dark army, she will fall into despair and her beauty will be gone."

"Wait, what?

"The Sorcerer's Society are increasing their attacks on Icester's borders. If I turn Prince Jasher and Princess Talia over to them, they will spare Maxia. As a bonus, my daughter will be crushed."

The Huntsman wanted to say something, anything, but he stopped himself. He knew the queen would hear no rhyme or reason. Though he loved her, he could see that jealousy and bitterness had overtaken her.

"You," she said interrupting his thoughts. "Did you get the information I wanted? When do Jasher and Talia leave? I'll send spies to follow them and report their location back to me. I'll use another magic mirror to contact Fabius Thorne and arrange a trade."

When he said nothing, she frowned. "Well?"

"Noon," The Huntsman lied.

Rhodesia smiled. "In that case, we have all night and all morning. Close the door."

Chapter 28

At the palace stables, Ezri Snow gave Jasher and Talia two beautiful horses for them to ride to Denoka.

She handed Jasher a map. "Denoka is only a day's ride from here. The border to Craih is not as protected because of the pirate activity, though it will be dangerous. Rumors of strange creatures haunting the forests are everywhere."

She paused, clasping Jasher's hand. "Be very careful. Emperor Midas has begun his siege on the lands of Icester to the west as you know. The attacks have been relentless. His armies of dark forces are overwhelming human, dwarf, and even elvish armies. Some kingdoms, when they see the banner of the golden hand, just surrender and now pay tribute."

"I will be careful, Snow," he assured her.

Talia popped up in between them. "Oh Heavens, I'll just be waiting outside," she said as she guided their horses out of the stable.

When Talia was out of sight, Princess Ezri suddenly grabbed him and pulled him into a hug. "I love you, Prince Jasher," she said. "You are my greatest friend. Return to me safely."

Jasher stroked her hair. "I love you too." He touched her cheek one last time. He turned to leave and headed for the entrance to the stable, when he heard a cry behind him.

Jasher turned around and Snow ran to him and embraced him more fully.

"Don't go," she pleaded before she kissed him. "Please, stay here with me. I can't... I can't lose you. If mother hadn't forbidden me to go..."

He felt her tears fall on his tunic. He rubbed his fingers through her dark hair and pulled her in close.

Jasher pulled her away and wiped her eyes. "Like we said, I'll return to you or you'll find me."

Snow nodded and then pulled out a satchel. "Take this. It's from Teysha. Your father left it here as a gift to my father. He would want you to have it. It's light, made of black metal chain-mail. Its gauntlets are made from dragon scales, better than any shield."

Jasher lifted the bag and put it over his shoulder. "Thank you." He did not want to leave her, but now he had to. His sense of duty called to him.

He walked out of the stables where he found Talia waiting for him. She was already mounted, smiling with a reassurance.

Jasher mounted his horse and took one more look back. Snow had not yet come out of the stable, but he waved anyway, hoping that she saw it.

They started in silence. As they rode away from the palace, Talia gave him a curious look, "Um, Captain are you..."

Jasher held up his hand. "Yes, Talia, I'm ready to for this. We will reunite us all together."

She laughed at that. It was a pretty, girlish laugh. "Oh Heavens, Jasher! I think all seven of us are going to be best friends! It's so good to be with you again!"

Jasher smiled. *"It is good to be with you again,"* he thought.

Princess Snow stood at the stable until they were out of view. She prayed to the Creator, "Please, watch over them. May you protect Jasher and all of his friends. Help him to lead them and guide them."

She had tears in her eyes as she sighed, "Oh, my prince..."

Chapter 29

Denoka was a seedy pirate town. It had been this way for as long as anyone could remember. Though, at one time in history, Denoka had been a single city kingdom that was known for their golden halls, but now it stood as a port that held no allegiance to any one kingdom, not that any would want it. It was dirty and filthy, and you could smell the stench from a mile away. The residents rarely bathed, if at all.

Even the physical layout of the city was a testament to its corruption. The buildings piled onto each other like a bookcase filled with too many books, one on top of the other. It was a favorite place for gamblers, thieves, outcasts, and murderers, for no one dared, except maybe the bravest of bounty hunters, to enter in to claim them. Those who tried either ended up dead, killed, died in vain, or gave into the corruption.

The citizens walked about, most armed to the teeth. The few good people of Denoka just wanted to escape and find refuge in any city but the one they lived in.

Jasher, right now, felt guilty about bringing Talia to such a vile place. He longed to return to Maxia, to the comfort and safety of someone who loved him. However, he knew the path that lay before him, and he would not turn back. He tried once more to convince Talia to stay at an inn outside Denoka where she would be safer, but she refused, insisting on staying with him. He admitted to himself that he admired her courage. Despite Talia's sweetness and almost enchanting naivety, she was truly a noble girl. Being at her side brought a feeling of welcomed familiarity.

As they approached the city gates, Jasher was happy he convinced Talia to at least wear a brown cloak they purchased at a shop on the way there. He knew that a disguise was necessary, especially for one as beautiful as Talia Rosebriar.

At first, she refused to wear it because it was not fashionable.

"What do you mean by 'not fashionable?'" Jasher had asked her.

She furrowed her brow. "Unlike your new armor, it's just simple brown and it is not a great style of stitching. Besides throwing parties, I'm pretty good at sewing, you know? However, no one will let me near a spindle for some reason."

Jasher cleared his throat. He remembered Father Tyroane telling him he would have to guide them. This was his first taste of it. He kept in mind that Talia was young, and though she had been trained well at the school she attended, she was still in need of a guiding hand.

"My dear Talia, this is a disguise," he explained. "You are indeed beautiful of mind and spirit, and that is why you cannot be yourself, remember?"

Talia gave a disappointed look, but acquiesced. She put on the brown cloak as they approached the gates of the city.

As soon as they entered the gate, Jasher felt a stone's presence. He informed Talia, and though he could not tell what it was, the presence got stronger. It felt even stronger than when he felt Talia's bracelet. He speculated on the reason for that only briefly. While the space stone was helping him home in on its whereabouts, he had trouble locating a specific location.

Jasher felt this to be rather likely. Denoka definitely had that effect. It seemed that everywhere they went, people would stop and stare, contemplating on whether the two were worth robbing.

Jasher found that though he and Talia had not spoken since she was a mere child, he found himself comfortable with her, as she seemed to be with him.

She told jokes and would make humorous observations about some of the more interesting people they would see. As a man with a hook walked by, she asked, "Do you think it's enchanted?"

"His hook?"

"No, Prince Jasher, his rotting teeth. Of course, his hook!"

"Uh, I doubt it."

"Must make it easy to catch fish. He does not even need any string."

While the joke was corny, it made him smile.

He soon realized there was a pattern to her joking. She would do this when he would tense up. Yet, her humor was so genuine that he could help but find it enjoyable.

Jasher finally asked her, "Why do you seem so cheerful, Talia? We do have a daunting task ahead of us."

"Jasher, I know I am young, but I have seen what fear and hopelessness does. I have seen friends die and have held their hands. If there's one thing we need, it is joy. If I have to bring it alone, then so be it!"

Jasher understood and said with a smile, "You do bring joy, Talia. I have a feeling we will need this on this journey."

They searched the ports for what seemed like hours, but when Jasher saw the sun was setting, he decided it was best to find an inn. The place was crawling with unabashed-crime bad enough during the day, but he knew the true villains would come out at night.

It frustrated him they had to stop their search because of the night's sky because Jasher could still sense the presence of the space rocks. He knew they had to be close because their presence was getting was very powerful.

They found a place called "The Hunting Bee Inn" that, while seedy, seemed to have the best smell of the places they had been searching before.

Jasher found himself puzzled over the name. "That's an odd name for a place like this."

Talia wasted no time in offering an explanation. "In the valleys in the west, there are honey bees the size of finches called Hunting Bees. They scavenge honey from the trees in the valley called Sweet Trees and put them in the pears that grow on the trees. The honey allows the trees to grow flowers that produce the pollen that bees have in their hives. It is a very interesting cycle."

Jasher could not help but chuckle at her quick answer. "That sounds fascinating." He was sincere. Anything he could learn about Icester would come in handy later. "These valleys could be a place to find food. I wouldn't want to go against bees that are the size of small birds though," he told her.

Talia further explained, "Unlike most bees, they are not aggressive. Just never touch a pear that has a bee on it, or it and its hive will go crazy. It is the strangest thing, but they are the sweetest fruit you can find. They make great desserts!"

They stood outside the inn and heard the sound of a piano and laughter inside.

Jasher immediately knew how he wanted to approach this. "After I get us a room, we go straight there. I do not wish to make the natives restless. I will get us one room and tell them we are siblings. I volunteer to sleep on the floor."

"Oh Heavens, your nobility is heartwarming, Jasher, but I am hungry and wish to feast," she said planting her feet. "We shall have supper, then go up to our room. And yes, sir knight, I shall allow you to sleep on the floor, but I will give up a pillow." She giggled at that.

Jasher looked at her, not finding this situation funny. "Talia, with all due respect, you've been at an all-girls school for the past ten years. The world is—"

"Full of rainbows, sunshine, and good deeds," Talia interrupted, "but also of clouds, fires, and evil." Talia did not appreciate Jasher's scolding. "Yes, I know. Jasher, with all due respect, you don't know what I've learned or the places I've been. You can be my leader, but you cannot be the angel on my shoulder."

Jasher was thrown off by her bold comments. They were unexpected. At first, he founded himself offended by them. After only a few moments, he realized she was right. He could not treat her or the others like children if they were to fight for their homeland. "Very well, we shall feast. All I ask is you keep your cloak on. Agreed?"

"Agreed," with that she took the first step forward leading the way into the inn.

Jasher was quickly behind her, with a hand on his knife.

Chapter 30

Jasher booked a room for both of them before they grabbed a table in the dining room. They both gave their orders to a scantily clad wench and then began drinking their ginger tea.

The place filled with a bountiful amount of loud yelling, and even some brawling, but the action here stayed rather light for what Jasher was expecting.

Their orders quickly arrived, which made Jasher a bit suspicious of the meal. Talia ate some fish and kale while Jasher ate beef and mashed taters. The young princess seemed to enjoy hers more than the Dragon Prince, who winced at the overly-salted beef and stale potato.

As the waitress took away their plates, a group of six men came into the dining room. When they walked in, most of the customers got really quiet. They were all tall, muscular men, dirty, grimy, wearing animal skin hides that were too small for them. All of them were graying, except for the one Jasher guessed to be the leader. He had a round, bald head, his face littered with stubble.

He approached Jasher and Talia's table. With a big, deep voice, he spoke, "I am Huxson. This is my table. My mates and I share it along wit the one next to it, Bowie."

Jasher stood as he said, "Our meal is done. We are leaving." Normally, he did not abide bullies, but since they were trying to avoid notice, he decided a tactical retreat was in order. Talia followed suit, with both of them stepping away from the table.

Huxson held up a huge hand. "Bowie, lad!" He exclaimed, and the dragon prince stepped back. "You rented it, you have to pay a fine. That's what I say, Bowie. After all, this is my table."

Jasher had some concern. This man was already intoxicated. He could smell it on his breath. He once again noticed the fact that Huxson stood high over him, his mass exceeding Jasher's by a plentiful amount. He and his friends would be tough to fight, but neither he nor Talia did not have money to spare, especially in the road ahead.

"Look, sir," Jasher said. "My friend and I are new to Denoka, just passing through. We are now going to our room." He nodded to Talia, who followed as Jasher again stepped away from the table.

"Bowie!" Huxson yelled out again. He reached out and grabbed Talia's arm. Her hood fell off and her hair fell to her shoulders.

All of the men began to whistle and make crude noises. Talia pulled her hand free.

"Well, I'll be," Huxson said with an excited growl. "She's a young and fresh one, eh, Bowie? I'll tell you what, my mates and I will let you go for her."

Talia gave Jasher an annoyed smile and before he could stop her, she turned to the fiend. "Oh Heavens, I do smell fresh, don't I? You could too you know?"

Huxson and his men looked at each other, confused.

Jasher swallowed hard and placed his hand on the knife Abigail had given him. He did not want to draw the blue blade here, though a sword would give him an advantage, but he knew word would surely reach the ears of Midas' spies.

"If you touch her again," Jasher began. "You will lose a finger." Huxson and his pals, amused, mockingly *oohed* and *awed* at Jasher.

Talia forced a chuckle, and cheekily replied, "Don't do that, Jasher. Nine fingers is not enough for them to count."

"Well, Bowie," said Huxson ignoring Talia. "We outnumber you six to one."

Jasher drew his knife while Talia pulled her staff apart, revealing her two short swords.

"Oh Heavens, two against six. The odds are not in your favor, skipper. Trust me, these daggers will do the trick. They are my own handiwork."

Huxson pulled a small axe from his belt, brandishing it with a smile. "I donae think so. The odds as you say, are in our favor."

He swung first and both Jasher and Talia dodged. His inertia was so strong, that he lost balance and crashed onto the floor. One of Huxson's pals quickly drew his dagger, and swung it at Jasher, who blocked the blow with deft skill, and then kicked, sending him across the room. Talia blocked a blow from the next and then cut off his belt. The man yelled in rage, ready to cut her, but Talia swerved so quickly she looked like a blur. She struck the side of his head with the blunt end of her right-hand knife, sending him down.

Huxson got back up in a heartbeat, two more of his thugs ready and willing to join the fray. Huxson swung his axe at Jasher, who once again dodged. The third thug ran up to punch Jasher, but the Dragon Prince punched the man's throat and then kicked him in the knee, sending him down. As he fell, Jasher knocked him out cold with a quick hit of his knife's handle. The fourth one swung his fist at Talia, who swiftly kicked her attacker in the crotch. He let out a squeal and fell the on ground, passed out.

The fifth and sixth pulled out miniature crossbows and were about to shoot Jasher and Talia, when an arrow struck each of the crossbows.

Jasher and Talia readied themselves for what was about to come.

The two of them, and their last two attackers, turned around to see a woman in dressed in brown trousers, and a green blouse with matching brown gloves. She seemed somewhat familiar Jasher.

The men turned their crossbows on her, but the hilt of a sword, swung from behind the inebriated combatants, caught the fifth's neck right on the spine. The swordsman watched the man fall, knocked into a daze.

"Now, that's not very nice is it," asked the stranger.

This man stood almost as tall as the lady. He wore a white pirate shirt, blue trousers, rough skin boots, and had shiny white teeth. Though he looked twenty, Jasher could tell he was in his late teens.

Huxson suddenly stood up and looked rather worried. "Connor, oh man, I'm not trying to cause any trouble. It's just this Bowie..."

Jasher's ears perked up. He looked over at Talia who nodded.

Connor interrupted Huxson's babbling. "This is my favorite inn, Huxson. They serve the best swordfish. Now, you and your men go to the pub down the street and cause no more trouble here. Remember what happened when you tried to get my lady friend's attention?"

The lady archer gave a grin and perked up an eyebrow. "Yes," she said. "Remember?"

Huxson swallowed hard, cowering before the man whom he dwarfed, helping his friends up and then all six of them stumbled out of the inn as they began feeling their combat injuries. "Yes, Connor," he said as they left. "We'll be on our way. No problem whatsoever for you or Belle."

When Jasher heard the name, he knew it was true, and as the sailor turned to leave, he had to stop him.

"Wait," he said. "Thanks for the help."

Connor waved this off. "Huxson and his lot get rowdy after they drink. They made the mistake of flirting with Belle, here. When she told them to leave and they didn't, they learned a very hard lesson. We've had no trouble from them since."

Talia voice rang out. "Oh Heavens! Connor and Belle! I don't believe it!"

Belle took a step back, confused by Talia's excitement. "What're you talking about? Have we met?"

Jasher looked at Connor's wrist and saw his bracelet. He looked at Belle. "I take it, you have one with that stone on it as well?"

Belle stiffened at the questions. "What is this, twenty questions? What's it to you?"

Talia held up her wrist showing them hers. "We do know each other, from a lifetime ago."

Jasher barely lifted his sword from the scabbard, revealing a hint of the blue blade. "That's why my senses were so strong. There were two of you here. Connor, Crown Prince of Seayarn. And Belle, Crown Princess of Kalataya." He slightly unsheathed his sword, briefly exposing the Blue Blade.

"Jasher and little Talia?" Connor exclaimed, "Oh, thank the sea!" He suddenly embraced Jasher, surprising him with this show of emotion. He did the same to Talia, who welcomed his hug with an equally enthusiastic embraced.

115

Belle stood and watched. She avoided a hug from Talia, pushing her away, turned to Jasher, and said, "So, you have returned, Prince Jasher, still looking younger than us. Are you here to lead us back to our beloved Craih?" She said it with no excitement and almost with an annoyance.

Jasher nodded. "Yes. We are now four royals, but there are still more to find. Philip, James, and Rapunzel are still out there. We have a lot of ground to cover."

Connor said, "Yes, we do, but first, let us go back to my ship. We will go in my quarters and catch up."

Belle grunted. "Yes, sounds thrilling."

Jasher saw how she crossed her arms when she realized who they were. While Connor seemed excited to see them, Belle seemed distant and unsure of the whole situation. He could not put his finger on it, but it almost seemed that she was disappointed at their reunion.

Talia exclaimed, happier now than she'd been since the wars began. "I can't believe it! We're going to be reunited! Oh heavens, the prophecy is coming true! We should throw a party! A party on your ship."

Belle looked completely passive. "No parties. There is not time for that."

Connor said, "Oh, come now, Belle..."

"This is not the time." Belle shot Connor a strong, stern look.

Jasher started to get rather uncomfortable. This reunion hadn't gone the way he had envisioned it. Of course, he was not really sure what to expect, but Belle's attitude about the situation threw him quite off balance.

Connor motioned out of the inn. "Very well then, we shall head this way back to port."

As they headed out, Jasher looked at the knife his sister had given him. He chuckled and said, "Your first battle, eh? Well, from now on, I shall call you Bowie."

"Oh Heavens, I love that name!"

Chapter 31

As they boarded the *Fiery Wing*, Jasher could see the crew staring at him and Talia. The Dragon Prince could not tell from their expressions if they were happy to see them or not.

A bearded man in a striped shirt and a hook for a hand approached them. "Dragon Prince Jasher, you have returned," he said as he bowed. "I am Captain Hull."

Jasher nodded. "Thank you, Captain. On the way here, Connor and Belle filled me in on your fight for Craih on the high seas."

Hull said, "Twas nothing, Dragon Prince. We a'least coulda see the sun on some days, but that there Continental Army at our home, they had not even seen a sliver of light through that toxic cloud."

Belle interjected. "Forgive me, Captain, but we have much to discuss with Prince Jasher."

Captain Hull slapped himself on the forehead. "Of course, mi lady. You may use me chambers."

He motioned to a set of doors behind the pilot. Connor thanked him and then led the other Royals into a room decorated with Craih banners with a single table in the center. The four of them gathered around a table, each taking a seat.

Talia spoke up first. "Oh Heavens, so where have you two been?"

"I was raised on another ship, the *Saint Mary*," Connor replied. "The monk bringing me to safety had an encounter with an Orc before the shipmates rescued me. He died, so the captain and his wife decided to take me as their own son. He was a proud captain in the Seayarn navy and though he wanted to go back and help his people, he and his wife decided that it was important to keep me safe."

"They raised me as a sailor, teaching me mapping, sword fighting, how to cook, how to survive in the wild, and above all, take care of a vessel. I miss my parents greatly, but the Creator provided me this family. For the last ten years, we've become buccaneers, fighting for freedom on the seas."

He paused for a moment, wiping his right eye. "Unfortunately, my parents were killed when the *Saint Mary* was destroyed by one of the Sorcerer's Society's naval ships. We later stole this vessel and renamed it the Fiery Wing. Hull was my step-father's first mate. He took command and we've been doing this ever since."

Talia said, "What a wonderful story. Belle, will you?"

Belle held up her hand. "I don't do backstory a whole lot, but since you told us your story and Jasher's... twice on the way over here, I will oblige. I was raised in a village along the border of Revenant. They never told me the truth. I learned of it a year ago. I left the castle and six months ago I ran into Connor in Denoka. I joined the crew of the *Fiery Wing*. That's all there is."

Talia's knees bounced excitedly. "What castle?"

Belle grimaced. "Excuse me?"

"You said that you left a castle."

Belle grew quiet and then said, "None of your business."

Connor decided to break the awkwardness. "Do we have any idea on the direction where we can find the other three? James, Philip, and Rapunzel must have some sort of clue that can bring us to their locations."

Jasher shrugged. "We only knew to come here, Connor, because your cousin recognized some tall tales about you. I'm not sure of the range these space stones work. For the most part, I have a rough idea and it only seems to operate if I'm in the general vicinity. I didn't sense the two of you until I was almost to Denoka, and I didn't feel Talia until she was actually in Maxia's capitol. We can't count on what direction to go."

Talia held up her bracelet. "Maybe we can with this."

Belle asked, "What do you mean?"

"I learned a few things in the school I was part of," Talia explained. "Besides, fighting, I studied magic. Apparently, I have quite the gift for mysticism."

This did not impress Belle. She asked sarcastically, "Can you sew too?"

Talia stroked her chin and answered head on, "Actually no. I wanted to learn, but my parents would never allow me. If I even looked at a spindle, they would fly into panic."

Belle was slightly displeased her ribbing seemed to bounce off Talia, not annoying the younger girl much at all.

Connor said, "Okay, so can you tell us how to find James, Philip, and Rapunzel?"

Talia told them, "Give me your bracelets." They handed them to her. "Now, Jasher, you can sense it because of your unique connection with these stones. Give me your hands. I'm going to try to tap into your energy to see if we can at least get a general idea where they are."

Jasher asked, "How? The space rocks are like me, immune to magic."

Talia waved this off. "It's true for direct magic, but indirect, not so much. I'm going to try to just create a bridge from these stones to the others and back to you. I might not succeed, but it's worth a try."

"I suppose it is, but before I do this, do you swear that you are using the mystic arts of magic, and not tapping into the sorcery realm."

"I swear!" Talia proclaimed this proudly.

Jasher held out his hands. "Your word is good enough for me."

She took them and placed the bracelets in his palms.

Belle was doubtful. "Have you ever done this before?"

Talia shook her head. "I've practiced several other similar enchantments. I've not done one for location, but I observed a master do it once. I believe I can remember."

Jasher said, "Good enough for me."

Belle folded her arms. She doubted the young one's ability to accomplish this mystic performance.

Talia placed her hand on his. She began to slowly and quietly whisper. Belle and Connor could not hear what she was whispering. To the others, it sounded as if she was just mumbling.

Jasher closed his eyes and suddenly, his scars began to glow with their bluish light as the stones began to glow with a matching color.

In an instant, he saw James, Philip, and Rapunzel all grown up and wandering forest within Craih. They were all close to one another in a dense forest that was covered in a strange fog. He could not get a precise location, but he saw where they needed to go. The journey would not be as far or as long as he first anticipated.

When the enchantment stopped, his skin turned to normal. He did not know his scars had glowed and when he saw the surprised look on Connor and Belle's face, he asked, "What is it? What happened?"

Connor shook it off. "Uh, nothing. Did you see anything?"

Jasher nodded. "Yes, they are all located in the same general region of Craih. They are fortunately not far from Denoka and all within close range of each other.

Belle said, "They hid us all within the same region except for you and Talia. It's a surprise we never realized how close they are."

Jasher nodded. "Are you two in with me and Talia? It means leaving the sea behind, but if we do, we will restore our kingdoms and avenge our parents."

Belle crossed her arms. "Of course, I'm in, fearless leader. We were told how you were made our 'Captain.'"

Connor nodded. "You see, I've wanted to avenge my parents since I was taken from them. So yes, Jasher, I'm in."

Talia said excitedly, "Oh Heavens, at last, all seven royals will be united."

Jasher nodded. "Good, then let us leave Denoka in the morning. We've got a long journey ahead."

Omri and General Bloont stood at the foot of the base camp on the outskirts of Revenant, observing as Emperor Midas' troops sharpened their swords and ready their shields. Soon they would be off the battle at the front lines. They were starting to paint gold hands on their armor and flags to let the kingdom of Icester know that they were coming.

A messenger hawk flew down and landed on General Bloont's arm.

The vampire took the message, and brought it to Omri, "Sir, permit me a word?"

Omri simply nodded his reply.

"I've received word that a man was spotted with a blue sword in Denoka. He was with three companions. One man and two women," General Bloont continued.

Omri smiled, revealing his yellow teeth. "Hmm, and then there were four."

He paused for a moment. "Excellent. I need a hunting pack of your finest werewolves."

Bloont hesitated, then spoke up, "Sir, if I may speak freely."

"You may," Omri said as he licked his lips.

"Surely this is just a rogue human whose painted his blade," said the vampire. "These are probably the fakes that the Continental Army created to rally their troops. Why risk yourself? I mean, we're at war. You are one of our greatest leaders, and the emperor's adopted son. You could be captured. Or worse."

Omri gave a wicked smile. "Your loyalty is noted, General Bloont. I must do this to prove it is a fake. No doubt, stories of this blue sword-armed warrior has reached the Continental Army. I will stamp it out with the wolf pack you provide. Because that is what I must do."

General Bloont nodded. "In that case, sir, instead of a wolf pack, I remember you mentioning you wanted the best bounty hunters. I might have a group that would do the trick."

Omri turned to face him. "I'm all ears."

Chapter 32

Connor shook hands with Captain Hull. "Thank you, sir," the sea prince told his skipper. "After my step-parents died, you took me in and taught me even more. I will, miss you, sir."

Captain Hull pulled out a sheathed sword. "Take dis, Prince Connor."

Connor took it and drew it, revealing a beautiful silver saber.

"Your shipmates had it forged in Denoka," explained Hull. "We a'wanted you to 'ave it. The *Saint Mary* is engraved on one there side wit' the *Fiery Wing* on the other."

Connor immediately tied it to his belt and then he saluted his captain.

Captain Hull saluted back. He turned to Belle. "Me lady, I know yer not as, uh, sentimental as Connor, but we a'made you this just'n case." He handed a brown quiver, engraved with flaming wings.

Belle gave a brief side smile. "Thank you, Captain Hull. For this and for taking me in, even if I was seasick for a week."

Captain Hull then approached Talia. "Thank you fer findin 'em. We're sorry to see 'em go, but we understand."

"Oh Heavens," and then she blushed.

Captain Hull bowed to the Dragon Prince. "Me Lord, we a'welcome yer return. We'll be sure and tell of yer return and that the Sorcerer's Society, they scant got a chance."

Jasher lifted him up. "Thank you. Thank you for everything. By the Blue Blade, I will set Craih free."

After that heartfelt goodbye to their shipmates, Connor and Belle departed.

Belle asked Connor, "How do you feel?"

He replied, "Like I'm losing my home, but I know I'm gaining another."

They bought horses for each of them, and a donkey for supplies, they decided it was time to depart the seedy port-town of Denoka. The longer they stayed, the more likely some of Midas' spies, or worse, bounty hunters, would find them.

As they passed through the city gates, they headed west.

Jasher was relieved when the stench of Denoka was long gone. He allowed himself a sigh of relief, said a quick 'thank you' to the Creator under his breath.

Along the way, he took a chance to speak with Connor. He wanted to assess the sea prince's experience and the young buccaneer was more than happy to share.

Jasher asked, "Have you ever been against the wall?"

Connor smiled, "Only once, but I escaped. Why do you ask?"

Jasher raised an eyebrow. "You've never been in a no-win situation?"

Connor let out a laugh. "I don't believe in those. If my life hung by a thread, I'd just cut it. Surely you have never encountered this."

Jasher said, "Well, when I was apprenticing for the army, and we ran into some thieves, we were pinned down and could not get out. My entire team could have been killed. With the help of Commander Bearskin, we rallied and made a stand."

"So, how did you get out of there alive?"

"We got out thanks to some well-timed reinforcements."

Connor laughed even harder. "Then that is not a no-win situation. There's no such thing. You can always find a way out."

Jasher decided not to belabor this conversation, but realized when he looked at Connor, he saw a man who was fuller of stubbornness and rashness than courage. Connor fancied himself a swashbuckling rogue who enjoyed heroics as a sport more than a duty. Jasher could not help but wonder if this would cause trouble for them in their quest.

The sun setting in front of them revealed that they had spent a whole day of traveling. Stopping once to ask for directions, they realized the next village was at least a few hours' ride. Thus, Jasher decided to let the horses, and themselves rest for the night.

They found a nice little cove of trees and settled down there. After they made a fire and laid the horses down, Belle was fashioning arrows from some limbs she had found. She looked up at Jasher, who had his cloak on and he seemed to be hiding in the shade from the trees.

"Can I ask you something, Captain?" she asked. Jasher just nodded in reply. Belle said, "You told us stories about after your wish came true, how you worked with knights, detectives, and all manner of warriors to learn skills. I remember a story about how you single handedly collected a bounty for a known murderer. For us, it seemed so astounding, but you were so young. Now, seeing you here, and me being taller, they seem a bit like tall tales."

Talia exclaimed, "Belle!"

Belle ignored her. "So, are they true, Fearless Leader?"

Jasher gave a meek smile from beneath the trees. "Yes, everything I told you was a real circumstance. They were not what I'd call tall tales. It is true that I was young, but my circumstances were... different than most of yours. Anyway, I will admit, some of the stories had embellishment. After all, a wise man once said that all stories need embellishment to make them more entertaining. For instance, the spinning-round kick did not get its name after I knocked out a rampaging boar."

Connor laughed. "Oh, yeah, my favorite was the story of how you wished upon a star. We had you tell it at every one of your birthday parties."

Talia laughed. "Yes, sometimes twice."

Belle asked, "So, Captain, how did you take out the boar?"

Jasher laughed. "I stuck it with spear." He paused for a moment and then stood up. "I'm going to get some more wood. I will return momentarily."

After he was out of sight, Talia looked at Belle. "What was that all about?"

Connor said, "Yeah, you've seemed quite frustrated since we reunited."

Belle replied, "Our captain was put in some ice capsule for ten years. It kept him from aging. One would think that High Priest Tyroane would send him off to be better trained. I'm not sure if the priest knew what he was doing."

Talia said, "He was very wise. We all miss our parents and we all mourn. I think you are being too harsh on poor Jasher. He had to put what he wanted aside to come and find us. He is our leader and we must trust him. Think about what it is like for him. To him, everything happened just a few days ago. We've had ten years to mourn and to prepare. He's thrust back into the action with barely anytime to rest. We need him, we need him to avenge our families."

Belle thought before replying. "I always wanted to avenge my family. When I heard that Midas had turned them all to gold, I could not believe it. I will follow the captain because it is my duty. I don't have to like it though."

Connor and Talia considered trying to convince Belle out of that way of thinking, but they chose to remain silent.

What they did not know was that Jasher heard every word and it weighed heavily on his heart.

Chapter 33

The next morning, Talia awoke and realized Jasher was not among them. She stood up quickly. Fear started to grip her heart. *"Dearie, please tell me he did not run off on us!"* She laughed at herself for even entertaining that thought.

She was about to awaken the others, but then she turned and saw him lying under roots of a tree close to them. She shook her head.

Walking over to him, she pushed on him. "Oh Heavens, Jasher," she said. "It is time to wake up."

He yawned and stretched, but then bumped his head on the root. "Ow," he said rubbing the top of his head.

Talia chuckled at him. "Oh Heavens, why were you sleeping under the roots?"

Jasher answered as he crawled out from under them. "I was cold, and I found it warmer under there."

Talia shrugged, accepting his answer.

She looked over and saw Belle and Connor were starting to stir as well.

Jasher called out to his charges "Let's eat a quick breakfast and be on our way. I believe that Philip is nearby."

Talia thought about this, and then some up, "Let us stop for breakfast in a valley close by. I want to show all of you something."

After saddling up, the royals pressed on until Talia led them to a valley. It was filled with large trees that were higher than some castles the royals had seen. They were filled with branches of fruit and leaves until about two feet above the ground. Flying all around were bees the size of finches: The Hunting Bees.

Talia smiled. "Jasher, welcome home."

The Dragon Prince looked out over the valley they had entered. Though he had not been to this particular region, he could feel it. It was Craih's lands. He breathed it in and then a shadow fell over him.

He realized the sky was blocked by a giant cloud in the sky. The sun was completely masked out and Jasher sighed in agony as he realized that his people had not seen the sun in a decade. Only hazy sunlight could make it through.

"Where are the patrols of the dark army," he asked.

Belle said, "We're on the other side of the Giving Forest. For some reason, those armies do not cross it. No one knows why."

Suddenly, a giant bee flew in front of Jasher's face. He was about to swat it when Talia said, "I would not do that if I were you. Take a look."

The Royals watched in awe as bees flew from hives unseen and hooked onto the fruit of the tree. The Hunting Bees would sting the fruit, and then fly away.

Connor was the first to speak. "That is one of the most spectacular sights I've ever seen."

"Yes," Belle agreed. "They're working in perfect harmony."

Jasher looked around. "Where's their hive?"

Talia got off her horse, smiling as she watched the Hunting Bees as she answered, "Their hive is located in the caves on the other side of the valley. These bees are unique to this area."

Belle asked, "Could we try one of the fruits?"

Talia nodded. "Yes. Just do not touch a fruit that has a bee on it. The bees will go crazy. Otherwise, the Hunting Bees are totally harmless."

"This is a good a spot for our breakfast," Jasher said. "Yes, let us enjoy some of this delicious looking fruit."

They all dismounted and approached the trees, carefully avoiding touching any of the bees.

Belle was the first to pull a fruit off the tree. She took a bite and proclaimed, "This is the best fruit I have ever tasted."

The rest of the group quickly agreed. They sat under the trees, and all seemed very quiet and very peaceful. Each one of them enjoyed every bite. Time seemed to move by so slowly. For these moments, they forgot about their troubles and their quest, as they ate together. These royals would enjoy these moments, which would seldom happen, and they all knew it. For this brief respite, the worries of tomorrow seemed to just fade away as the Hunting Bees injected more of the fruit with their honey.

After they had sat there for some time, Jasher stood. "Being the leader is tough with very hard calls, and here's a hard call I must make. It is time to press on for I feel Philip is nearby."

They all let out some murmurs, but no one protested. They knew him to be right.

"Wait," Connor said, "Before we go, I must have one more."

He reached for a fruit that was directly above him, but the tip of a double-edged sword stopped him. It did not stab, merely gently tapped him to stop him from reaching up.

A new voice warned, "I would not touch that one, friend." A man came out from behind the tree.

Connor looked up at the fruit. A Hunting Bee was seated on it, injecting it with honey.

The sea prince said, "Thank you, sir. That would've been unpleasant if they all swarmed upon us."

The young man nodded. "Yes indeed."

Belle asked, "Who are you?"

The young man bowed. "I am Crown Prince Philip, of Sheyer."

Talia let out a squeal of delight and tears streamed down her face. Connor put a hand on his shoulder. Belle walked up and shook his hand.

"It is good to see you, brother!" Jasher approached him and shook his hand.

Philip held back tears in his eyes. "I have for a long time wished to lay eyes upon you once again. I knew this day would come and I knew this would lead you to me, Prince Jasher." He lifted up his wrist where they saw a bracelet. "I heard you say you felt me nearby. I was closer than you thought."

Prince Jasher took a moment to look over Philip. He was six foot five and clean shaven. He still had the short red hair, but his freckles were gone. He had those same green eyes he had as a kid. He stood up straight and tall, almost at a military pose.

He wore some kind of brown animal-hide trousers, and chainmail armor that had a black vest. He wore black gloves, and boots to match. He had a thick belt, and he carried a long sword.

Belle asked, "How did you find us, Philip?"

"I grew up in a military barracks not far from the Giving Forest," he replied. "I was a squire under Captain Makeda of the Order of the Blue Lacies. We have been leading a resistance in this area against the forces of the dark army."

"That's pretty brave," Talia said.

Philip turned to reply, but he stopped when he saw Talia. He swallowed hard and gazed upon her beauty. He stammered something before Belle said, "Well? You haven't answered the question."

Philip snapped out of it. "Oh, yes, well, after the bracelet glow, I set out. I bought some supplies from a local merchant who told us that a band of young people were heading toward the Giving Forest. He mentioned that one of them had a blue blade named Alilth, and that they were looking for more companions. I had not heard of Alilth, but I had heard of the blue blade. I hoped it was all of you. The merchant knew this was a popular stopping point for anyone heading into the Giving Forest area." He grinned. "It paid off."

Jasher walked up to him and shook his hand. "Crown Prince Philip, the giver of my leather belt. The Creator has surely shined down on us! We are now five!"

The five royals all gathered around each other. They briefly celebrated, for they all knew that the only two of their company left to find was Rapunzel and James.

Chapter 34

The five Royals entered into the area called the Giving Forest. Scattered around its borders were villages and trading outposts. It ran along the border of Craih and Icester, with small villages yet untouched by the dark army, though they still felt the effects of the war.

Many described the Giving Forest as a place of magic and everyone wandered in to catch a glimpse of a wisp or a fairy. Because of this, no village or town existed inside the forest itself, for fear of unbalancing the delicate nature of the magic that existed there.

However, Jasher could sense something was wrong as soon as they crossed into it. The Giving Forest was supposedly full of game, but he saw not one deer, rabbit, or squirrel. He could hear insects and frogs, but those were the only sounds he detected. He did not even hear a bird chirp. The looming silence felt almost sinister.

This made Jasher suspicious and curious, so he looked all around, and he quickly spotted something else. There seemed to be a mysterious fog coming from the center of the Giving Forest. He had never heard of such a thing. Of course, he had never seen a sky blocked by a huge plume of smoke.

They passed through a few villages, but found it odd as the populaces seemed afraid, and would hide as the five passed through.

Belle spoke first. "Friendly bunch," she muttered.

Frustrated, Talia replied unhappily, "This makes no sense. I've been to these parts before, not these villages specifically, but nearby. I've never had any sort of greeting like this. It has all been very pleasant."

Connor nodded. "You'd find more cheer at a funeral."

Philip added nothing to the conversation. Normally he would have said something, but he had his hand on the hilt of his sword. He found himself needing to be on guard. He carefully observed each villager as they passed by, not knowing what to expect.

Around midday, they reached the village of Oakwood. It was a small, typical village that dotted the borders of the Giving Forest. They had a blacksmith, a medicine man, a priest, a tavern, and a school. They saw no inn or any other sign that they welcomed strangers.

Jasher could feel the space stone's presence. He found it strange that, now that he had made contact with the others, their presence had faded away. He could still sense them, but they were not as strong as when he first felt them. However, this new feeling felt incredibly powerful. He knew that either James or Rapunzel would be close, but he could not figure out whose presence he felt, as he had with Philip. He wondered if the fog somehow caused some sort of disruption.

As they walked through, they realized that the people in the town behaved in a peculiar manner. No one seemed to be talking, and all of them were walking by as if in a daze, but this village differed from the others they had passed. The people in those villages just seemed afraid, but these people almost seemed out of place in their own homes.

Connor asked, "Is it just me or does this seem a tad creepy to anyone?"

Philip nodded. "Yes, this town does have a strange feeling to it."

Talia did not respond but she had become slightly agitated and seemed to fidget.

Jasher at first could not place what they were feeling, but then he realized, "There are no children."

Belle swallowed hard. "That's not disturbing at all." Her usual sarcasm came out more serious this time.

Talia still said nothing, which had so far been uncharacteristic, but began to breath heavily and she could feel her heart beating faster.

Belle could tell something was bothering the young one. "Talia, are you okay?"

Talia nodded rapidly in response. "Oh, um, yes, I just need something to drink. Tea, preferably."

Jasher pointed to the local tavern. "That one will do."

They tied up the horses and walked into the tavern, which out-paced every other tavern they'd ever visited in its quietness and its deadened activity level. None of the plentiful customers were singing or laughing, and even the piano player played a somber song about defeat in battle and lost love. It affected the mood in a most unusual way.

Connor shook his head. "In all my travels, I've never seen a village like this."

"Oh my, they could really use a party." Talia normally mentioned parties with a smile and excitement, but this time, she seemed to force it.

When the barmaid came to their table, she asked, "Hi everyone. My name is Maris. I'll serve you. With the war, we don't get many visitors. What'll you have?"

They gave their drink orders and Jasher asked, "Where are the children?"

A tear came down the barmaid's eye as she stumbled over words before saying with a broken voice, "The Pied Piper got them!"

Belle asked, "Piped Piper? What do you mean?"

Maris explained, "A year ago, we had a vermin epidemic. It was bizarre, rats were everywhere, but these were different. They were large, some of them the size of a deer, elk."

Philip said, "Giant rats, that does not sound pleasant."

The barmaid continued, "Then this man appears calling himself the Pied Piper. He said he heard about our plight and offered his help for a small fee. We hired him immediately and he played this magical flute and danced the rats away. We were so happy. However, when he returned, he wanted ten times his payment. We could not afford it, so he told us he would make off with our, with our... children!" The barmaid fought back tears, cleared her throat, and continued. "We never believed he would do that, but he did. We couldn't hear the music, but one by one our children started vanishing. People who saw last glimpses of them saw them dancing off into the woods. Even children as old as sixteen were affected. We don't know what to do!"

Connor asked, "Hasn't anyone gone looking for them?"

She nodded. "Yes, of course we have, but to no avail. Men, who had known the forest for years, would end up going in a circle and returning, or end up in a neighboring village that also borders the forest. The Pied Piper has done something to the woods to make it seem as if it is a maze. No one can venture in it! We don't know what to do! We just don't know what to do!"

Tears began to form in Maris' eyes. She excused herself quickly and rushed away from them, leaving behind a pitcher of water,

The five Royals sat, absorbing what the she had told them.

Belle broke the silence. "How can one man do this? It is unconscionable."

Talia said, "I know how, as in what kind of technique. Whoever this Pied Piper is, he's cast a spell of confusion and doubt. It's starting to affect us as well. I wasn't sure until she told us her story, but that definitely confirms it. I'm not sure how he was able to weave so much dark magic, but it would not surprise me that, if we stay here much longer, we will be just as affected by it as these villagers are."

Connor exclaimed, "Wait, you said it's affecting us?"

"If it has not yet, it will eventually."

Philip agreed, "Yes, I have been feeling on edge since we started in on these villages. It is curious why my knight troop did not hear about this. Perhaps news has been slow to spread since this fog."

Jasher looked around. "It is curious, but I've felt not a single thing since we came here other than the general atmosphere of the place."

Belle raised an eyebrow. "It must help to be immune to magic."

Before Jasher could respond, a young man suddenly walked up to the table and pulled out a dagger which he immediately stabbed into the table. At first, it made all them jumped, but then the royals all looked up at him. Connor and Philip both reached for the hilt of the swords while Belle reached for her bow string that was around her chest.

Philip made the first move by standing up and asking, "May we help you, good sir?"

This man stood tall and the ladies were quick to notice his muscular physique. He demanded, "Which one of you made my sister cry? Which one?"

Talia said, "Sir, I don't think you..."

"Hold on," he interrupted. "She's going through enough with my niece vanishing. That took enough of a toll on her. Now, you lot roll in. Which one of you boys got frisky with her, huh? I will not stand for it, I tell you!"

Jasher looked at the young man's wrist. He spotted a familiar bracelet and said, "Prince James of Monokilin. It is you. It must be."

James' eyes widened. "Do I know you?"

Jasher set his sword on the table. "Yes, I believe you do." He partially unsheathed it, revealing his blue blade.

James said, "Wait so...I don't bloody believe it! You five are also royals!"

Connor nodded. "Yes, James, yes we are."

James shook his hand, then Philip's, then Jasher's, then Belle's.

Belle shook it firmly. "Thanks for not hugging."

He replied, "You have a firm handshake. It is refreshing."

Belle turned her head away, so no one could see her blushing, but it was too late, Connor saw and was not pleased by this.

Talia, however, needed a hug. She immediately stood up and gave him a big one. He accepted it awkwardly and he sighed in relief when she finally let go of him. He straightened his shirt.

Jasher said, "Tell us about yourself and your village.

James pulled up a chair. He explained, "I grew up in Oakwood. My adopted parents, the sheriff and his wife, died two years ago. Now I live with my older sister, called Maris, and her husband, the new sheriff Wesley, and their daughter Red, uh, Naurice." He motioned around the tavern. "I work here to help out the family."

James took a moment to pause before continuing. "I'm sorry about my first impression but what is happening here is heart wrenching. I grew up in this village and what happened here, it's almost too much to bare."

Jasher said, "I'm sorry that we've come at such a bad time. I know it was not how you wanted to be rejoined with your fellow royals."

James shook his head. "I'm not leaving. Not until we find the missing children."

Jasher nodded. "I thought you'd say that. That's why we're going to help you."

Surprised, Connor said, "We are?"

Belle could not contain her annoyance. "Didn't you hear what Talia said? We are also being affected by this spell of confusion. We can't just wander into the forest. We'll get lost too. James, here is probably already affected."

James nodded in agreement. "I've tried going in before, but I got lost like everyone else."

Talia agreed, "I hate to say it, but they're right. I can tell that this is a very strong spell. It would take me forever to try to learn how to break it."

Jasher replied, "It is not affecting me. Any direct attack against me will bounce right off. Whatever it is, my immunity is working. That means that this spell is meant to directly affect whoever it touches. We will go into the forest and search for this Pied Piper and the children."

Philip nodded. "Jasher is right. These people need our help and if he can lead us through whatever is causing this, we can do it."

Belle crossed her arms. "Well, I guess that means we are going."

James said, "If you help me catch him, of course I will join you on our quest to restore freedom to Craih."

Jasher declared, "Then let us prepare to enter that corrupted forest."

Chapter 35

Maris stood with the royals outside the entrance to the deepest parts of the forest. "We counted ourselves fortunate that the Orcs do not travel this far. Before the rodents came to the Giving Forest, it was beautiful and full of life, but now it is dank, and no one can seem to go deep inside. Without the sun, it's even more impossible. We cannot even hunt there for the animals seem to be elusive. More than that, it's almost as if they are disappearing. Only the vermin and insects remain. I have never seen so many disgusting creatures."

The royals stood listening to her intently. None had heard of such a thing, besides James, of course, who had barely said a word since they left the tavern.

Connor, who had previously seemed eager for adventure, just stared deep in the woods and kept gulping. Philip stood tall, like any knight would, however his hand stayed clinging to his sword. Talia sweated, and her natural cheeriness seemed forced and shallow. If the others paid attention, they would have noticed that she hadn't mentioned some dessert for some time. James just glared into the forest as if he wanted to conquer the whole forest to himself but did not know how. Belle peered into it. It seemed to go on forever, and for a brief moment, she felt claustrophobic. She could see fog rising, but from what, she had no clue. She found that more worrisome than anything else.

Jasher noticed their ill feelings. He looked at each one of them and raised an eyebrow. Not a word was spoken.

"Is everyone ready?" Jasher asked, breaking the silence.

Philip quickly nodded. "Yes, uh, Captain. We are ready and willing."

Though a most sincere response, Jasher could feel the hesitation emitting off of the prince charming.

"Well," Belle said, "perhaps we will be able to traverse it. I've seen darker woods than this." She said this more for self-assurance than for that of her companions.

James nodded. "I am ready to rescue my niece."

Connor grinned, showing his white teeth. "Have no fear, dear Maris," he said addressing James' sister. "We will find your daughter Naurice, and all of the other children. It's what we do."

Talia stuck her hand through the entrance of the forest. "It feels very strong, whatever it is, but I believe we are ready. There's not much we can do to prepare anyway."

Jasher nodded. "Then let us go."

He stepped in first, and where he stepped, the fog seemed to clear away, but would return when he stepped forward into a new place. It was as if a perfect circle of clarity surrounded him. The others followed, and though they were right behind their leader, it still seemed as if they were stepping into a nightmare.

The fog that permeated it seemed to get denser as they traveled along the trail.

Everyone except Jasher seemed to be disoriented and out of sorts. At several points along the trail, one of them would motion to a different route and want to follow it. Jasher had to point out several times that it was the way home or perhaps to a different village. However, it seemed the deeper they got, the more the others, even Talia, who was normally supportive, seemed to want to turn back or take an alternate route.

Jasher remembered High Priest Tyroane's words about being patient with them. This was definitely testing his patience, but he knew it was the spell of confusion that was making them act this way. It had begun to affect them.

At one point, Belle shouted in frustration, "We are going in circles!"

Jasher replied calmly, "No, Belle, we are not. I have been marking the trees to be sure we are not lost." It was true, he had been using his Bowie knife to mark the trail.

Connor scratched the back of his head. "No, no, no, I agree with Belle! We are lost! Remember what James said about others leaving markers?"

Jasher turned around. "It is not so. Talia, have you found an enchantment to break this spell?"

Talia glared at him. "What? You think just because I know mysticism, that I can just conjure up anything I want? You should've gotten a witch for that! The five rules of magic are: you cannot come back to life, you cannot go back in time, you cannot force someone to love you, you cannot permanently shape shift anyone or anything, and you definitely cannot be all powerful!" Talia's outburst shocked Jasher, who could not muster up the words to respond.

Belle asked, "What does that have to do with anything?"

Talia pointed to Jasher. "He expects me to move mountains!"

Jasher wiped his face in frustration. "Talia, you must understand..."

"I don't think so!" She interrupted.

Philip blurted out, "Hey, you are all using a pretty harsh tone with our leader."

James chimed in, "I just want to find my niece! My life was totally fine until the rest of you rolled in and had me wander into this forest!"

Belle pointed at him, "How dare you! You knew this day would come!"

James bit back, "I did, but I thought I would be ready! Well, I'm not!"

Connor laughed. "I should be the navigator on this one."

Philip raised his voice, "Jasher is our leader! We go where he wills!"

"I'm tired of all this," Belle yelled back. "We should go our separate ways and choose our own path back to our kingdom!"

Jasher kept trying to jump in, but their arguing was making it near impossible. He then suddenly realized that the fog got thicker as they fought.

"That's it," he thought. The fog is being fueled by our frustration, not the other way around. The more agitated we get, the stronger it gets!

He pulled out his blue blade, and he slammed it into the ground. A blue wave came from it and it briefly cleared the fog away. The others stopped fighting during that interruption.

Jasher said, "Listen to each of you. It is true we don't know each other that well anymore, but we are on this mission, so we have work together. Our arguing is what is fueling this fog. We must stand together, or we will rip each other apart. We all have doubts, but we will take them on as a team."

Suddenly, they heard some sort of flute playing in the distance. At the same time, Jasher felt the presence of a space rock. He knew it had to be Rapunzel but unfortunately, she would have to wait. They had to find these children. The others were already affected by the fog and he did not want to give them another reason to argue.

He asked, "Do you hear that flute?"

They all nodded in reply.

Jasher added, "I think we found our Pied Piper."

Chapter 36

The Royals approached a small opening in the forest where it split into a valley of sorts. The music grew louder as they got closer to the high rise.

At that moment, James came to a realization. "This is the Low Peak Valley. It is remarkably easy to find and yet none of the search parties could get to it."

They came to the edge of the forest and looked down into the valley, and there they saw four giant rats at each corner of the valley each of them playing flutes. A large fire blazed in the center of the valley. Around it, there were children, at least two dozen. All of them were dancing in a circle, and to everyone's surprise, the fog that had been creating a confusion spell in the forest and spreading into Oakwood, and possibly other villages, was coming off of them.

Talia exclaimed, "Oh Heavens! It all makes sense."

Belle asked, "What do you mean?"

"Children are by nature afraid of things because everything is new," Talia explained. "The magic flutes or pipes are lifting off those inhibitions, and from that, the Pied Piper is making a fog. The children's own energy creates the spell."

James growled. "That Pied Piper must do this everywhere. He brings the rodents, then chases them away promising a modest bill, then demands more, and then uses his magic to dance the children off. More than likely, he would return to the village demanding ransom, forcing the parents to pay. He's been using this beautiful forest for his hideout. He is a fiend."

Connor patted the hilt of his sword. "That's what we're here for, to fight off fiends. There's only four giant rats, we can take them."

Jasher stepped forward. "James, Connor, you two and I will head down there. Belle give us some cover fire. Talia, you get to children and try to break off this hypnotism. Philip, you make sure Talia gets there safely."

Philip drew his sword. "You got it."

Belle pulled out an arrow and readied her bow. "Finally, some action."

James drew his short sword. "Let's do this."

Jasher turned to Belle. "As soon as we are down in the valley, shoot the rat nearest to us."

Belle nodded. "Got it."

Talia realized, "The spell, it doesn't seem to be affecting us anymore."

Philip nodded. "Perhaps it is because we have thrown off our childish fears."

Jasher agreed, "Yes, faith is a far more powerful tool than fear. Now, let us go!"

Jasher, Connor, and James began to steadily climb down the hill. They saw a bright green tent on the other side that they had not noticed before.

To their surprise, the Pied Piper himself emerged from the tent. He was not what Jasher expected. He stood short, with an almost-skeletal figure, and had long greasy brown hair. He wore a bizarre, round hat, green-colored blouse, yellow trousers, and green shoes. He was a smoking pipe and with each puff, a different smoke was coming.

A fifth giant rat approached him and handed him something.

The Pied Piper said, "What's that? Doamer Town left a note on the edge of the forest? They are ready to give payment to me?" He let out a chuckle. "I'm not surprised. I guess it is time for me to back to Oakwood and make my demands."

Jasher, Connor, and James got down to the bottom of the valley.

Jasher looked up at Belle and nodded. She aimed at the giant rat nearest to them, and fired, hitting it right in the heart.

The other rats turned toward them, squeaked low squeaks of protest, and then rushed at the three men.

Belle took the one nearest to the Pied Piper just to make a statement and the message was received. The Pied Piper took cover.

Talia and Philip slid down into the valley and headed for the children who were still in their hazy dance.

Connor took out a rat with a slice across the stomach, and then a stab in the heart. James' attack came next. He cut off his rat's tale and gave it a quick slice across the neck. Jasher stabbed the Blue Blade into his rat's stomach and then pulled up, slicing through bones and puncturing the lungs.

Talia was observing the kids as they continued to dance though the music had stopped. They were caught up in whatever spell the Pied Piper had placed on them.

The Pied Piper laughed, and mockingly told Talia, "You'll never break this spell, young enchantress! It took me years to sew it!"

Philip drew his sword, standing ready to defend Talia. "You are a foul man!"

Talia ignored them, and it dawned on her, "It's a homemade spell!" She said a silent to a prayer to the Creator, asking for his guidance. She started to whisper, creating an enchantment to unravel the spell. Suddenly, the winds started to pick up, and it began to blow the fog away. Then a vortex came down upon the fire. All were stunned and shocked by what they saw. Suddenly, the vortex just stopped, and the fire was snuffed out.

The Pied Piper was shocked as the children began to come out their haze. Some of them fell to the ground, tired. Some of the younger ones began to cry and were begging to return home. Philip and Talia began the task of comforting them.

Jasher, Belle, Connor, and James approached the Pied Piper with their weapons drawn.

The Pied Piper pulled his flute, but James raised his sword. "Don't even think about it. We've got you surrounded, and your evil spell is broken."

The Pied Piper dropped his flute, but then let out a whistle. They heard a rustling in the trees.

"Did you really think I only had five rodents at my side?"

Suddenly, at least fifty rodents came out from behind his tent and began to surround the five friends. The five gathered in a circle bracing themselves for a fight with an army of giant rats.

The Pied Piper laughed almost manically. "You younglings are great fighters, but I doubt even you all can take on fifty giant rats. Even if you could, you would not risk the safety of the children."

Talia screamed at him, "You wouldn't dare hurt the children!"

The Pied Piper laughed again, this time with a more sinister touch. "You want to take that risk?"

Then they felt something. The winds began to pick up again and they heard a whispering voice in the wind. All of the rats stood at attention, then all turned around and began to leave.

This shocked the Pied Piper. He started whistling again, but this time, they paid him no attention.

Then an even more surprising thing happened as the rats began to shine, and they turned into deer. It took them a moment to realize what had happened, but when they did, they started to frolic into the woods.

This almost brought the Pied Piper to tears when he saw this. "It can't be!" He screamed. "It can't be! No one could've been able to break that spell!"

"I'm sorry, sir, but you are wrong."

They turned around to see a young-looking girl coming out of the woods carrying a heart-shaped staff.

The Pied Piper's jaw dropped. He couldn't believe his eyes. He quickly regained his composure. "The girl of the forest! The girl who commands animals! The one raised by fairies! You're a ghost!"

The girl chuckled when she heard this. "I'm not a ghost or a wisp. I am Rapunzel. I live here in these woods. I've been trying for months to track down the one who had made the fog and caused the deer to vanish. However, that spell of confusion affected me and the fairies as well. Thanks to these six brave souls, I have told the animals who they really are, and sent them back home."

"You are Crown Princess Rapunzel of Osterburg," Jasher observed. "How I've missed you."

Rapunzel looked at him curiously, but then she saw the blue blade. She smiled, and tears filled her eyes. She ran right up to Jasher, and then stopped right in front of him. She hesitantly lifted her hand, and then halted looking at him for permission to continue. He smiled and nodded, she reached up and felt the scar. When she saw it was real, she grabbed Jasher in an embrace.

"At last, my brothers and sisters!" She cried. "I have found you!"

The Pied Piper tried to slip away, but Philip raised his sword. "You aren't going anywhere."

Talia looked around at the deer as they frolicked away. Only the ones they had slain remained dead rats.

Jasher's voice interrupted, "Talia, it is Rapunzel!"

Talia let out a squeal before running to Rapunzel. "Oh Heavens! My dear! How I missed you so much!"

Jasher grasped them and said, "At long last, we are seven."

Chapter 37

Porlem played a sweet song on his stringed instrument as Emperor Midas lay down in his bed at the castle in Grandfire City. When he was sure that his emperor had fallen asleep, Porlem stood up, and went to his own bedroom situated down the hall from his master's bed chamber.

Porlem exhumed loyalty to Midas. He had his misgivings about how Fabius Thorne had sway over him. He did not like Thorne or the work that he did.

He feared that since most of the orcs were overseas at Icester, that they could not handle the Continental Army that had gathered at Craih.

Thorne saw Porlem in his crystal ball. He saw him, and he heard his thoughts. He heard everything from the former Church of Craih at Grandfire. The place that now stood as a tower for him and his servants of the Sorcerer's Society. Eunuchs have such weak wills. He knew that Porlem was the only person who was closer to the emperor than Thorne himself.

The Grand Mage was disgusted by this show of weakness in Midas.

"How long do we have to put up with him?"

The voice came from a scarecrow in the back, the sorcerer known as The Wicker Man. His potato-sack skin, red blazer, trousers, pointed shoes, and straw hat with a scythe sheathed to his back.

Thorne snorted at his question. "Right now, we need Midas' men. We've tried covertly to convert them to vampires or werewolves, but all died rather than become undead. If this were not the case, I would have killed him long ago."

"That does not answer my question." The Wicker Man said this more forcefully.

Thorne fought the urge to swallow nervously. Of all the members of his Inner Circle, he feared the Wicker Man. His power was legendary as well as his cunning. He was a psychopath, who would kill for fun and one of the few that even killed women and children.

Right now, Thorne was confident in the fact that he was more powerful, but he would have to stay vigilant in case a day came when that changed.

Fabius turned to answer his question. "Once the Seven Royals are captured and executed, we will have no more use for him. Craih will be broken and we will have won."

The Wicker Man asked, "What do you intend to do?"

Thorne laughed. "I will dress Jasher in his father's armor, not the cliché of stripping him down, I want him prim and proper."

"Why not execute him, naked, with his own sword?"

Fabius waved this off. "No. I want them to see us kill him looking strong. This way, they can see that we will win when they are at their full strength."

The Wicker Man picked up the crystal ball. "They seem to be eluding us. Our mirror spells, crystal ball, and diviners have not been able to find them. How is this possible?"

Thorne stared at it. "The world is too big. We cannot just snap our fingers and find them. However, I am concerned. Omri will find them. He knows Jasher. Probably better than anyone."

The Seven Royals brought the kidnapped children to Oakwood and sent word to all of the villages, and parents were flocking there. With the spell broken, the villagers living in the Giving Forest returned to normal. As they watched their children return, there were tears and cries of joy as the families were all reunited.

James watched with a smile on his face as Naurice was returned to his adopted sister Maris. The three of them embraced. He held them tight, but he fought back tears, knowing that he would have to leave them in the morning.

The Pied Piper wept as Philip threw into a prison wagon.

"Stop your crying. You bring shame to yourself," Philip said with disgust. "Have some dignity if that's possible for you."

"You'll never find the loot," the Piper said through snot.

"We already found it in your little camp," Philip replied. "You aren't very good at hiding without magic." He slammed the wagon door shut.

Belle and Talia was standing several feet behind them.

Talia said, "Isn't he a prince charming?"

Belle looked over at Connor, who was sharpening his saber.

"He is handsome, if you're into that."

That night, the villagers threw a feast with dancing and music to celebrate the return of the children.

Connor danced with Belle and Jasher noticed how close they held each other.

Encouraged by all of this, Philip walked up to Talia. He said, "It would be my honor if you danced with me, my dear."

Talia took his hand. "A prince charming and knight wishes to dance with me? How could I refuse that?"

The two of them began to dance. They danced so beautifully, and their eyes stayed locked the whole time. They were in sync and their hearts beat faster and faster as they danced.

When the song ended, they realized everyone stared, watching them. The crowd gave them an applause, a happy one. Both Philip and Talia blushed.

Unbeknownst to both of them, each was feeling a slight touch of admiration in their dance. They soon began another dance, their smiles even broader.

Jasher watched with a smile on his face. James walked up to him.

"My Captain, thank you for helping me. I have not seen the village this happy since the days of the smoke cloud."

Jasher smiled. "You and your village are welcome, Brave Woodsman."

James grunted. "I see you've been talking to my niece. She started calling me that after I rescued her and my adopted grandma from a wolf."

"I'm sure it's a worthy name." Jasher smirked.

James said, "Sir, I am prepared to go with you, but allow me to spend one last night here with my adopted family. Let me read my niece a story and tuck her in. I swear I will leave with you in the morning."

Jasher nodded. "This is acceptable."

"Thank you, sir." James nodded in appreciation. "It is good to see you again."

He started to walk away and then stopped. "Strange."

"What is, Prince James?"

"To my knowledge, no one has soon you outdoors at night." Then he kept walking.

Jasher felt a twinge of guilt as he looked upon the sky. The cloud blocked out the moonlight, shielding him from the strange glowing ability.

He spotted Rapunzel sitting by herself. She sat, enjoying some juice, and though alone, she seemed to be having a good time just observing.

Jasher approached her, and she shifted nervously when he approached, but relaxed when she realized it to be him.

"Oh, Captain, what can I do for you?"

"I was just wondering, where have you been all of these ten years."

"Oh, well, here in the forest. I was raised by the fairies here."

"That spell, where you turned the cursed animals back into their true form. I see they taught you their magic."

"I've always had this gift for animal whispering and magic. I'm told I'm a prodigy. I just sort of knew how to do it, my Lord."

Jasher laughed. "Oh, Rapunzel, I am no lord to you. It is true I am your captain and if you wish, you may call me that, but otherwise I am just Jasher."

Rapunzel blushed as she smiled. "Okay."

Jasher motioned to the party before them. "Would you care to dance?"

Rapunzel shook her head. "Oh no, but if you would care to, I would really like to talk with you some more. I have missed you so."

"I would like that as well."

Chapter 38

James his niece a hug as the other Royals waited for him at the edge of the village.

She cried, "Why do you have to go," as she clutched his giant chest.

"Because, Red," he replied. "I have to save you. No more fear of Orcs or wolves in the forests. It'll be sunlight and joy."

She released him, still wiping away tears as she backed away.

Maurice gave him a hug. "We knew this day would come. Go save Craih. Go save us."

"I do this for you," he said. "I can't promise what will happen to me personally, but I know my friends and I will do whatever it takes to show you the sun."

He released his sister and slowly climbed onto the horse the village had provided him. He followed the others as they entered the Giving Forest on their own borrowed horses.

James took one last look at the village of Oakwood. He waved to them and then turned forward. In the moment, he felt an overwhelming sense of loneliness as he rode with the others. To him, they were all strangers and the village was what he had known as his family. However, he had taken an oath and he would not run from his responsibility.

After about an hour of riding, the Seven Royals stopped along the road briefly for a rest beside a stream where they ate and drank in silence until Belle finally said, "Where do we head from here?"

Jasher thought for a moment. "Should we stay within the Giving Forest until we find a resistance troop?"

Philip shook his head. "Before I left, my captain told me that my order was headed away from the forest to assist another group. They were the last ones in this area."

Belle said, "If that is true, we could go through the Shadow Marsh."

Jasher scratched his head in thought. "I do not believe I've heard of it."

James explained, "It is not a natural marsh. It was created by the dark mage known as the Wicker Man. He created an environmental barrier to keep out invaders from other lands. That is how this side of the Giving Forest survives with minimal raids."

"Has anyone tried?" The Dragon Prince remained unconvinced.

Connor sighed heavily. "We'd be the first."

Philip said, "It be a dangerous crossing. They say a great evil lies in the Shadow Marsh."

"Are you sure it is safe?" The question came from Rapunzel. "Could we go around it?"

Belle said, "We could, but it would take at least a week."

Jasher asked, "Going through the Shadow Marsh, won't that put us close to Revenant?"

Talia nodded. "The dark army took it weeks ago. They put a second smoke factory there, but it is not as developed, and the smoke is spreading much more slowly.

The Dragon Prince was not convinced. "That is risky. Is it worth it to take a chance on capture to spare us a few miles of travel?"

"They are fighting a war, not looking for seven traveling companions," said Belle. "Breezing past

Revenant is the last thing they will expect."

Jasher finally got frustrated and motioned to the sky. "Look up! What do you see?"

At first, no one answered awkwardly, but finally, Rapunzel said, "Uh clouds?"

Jasher said, "Yes! We have all been able to see the sun, not our people. That is how the vampires and orcs were able to invade our land in the broad daylight and overwhelm our kingdoms' forces. As long as we travel closer to that cloud, we move closer and closer to danger."

Talia agreed, "Jasher is right. We should head East and perhaps to find a ship to come in along the coast. It's closer now, anyway. Let's gain ground, not lose it."

Belle said, "Sir, I must protest. We have all been a part of this fight for ten years, well except for Talia."

Talia shouted, "Hey!"

Belle interrupted her. "Connor and I were at sea. Philip was with a knight squad. James and Rapunzel were in the forest protecting what they could. You were at some all-girls school and Jasher was asleep."

Jasher needed to put a stop to this. "Belle, your point is well taken, but the insults are unnecessary. Do you really think this is the best way?"

Belle said firmly. "Yes."

Jasher pointed to the others. "And the rest of you agree?"

James, Philip, Connor, and even Rapunzel all nodded in agreement.

Jasher said, "Then to the Shadow Marsh it is."

Omri wandered into a tavern where there was a lot of jolly drinking songs ringing through the establishment. He stood taller than any man in the room, but most people did not notice him because they were so drunk. He took a barstool at the edge of the bar, closest to the door.

The bartender walked over to him. "What can I get you?"

Omri licked his lips. "I'll have your finest wine." He then set a bag of gold on the bar.

The bartender picked up the bag greedily. "Is that all?"

"I'm looking for seven individuals. They are of interest to me. They are in their late teens, still children, and being led by a man in his late twenties. He carries a blue sword."

The bartender shrugged. "I know of seven individuals. The story goes that they were two, then four, then five, and now seven. One of them carries a blue sword named Alilth."

Omri chuckled. "So, the sword has tasted battle."

"What?" This confounded the barkeep.

"Never mind, please continue." Omri smirked.

The bartender just shrugged and explained, "The rumor is, they defeated the Pied Piper in the Giving Forest and broke his spell over the place. However, they are all children. Their leader is no older than any of them."

This interested Omri. "I see. So, they are all children?"

The bartender nodded. "Are you a bit deaf? That's what I said. However, they fight like seasoned warriors. It is said two were pirates, one a knight, two mystics, one a fighter, and their leader, they say he woke up from a deep sleep and slew a wolf pack. I would not oppose them." He set down the wine bottle and the glass of wine and then walked away.

Omri started to laugh to himself. So, he thought. *"The so-called 'Jasher' is nothing more than a child that is good with a sword. He's a fake and fraud. Jasher, more than likely, must've died or ran away a long time ago. The other six got this imposter and gave him the blue sword just to generate some gossip and give hope to the Continental Army on Craih. So be it! Once my predators and I find the seven royals, we will put an end to them."*

With that, he crushed the glass in his hand, yet his flesh did not bleed.

Chapter 39

The Seven Royals came to the edge of the Shadow Marsh.

Jasher drew his weapon, prompting the others to do the same. He took a step into the mud and saw he sank to his ankles.

He turned to face Rapunzel and motioned to her hair which he realized had gotten even longer. "Your beautiful hair might get caught in the mud."

Rapunzel closed her eyes and clenched her fists. The others looked on in amazement as her hair began to glow and it started to weave and tie itself into a braid that came down to her to the middle of her back.

When it was done, her hair ceased its glow and she relaxed, breathing out.

Jasher nodded with approval. "That'll do it."

He heard a snap in the trees. It would have gone unnoticed by anyone else, but it was just loud enough that it gave Jasher pause. He looked into the tops of the trees, but he saw nothing.

Belle asked, "Anything wrong, Captain?"

Jasher shook his head. "I don't think so. Is everyone ready?"

Everyone gave an acknowledgment as they headed into the swamp. He said, "Belle, you and Philip take point. I will cover the rear."

Philip started to chop vines away. "Aye, sir."

They heard a yelp and saw that Philip had fallen into some water.

Talia screamed, "Philip! Philip, are you okay?"

They all gathered around the edge of the pool.

Connor asked, "Come on, friend, show us a sign!"

Philip stood up and spit out the swampy water. He was in about waist high. "Yes, yes, I'm okay, though now I'll definitely need a bath. Whatever is in this is gross. The dark army did not waste any spells of yuck."

Rapunzel said, "I've never heard of such magic."

James replied, "I think it was a joke."

He reached in and helped pull him out the pond.

"Thanks," Philip said as he sat on the edge. "Is there some place dry where I can empty my boots?"

Belle raised an eyebrow. "We're in a swamp."

Talia pointed. "Wait, look over at that hill. It has caves in it. Maybe it is dry on the inside."

They turned to what appeared to be a hill, though it looked more like a giant dried mud-hill. It had many holes in it that led into tunnels.

Jasher nodded. "Let's look at it, but not wander too deep inside."

He headed toward it and the others followed.

Philip sat on the ground and started to dig mud out of his pockets and water out of his boots. "This is not what I had in mind when I became a knight."

Rapunzel suddenly sensed something. It was a voice, no several voices. At first, she thought it was a pack of animal, but then it grew to a hazy sound and she had to block it out. "Everyone, something's not right," she warned. "We're not alone in this hill. There are creatures here, but none like I've ever felt before."

James drew his sword. "Are they hungry?"

Philip had hastened to put his boots and tunic back on. He stood up and drew his sword.

Jasher saw something glowing in the darkness. He started to approach it and looked down at it. It was round, gel-like, and moving.

The others came up behind him.

Connor started to gag. "What is that?"

Rapunzel touched it gently. "It's an egg."

Connor repeated, "An egg?"

Jasher looked up and saw the tunnel. "Yes, it is an egg, and this isn't a cave."

"What is it then?" The question came from Philip.

"It's a mound." Jasher reached for his sword to prepare for what was coming next.

Suddenly, the ground started to crack beneath them and though they tried to scatter, the ground fell apart and they slid down a deep dark tunnel. It seemed to go on and on, but it finally ejected them into a large room where they landed hard on the floor.

Jasher grunted. He was sore, but uninjured. He called out, "Is everyone okay?"

James looked up. "If we are, we won't be for long."

They all looked up to discovered they were surrounded by ants, but not just any ants. These ants were as large as a person. They had large eyes and hard shells. Saliva dripped from their chompers as they hissed and screeched at the Seven Royals.

"Rapunzel, can you do something," Jasher asked.

Rapunzel focused on them as hard as she could, but she was met with a screeching reply in her mind's eye that forced her to take steps backward.

"No," she shouted back. "They're not thinking individually. They're all connected to a central mind or something. I can't access it without their queen."

Connor drew his sword. "Something tells me that is where they want to bring us, but I have a feeling we'll be covered in a sauce."

"Maintain some a circular formation. If they manage to separate us, we'll be picked off," Jasher ordered.

Belle looked around and spotted a hole. "Everyone, I found an escape route. It's right in front of me!"

The ants screeched and howled even louder and began to move forward.

Jasher followed that up with, "Okay, we have our goal. Belle will take the lead. Remember, no one gets left behind. We move when she says."

"They're getting ready to lunge," Philip called out.

Belle told them, "Slide under their legs on the count of three. One..."

The ants were almost on them.

"Two..."

The ants charged forward.

"Three!"

The seven royals got running starts and dropped down, each slip under an ant just in time to get behind them.

One jumped in front of Jasher who slashed its head with the blue blade. It cracked through the shell and the ant backed away screeching.

They managed to enter the tunnel with the ants in hot pursuit veering toward a light, but ants came out of the ground to stop them.

Philip, Talia, James, Connor, and Belle struck at the ants, but their swords could not pierce through the armor. Jasher swung and cracked one ant in the jaw with the blue blade.

Philip said, "Our blades won't pierce their armor!"

James called, "There's an empty tunnel this way."

He led the way as they jumped, dodged, and avoided as more ants kept coming up from the ground.

Connor jumped to avoid one coming up from below him. "They're popping out of the ground like weeds!"

They ran into a large domed room, but it was a dead end. They could hear the ants coming from the cavern.

Belle demanded, "What do we do now? We're trapped, and our swords can't pierce their outer shells. Even if Alilth is at least cracking, we can't do it with just one sword."

Connor looked behind them and noticed water leaking from it. "Hey! Check this out!"

Philip asked, "What's he on about now?"

Jasher walked up to the wall and felt it. He said, "This barrier is different. It's sealing something. The mud is packed with grass, hay, and sticks."

"It's not a wall, Jasher," exclaimed Talia. "It's a dam!"

Jasher stabbed a hole into it and water started to pour out of the hole.

"Everyone can swim, right?"

Rapunzel asked, "Captain, what are you planning?"

"If they dammed up the water, then it might be a weakness."

The ants started to run into the room and began to surround the Seven Royals. They increased their screeching and smacking.

"Everyone," he said. "Line up along the wall. We are going to slide again. Get ready."

The ants braced and then charged forward.

"Now!"

The Seven Royals dove, and the ants crashed into the dam. The impact caused the dam to start to crack and water started blasting out. The ants began to screech and holler even worse than before.

Jasher stood up and helped Rapunzel stand. "Let's get out of here!"

The Seven Royal took off just as the dam collapsed. Water began to flood into the chamber and the ants were doing their best scatter, but the water was overtaking them.

The Seven Royals were barely staying ahead of it. They backtracked through the tunnels and saw the exit tunnel. They dashed for it faster, but soon the water caught up with them.

It ejected them outside the mound and sent then landing onto the hard guard. They all laid still for a few minutes. Soaking wet and now in the humid air. No one said a thing, not even a grunt.

Chapter 40

Jasher woke up first and tried to stand, but every muscle in his body was aching. He forced himself to at least get on his knees. "Say something, anyone."

"What... what was that?" The comment came from Connor.

One by one they slowly started to stand up. Every single one of them were moaning from the pain.

Talia said, "Oh Heavens! Almost drowning can make a girl hungry."

Jasher stood up and began to wipe off the mud. "That was a waste of time."

Belle raised an eyebrow. "Are you serious? We're still closer to our destination."

Jasher pointed back to the mound. "How does that make any sense? We all almost died!"

"But we didn't", Belle replied. "Look you can see the smoke coming from Revenant and where it ends." She pointed to a large smoke plum in the sky and a sunlit horizon.

Jasher turned to the others. "Everyone, we must take a different path out of this swamp."

Belle's eyes narrowed. "Jasher, again I must protest. I think we should stay on this course."

Jasher sighed. He remembered High Priest Tyroane's words about having to be patient with his fellow royals, but that had become a chore.

"Look," he replied sharply, "I understand your logic, but once again, I must repeat that we would be heading towards our enemies, not away from them. This is not a good plan. We should continue to search for Continental Army insurgents, especially knowing there are bounty hunters and wolf packs out there looking for us. When I awoke in the Kurve, I was attacked by an Alpha. He was in the Kurve. The Kurve!" This made his fellow royals uneasy. "Don't you see? Not even pirates dare go into the Kurve, but Midas and his foul creatures will."

Connor shrugged. "We are strong."

Jasher raised an eyebrow, ready to respond, but James cut in first, "I understand what you are saying Jasher, but I have to agree with Belle and Connor. I believe it will be swift and silent."

Talia shook her head. "Oh Heavens, Jasher is right. Philip, what do you think?"

Philip gave a small smile. It pleased Philip that she had asked him. "It matters not what we think. He is our leader and we should obey his command. The men who risked their lives so that we might live gave us these instructions. Jasher is our leader and I intend to follow him."

Connor spoke up. "Perhaps we should put it to a vote."

Belle exclaimed, "That is an excellent idea! All of those in favor of staying in the swamp, put up your hands."

Belle, Connor, Rapunzel, and James all put up their hands. It was a four to three victory for that part of the group.

"I guess that settles it," Belle said, satisfied.

Jasher stood up and faced her. "No, it most certainly does not."

Belle glared at him, but Jasher just glared right back.

"Listen, Captain," she said with much contempt. "You don't know this to fight for is about. Some of us wanted to stay here and move on with our own lives, but we came. Why? Because we saw the suffering. You haven't."

"Look here," he said. "I am the Captain and do not think I have not seen battle. I will make these calls. It is not up for a vote. We are not a committee and certainly not a senate. There isn't time for that. Right now, we're soldiers, and we're heading into battle. We have to return home and aid our countrymen. I was placed in command. If you do not like it, that is insubordination."

Belle's face reddened. "We just voted," she repeated.

"Enough!" The scream came from Rapunzel, chilling everyone to the bone. No one had heard her say anything above normal volume, so it stunned everyone.

"It's my turn to speak," she said.

Belle started to interrupt, but James stepped in. "You had your turn. Now it is hers." he said. When he had heard her, there was something about that moment that made him respect her more. She was a quiet soul but had every right to say something.

Rapunzel thanked James with a smile that made him blush.

"Jasher is the leader and yes, I voted against him, but I wish I hadn't. Despite what you think, he has to decide. That's the only thing there is to it. Right now, wolf packs could be converging on us as we speak. Or worse, some nameless, faceless enemy we know nothing about is heading our way. We all may have had some hand in this fight, but Jasher fought enemies long before any of us. We must trust him. I know I do."

For a moment, the other six all stood silently, not knowing what to say.

Finally, Connor said, "She is right. We are wasting time here. Jasher, I..." before he could finish, a dart hit his neck. After a few seconds, he fell to the ground.

Belle was hit next. She gave a cry of pain as she fell to the ground. One by one, they were each hit, until they collapsed to the ground, not unconscious, but unable to move.

Jasher was the last one to get hit. He still managed to draw his sword and he looked around as he collapsed. The last thing he could make out was the smiling face of a werewolf.

A messenger hawk landed on Omri's arm as he rode on a giant boar. He removed the contents and read the message. He gave a sinister smile and looked up in the horizon where he could see Revenant.

"Well, well, it seems our journey is cut short, my friend," he said to the boar. "A wolf pack captured our seven targets and are taking them to Revenant."

The boar just grunted in response, almost as if he was disagreeing.

Omri laughed. "This will be my shining moment. I will have the six little brats and the imposter as Jasher's head on a pike and parade them around every city in Craih."

"That will break the spirit of the Continental Army," he continued. "Without the hope of the seven royals, their resistance fighters will fall like dominoes."

Chapter 41

Snow had nightmares of Jasher and his friends captured by a pack of werewolves. Though her mind told her it was just a dream, she knew in her heart that is actually happened. She could hear the throaty growls of the wolves, smell the stench of their fur, and see their slobbery fangs.

She sat up in her bed, finally awake, weeping from those horrible images. She remembered doing battle against werewolves in her days as an apprentice. Nothing could match their savagery.

"Oh, Jasher," she said aloud. "My love, you said you would return to me, but I have to know if you're alright."

Sighing deeply, she sat up in bed and walked to the window when an idea suddenly came to her.

"Mother's magic mirror," she said.

Not taking time to light a candle, she ran to her wardrobe and began to dress as quickly as the dark would allow. At once, she dashed through the dark until she came to her mother's dressing room. She opened the door to find it vacant.

She ran up to the mirror and to her surprise, she found it completely shattered.

Snow could not contain her shock and gasped in horror.

"Daughter, what are you doing here?" The voice came from behind her.

Snow turned around to see her mother standing in the doorway.

"Mother, what have you done? Father gave this to you before he died."

Queen Rhodesia's grew angry when she heard this. "It was my mirror and I chose to do with it as I please. Again, what are you doing here?"

"Prince Jasher is in trouble," Snow replied. "I can see it in my dreams. I must go to him."

Her matron shook her head. "That is an unwise thing to do."

"Why do you say that? I love him."

Queen Rhodesia walked up to her and slapped her daughter so hard it left a bruise on her face.

"Foolish girl," she said. "Love? Love? What do you see in that boy?"

Snow could not believe her mother's outburst. "Mom, why did strike me? I don't... I don't understand. I tried to pretend, but it is obvious. You have been harsh with me lately. Why? Ever since father died, you... you...."

"Quit your stammering, child," Queen Rhodesia ordered. "Your father could not see the big picture. I could! Your beloved is dangerous! Don't you realize that the dark army has seized Revenant! They are merely days away from our borders. If Jasher and Talia had not left earlier, I would have turned them over."

Tears streamed down Snow's face. "What? Why? Craih and Teysha have always been our allies."

Her mother screamed. "Shut up! You're just like your father! He was fairer than me! Why? You are fairer than me! Why? I don't understand why the mirror told me that!"

Snow swallowed hard. "Mother what are you talking about?"

Queen Rhodesia started laughing uncontrollably. "Your father," she said. "He gave me that mirror when I expressed an interest in exploring my magical abilities. Then one day, I asked, it who was the fairest of them all. It told me your father. Over and over again. I tried, I tried so hard to make myself more and more beautiful, but the mirror always said your father."

Snow interrupted, "Mother, that's not what the mirror is for. It's for seeing things and..." That was when she came to a realization. "Mother, what did you do?"

Queen Rhodesia drew her dagger, showing the apple on the scabbard. "I could not stand it. I wanted it to say I was the fairest, but it never did! I could not live with the bitterness, the pain, so I fed him that apple. The one with poison."

Snow screamed. "What! You did what?" She took a step forward, but suddenly, the drapes on the window came to life, wrapping her arms and legs, not allowing her to move.

Queen Rhodesia shook her head. "After your father died, it just told me you. You! You! You! No matter what I did! The mirror told me you!"

Her mother started to walk toward her. "This dagger is dipped in the apple poison. It'll just take a quick slice. After that, I'll use my magic to hurl you out a window. No one will think to look for poison. Everyone will assume that you flung yourself out the window after hearing of Jasher's capture."

"Capture? Mother, where is he?"

Queen Rhodesia laughed again. "He's been taken to Revenant where he will die!"

Snow struggled, but she could not move. Her mother moved closer and closer.

"Mother," she pleaded. "Please don't do this! The mirror, it was showing the hearts. Dad's heart was pure. It had nothing to do with outer beauty! If you kill me, you will never come back."

"Silence!" The Queen lifted her dagger, prepared to slice her daughter, but before she could, she lurched forward. She turned around, revealing to Snow that she had an arrow in her back.

Snow looked at the entrance and saw the Huntsman, and a crowd of servants who had gathered after hearing the screaming.

Queen Rhodesia yelled, "You won't stop me! I shall be the fairest!"

She tried to turn around, but the Huntsman fired a second arrow, this time, piercing her heart.

Queen Rhodesia fell to the floor, her face twisted in rage, her hand still clutching the apple adorned knife.

The drapes returned to normal, allowing Snow to drop to the floor. She ran to her mother and cried as she heard the servants whispering about the queen trying to murder her own daughter.

The Huntsman approached cautiously. "I'm sorry. I wish I could have stopped this. Like you, I tried to see the good that use to be in her, but I ignored the bad."

Snow kissed her mother, closing her eyes before standing up. She dusted herself off and wiped her face, realizing that now she was free. Ezri was saddened by her mother's death, but knowing the truth, it had made her more determined to find Jasher.

The servants began kneeling. One called out, "All hail the queen!"

"No," she commanded, stopping their bowing. "I abdicate my throne."

They all stood frozen. "But, your highness..." one stammered.

She lifted her hand. "I, Ezri Snow, daughter of the King and Queen Snow, hereby resign my right to the throne and pass it to none other than my mother's consort."

Snow turned to her savior. "The Huntsman."

"Me," he said with surprise.

"Yes, they should not be ruled by the daughter of the woman who tried to betray them, but by the man who saved them," she answered.

Snow took one last look at her mother, lying there on the ground, face contorted, then she saw something. Her mother's wand. Snow did not know much in the ways of magic, but she did remember one enchantment that her father told her about. She picked up the wand and broke it in half, whispering a plea for her mother. Energy came from the enchanted wood, surrounding her mother, until she disappeared in a swirl of light, leaving only the crown behind.

"Goodbye, mother," she said.

She looked up at the Huntsman. "Take care of the people of Maxia."

The Huntsman said, "I swear it."

Snow nodded. "Then there is a duty I must fulfill. One to my heart."

Chapter 42

Jasher was the first wake up from the poison. He found himself unable to move. He was in a small cell with bars at the door. He looked around and saw that the others in cells right across from him.

A Beta werewolf walked up to the cell door and growled at him, but Jasher showed him no fear. The werewolf sneered. "My cousin was Alpha pack that was sent to the island in the Spine."

Jasher chuckled as he said, "Then he died a foolish and needless death. Just like you."

The werewolf tried to slash him, but Jasher avoided it by leaning back.

A larger werewolf, presumably the new Alpha, yelled out from the entrance of the cell block. "That's enough! There'll be plenty of time for that when Omri returns to bring them to Craih."

The first werewolf grunted his obedience, and then turned to Jasher, "When we get there, you'll wish you had never been born."

Jasher rolled his eyes. "Who is Omri?"

The Beta grunted. "Overlord Omri is King Midas' adopted son, appointed as the ruler of Teysha. He is also Fabius Thorne's apprentice. He is very large, and one of the most powerful sorcerers in all of Craih and Icester put together, almost rivaling Thorne and the Wicker Man. You do not stand a chance."

"Why do you say that?" Jasher asked.

The Beta laughed. "For one thing, we've taken your sword and hid it in the vault." He smiled wickedly as he added, "Did I mention Omri killed Aikin and Abigail?"

Jasher clenched his fists. He had known of their passing, but not in the manner in which they were killed.

The werewolf laughed as he turned away. "You think you can take him. You'd have better chance of challenging the Creator, if He actually existed."

166

Fabius Thorne meditated in his room. He was a man of simplicity. His large room was round and painted completely black, even the wooden floors. In the center of his room sat the crystal ball. In the north part was a bed with a table beside it. That constituted all the furniture in the room. He had no use for anything else. Attachment and love was a weakness, and it was one that he would not allow to creep into his heart.

He remembered that his mother, who was a very powerful witch, had wanted to dethrone the former leader of the Sorcerer's Society and make herself Grand Mage. She had taught Fabius everything he needed to know about the dark arts and he was pleased for that. He heard the tale of how he destroyed a whole village to become Grand Mage. Of course, that was only a half truth.

He remembered.

The snow came down, covering the village. The then-Grand Mage, a large, oily man, who wore black robes, and a pentagram around his neck. He was completely hairless, and his skin looked as if it had been burned. He had a wand that he used to fight off Fabius and his mother. He cursed as he shouted all manners of spells.

Mother Thorne, as she came to be known in the society, was a beauty to behold, but a terror to know. She was tall, curvy, wore black boots, stockings, a skirt, black blouse, but had long waving blonde hair. Her eyes were red like fire.

Fabius remembered how he gave back-up to his mother and at last, they descended onto the former Grand Mage. His mother and he were weakened as they both blasted him with lightning, causing him to disintegrate into ash.

His mother stared down at the pile of ash and declared, "Now, my son, we shall take our place and rule the Sorcerer's Society together as..."

He shot his mother with lightning while her back was turned. As she turned around again, he struck her again and again.

She looked up and howled. "Fabius, why? I have taught you everything! I could give you everything!"

Fabius smiled wretchedly. "Why would I want you to give me everything, when I can take it for myself? Goodbye, mother. Thank you for giving me this power. Now I am Grand Mage."

With that, he struck her once more, and she, too, turned to ash.

Fabius was smiling as he glared into the crystal ball, returning to the present. A strong sense of self confidence rose up within him as he remembered.

Omri's face appeared in the orb, interrupting his prideful thoughts. "Forgive me, master, if I have disturbed you."

Though he was slightly annoyed, Fabius shook his head. "Not at all, my apprentice. Please, give me the news."

Omri licked his lips. "We have them, my lord. They have been captured and taken to Revenant. We just received word from the Alpha there. I am approaching quickly."

Fabius let out a laugh. "Excellent! I need not their bodies, so just bring me their heads, but most importantly, bring me the blue blade."

Omri explained, "Apparently, master, it has tasted battle. It is called Alilth now."

Fabius waved this off. He repeated the order, "Bring their heads and that sword here. I will parade their heads on pikes around Craih to show the Continental Army that they have no chance of winning against our might and our power."

Omri bowed his head. "It shall be done, my lord."

His face disappeared from the glow.

Fabius admired himself in the reflection of the crystal ball once again. However, it suddenly changed. Fabius paid close attention in case it was trying to show him something. It began to show him the past, present, and the future.

It started out showing him the beginnings of his rise. Never before had a Grand Mage had performed such a feat. In one day, he turned Midas' heart black and against his neighbors on Craih. Of course, Fabius had him do nothing that he did not want to already. All Midas needed was an army that could overwhelm Craih in an instant. Despite the ability to conquer Craih within just a few short days, the plan to make a home for his brethren had taken years. Sure, his own brethren in the Sorcerer's Society were eager to join forces with him, but it was other manner of foul creatures that he had to convince. It was tough, but he had persuaded the Orcs, Werewolves, Trolls, and several armies of witches to his side.

It showed him Midas in his throne room, once again weeping over the golden statue of his beloved wife. He would soon outlive his purpose, and Fabius Thorne would become the first ever Grand Mage to become an emperor. For now, he needed Midas to be a mascot to the soldiers of Gorasyum, as many had already begun to defect to the Continental Army. The only reason the others were still present was because they were loyal to Midas. For now, he needed a more human touch.

Suddenly, the image within the crystal ball changed completely. It seemed to fill with a black smoke that began to leak into his chambers.

"Well," he whispered. "It appears to be showing me the fires of our armies."

Fabius watched with awe as it overtook everything in the room, and then it turned normal once again.

Fabius laughed at this image. He picked up the crystal ball as he said, "I have seen my future. I shall soon be the one true emperor here on Craih, Icester, and then all over Paraina! I will make things turn to gold, not Midas."

Snow rode her horse hard and fast. She could feel that something was wrong. Jasher and the others were in danger. They had been gone a few days now, but since she knew they were at Revenant. Her only hope was taking shortcuts and hidden routes through the forests to catch up.

Chapter 43

The other Royals began to stir, and they soon began to rise in their cells.

"Where, where are we?" Rapunzel asked as she scooted close to James and hugged her knees to her chest.

Jasher said, "We're in a prison here in the once glorious city of Revenant."

"We've only known it at as under siege." Philip punched the cell only to shake his hand.

"Revenant," Jasher explained. "It was a city of education and wisdom, has been utterly ruined. The forest is burned to the ground. This castle we are in, it had no prison. The castle's once beautiful stone walls are now littered with burn marks and covered in broken arrows. A tower, once a lookout, stands in the corner as a beacon for weary travelers, but now, it pumps the foul smoke into the sky, covering the light of the sun, moon, and stars."

"What do we now, Jasher?" Rapunzel asked.

Jasher let out a sigh. "I don't know."

Belle let out a frustrated grunt. "That's not surprising."

Jasher had had enough. He turned to Belle. "Look here, if we had just gone with my plan—"

Belle's face lit up with anger. "Oh, ho, now it's my fault?"

Philip chimed in, "We should've followed orders."

"Wait a minute!" Connor interrupted, "That's not fair!"

James agreed, "Yeah, these werewolves caught us off guard."

Rapunzel tried to be diplomatic. "Yes, it was nobody's fault."

Belle pointed a finger at Jasher. "I don't know why you were chosen to be the leader. You obviously couldn't lead a horse to water! James, Philip, Connor, and even Rapunzel, we've been fighting this war for years. You've been asleep, and Talia has been at some school!"

Talia grunted. "Not this again."

Jasher replied to Belle, "I grow weary of your whining. It's obvious that you don't want to be one of us. Why don't you just go back to your village!"

Belle said, "My village was destroyed!"

Connor touched her shoulder, "Belle..."

She pulled away, causing his hand to drop. "I was raised in a village that offered no resistance to the dark army. Only one man stood up to them. The Duke of the region, who had been cursed by a witch and forced to take the form a great beast. The villagers rejected his call to arms, except for me. I moved into his castle with other members of the Continental Army. We fought the dark army in glorious battles, until a spy sent word, one of my step-sisters. They razed the castle, killing the Duke, and turning everyone into the village into the undead. I barely escaped thanks to the Duke. If I hadn't found Connor..." She grabbed his hand.

She turned back to Jasher, "I could still be fighting with him at sea! I was there! Where were you? Where were you?"

"Asleep!" Jasher shouted in response. He sighed and quieted before saying, "I was forced into a sleep and told to lead you all. I did not want to leave you. Upon awaking, I heard of our family's death and now I know who killed my brother and sister I should not have been gone, but I am here now. About the lost years, all I can say is, I'm sorry."

Belle weighed his words for a moment. She saw every rude word, every insult, every sign of disrespect she had brought on her the Royals, her only friends. It was here she realized the error of her ways. Jasher could not have helped in matters he knew nothing about. She realized her anger was not at the Dragon Prince, but herself, who survived while her friends died.

"No, I'm sorry." Belle's words shocked them. "I tried to blame you, Captain, but you, you are different. Not because you were away, but because we were able to move on, but to you, this happened mere days ago. I was unfair to you. Forgive me."

Jasher stood and approached the cell door. He called to them in the other cells. "Belle look at me! Look at me!"

She finally looked up to him.

"There is nothing to forgive," he said. For the first time, Belle had tears in her eyes.

"You are not the only one who had hesitation in joining," Philip said. "I did as well. Captain Makeda told me the truth about my hidden truth two years ago, knowing that the time was approaching. I felt conflicted, so I ran deep in the woods of a haunted forest without thinking. My adopted sister, Gretal, a fellow squire, followed me in and we found ourselves captured by a witch in a gingerbread house. She did not know, or she would have turned me in, instead, she prepared to eat me. Gretal managed to break out and freed me, but at the cost of her life. I slayed the witch, but it was too late, Gretal lay dying in my arms. My sister is the one who encouraged me to not run in her final moments."

He looked at Talia, seated next to him in his cell. "I listened to her and I'm glad I did. I fight for her memory and to save Craih."

"You know all of my tales and all about me," Jasher said. "I would tell all of my stories at all of our birthday parties. However, there is one tale

Philip pointed out. "The scar over your eye."

Talia asked, "Tell us, does it have something to do with your glow?"

Jasher felt a wave of embarrassment wash over him. "You know about that? How? The cape usually shields me from the glow."

Connor noticed the red on Jasher's face. "Do not be ashamed, Jasher. Belle, Talia, and I observed it when you connected with our bracelets."

James nodded. "I noticed it happen to you when we were kids. You were at a window in the moonlight when it happened. You ran into the shade and it went away. Does whatever power controls the stone, is that fuels your glow?"

"Yes, but it is a lot more complicated than that," Jasher said. "When I was a young child, I was frail and sickly, as you all know. My brother, Aikin, tormented me constantly, especially when there was talk of my father allowing him to supersede me. However, on the night all of you know about, with the space rock, it came to a head. This time, I tried to fight back, but in a rage, Aikin pushed me into a table and a vase broke over me. The glass scratched my eye. My parents chided him, but I was embarrassed. Embarrassed because I could not beat him, even though I was full of anger. Nothing could give me an edge. I was weak and powerless."

He took a breath before continuing. "I decided that I did not want to be king at that moment, and I ran. I burst through the door, and I ran into the woods. To my knowledge, no one followed me or came after me. You know about my exposure to the space rock, which helped me gain the strength I always desired, it gave me one side effect. When the moon is out, every single scar that I received before the incident in the forest, well, they glow. It is shameful to me. It reminds me of who I was and that I never want to go back. I won't go back to what I was. It sickens me to think that I was so weak and so frail that I almost lost my birthright because my bones would snap like a twig."

He looked at Talia. "Can you move the clouds?"

Talia said, "The sun will be rising soon, Jasher."

"Please, Talia."

Talia looked up in the sky and began to weave an enchantment. She wished she could make a larger one to take the clouds away completely, but with the smoke factory, it would be too hard to make. Instead, a small hole formed into the artificial smoke, and the moon shone into the cell. Jasher became fully lit, with each one of his scars lighting up. The one over his eye, the biggest gash, especially.

His fellow royals looked on with wonder as they saw the blue glow emanating from him.

The Dragon Prince explained, "Now, you know who I am. I may be strong, but I am ashamed of my past, for all I see is weakness and it is one that I cannot escape from. Whenever I try, the moon reminds me."

Belle was the first to speak up, "Jasher, you have no reason to be embarrassed. Wipe away the weakness."

She stood up and put her hand on her heart. "You see a reminder of weakness and frailty, but I see transformation. I see you have risen from a miry pit and are now planted on solid ground. If you can rise, then you can lead. You can lead us to our homeland and to victory for Craih. By life or death, I shall call you my captain, and I will follow you to whatever end. This I make my solemn vow."

Talia stood up after her and also touched her heart. "My captain."

James followed suit. "My captain."

Philip was next. "My captain."

Rapunzel smiled as she stood. "I got your back, Jasher, because I know you have mine."

Connor stood up quickly. "Well said."

They were all standing, swearing their allegiance to him.

"Oh, my friends," Jasher said. "Oh, my brothers and sisters. I swear, I shall..."

As he spoke, the hole that Talia had formed in the clouds had grown, only slightly, but in that instant, the full moon of Paraina's sister planet Quaraina shone. Its light went forth into the cell.

When it did, it threw Jasher to the ground. The glows from his body intensified and he cried out in pain.

James shouted in shock, "What is happening?"

Talia explained, "He's never been exposed to both moons before! He must've kept himself well hidden from their light! Both are affecting him."

"Is there anything we can do?" James asked.

Talia canceled the enchantment, but the small hole in the clouds stayed. It would not and did not seal. She then tried to move them, but that, too, proved to be a failure.

James and Connor even tried to physically block the light, but the window was too high.

Jasher's eyes suddenly turned the same blue and as he did, his scars started to heal and vanish from his skin. All of them except the one over his eye.

Chapter 44

Jasher stood in an unfamiliar place. He couldn't wrap his head around this location. He looked around the unusual locale and saw it to be a valley surrounded by seven mountains, and a beautiful field. At the edge of the field sat a lake.

It felt strange. He felt so peaceful. The air caused goose bumps all over his skin. The air smelled fresh and gave him the feeling that it was purifying his lungs. He breathed it in and then slowly exhaled. His could see so clearly and vividly.

Jasher had never felt anything like this. It was as if he had been in a dream, and then had woken up. For a moment, he thought he might be dead, but if that was true, why did he feel so alive?

"Where am I?

A voice boomed in response, "Don't you know this place?"

Jasher looked up and saw them. There were seven figures, each standing on the peaks of a mountain.

He gasped as he realized, "This is the valley before my city, Grandfire City, but where are the buildings?"

Jasher almost fell back when he saw a great dragon laying before him.

The Dragon explained, "I am the leader of the dragons. You may call me Shade. You are in the Overworld, young Prince Jasher, but you might also call it, the Spirit World."

Jasher looked around in wonder. He had never seen so much beauty in all of his life. It overwhelmed him, but at the same time, it brought him peace. He nearly tripped when he noticed he had no shadow. There was no sense of gray or darkness. It was light, pure light.

The Dragon laughed at him. "Yes, there are many surprises here, my friend, besides not having a shadow."

"How did I get here?" Jasher asked Shade as he faced him.

The Dragon snorted "You have a rare gift, Jasher. The space rock you encountered unlocked capabilities that every human has, but has forgotten it, or written it off as only for mystics and sorcerers."

Jasher's face exuded curiosity, and the Dragon noticed this.

"Jasher, the space rock gave you an immunity to magic. No direct attack or even blessing can affect you. Only acts of true love can pierce through that. You see, you can use your powers with an advantage. You are not canceling the magic out, you are absorbing it. The moon's glow is merely a side effect to what is happening. It shows the energy that is inside you. The second moon, however, enhanced this effect, allowing you to cross into this world."

Jasher realized he was glowing. "Absorbing all that magical power? I've been holding it in for so long."

The Dragon nodded. "Yes, you have absorbed it in a powerful way. Now you can channel it as a cosmic energy."

"Cosmic energy?" Jasher raised an eyebrow.

The Dragon smiled, revealing his sharp teeth. "Cosmic energy is the foundation of the universe. You see only matter, space, and mystic, but Cosmic is none of those. It is the power that is inside you. Many generations ago, humans used this power. However, teachings prevailed that it was only myth. The space rock unlocked it inside you and gave you this unique gift."

Jasher felt the scars. "All of this time, I thought they were a reminder of a painful, weak past."

The Dragon shook his head. "No, Jasher. It is a symbol, a sign, of where you are going, not where you have been."

"How do I release it?"

"For now, use your sword as an instrument to channel it. You can summon Alilth the Blue Blade to you since it is made from the same space rock. Use it like a muscle and with practice, it will become stronger."

Jasher said, "Thank you. Thank you for revealing this to me."

The Dragon let out a laugh. "Now, return to your realm. You and your allies must return to Craih and defeat Fabius Thorne or he will put all of Paraina, not just Craih or Icester, but all of our beloved planet in a deep and dark shadow."

"Dragon, you must help us."

The Dragon reached out toward him. "We want to so badly. Thorne, however, saw this coming. He put toxins in the smoke that can kill us instantly. For now, we are forced to stay at the top of the mountain."

Jasher bowed to the Dragon. "Thank you, Dragon."

The Dragon seemed to form a smile. "Do not fear, for I shall bestow on you, this one gift."

His claw reached out and touched his forehead.

Jasher was in his cell, when he suddenly stood up, eyes still glowing, and he reached out his hand. He could feel the Cosmic energy pulsating through his body. It was invigorating. He gave a smile, and he called the Blue Blade. "Alilth! Come to me!"

The sword was strapped down in the vault next to them, but then it rose up, crashed through the wall, and landed perfectly in Jasher's hand. The rush caused an earthquake that swung the cell doors swung wide open.

"Clear the room!" Jasher commanded.

The six obeyed and headed into the armory where they found all of their weapons. They all smiled when they handled their weapons. Rapunzel found the Bowie Knife hidden behind her staff.

Jasher aimed Alilth carefully, and fired a blast of cosmic energy from himself, which he channeled through the sword. It went through the halls of Revenant, disintegrating any werewolf or orc that came in contact with it. The cosmic energy burst through more walls of Revenant and struck the smoke factory, causing a massive explosion. The smoke ceased, and all of the orcs, vampires, and werewolves coughed as the dust rose up.

Suddenly, however, the smoke in the sky started to dissipate and the sun began to rise in the horizon.

The orcs screamed in terror as their skin began to burn. They fled, but it was too late. The vampires began to crumble into dust as their old age took them.

It was at that moment that the human slaves took up the arms dropped by the Orcs and began to attack the now-outnumbered werewolves who could not even retreat. The

Alpha looked on in terror and disbelief before he was struck down by a simple slave that he had previously been whipping into submission.

As soon as they had killed the Werewolves, the people retreated into the forests headed back to their villages.

Jasher collapsed from the energy he released. The six ran in to check on him. Philip and Talia helped him rise as he assured them, "I'm alright."

Talia exclaimed, "Oh Heavens, that was incredible!"

Connor agreed, "Amazing, simply amazing."

James said nothing. For once, it was because he was speechless.

Rapunzel kept stammering before she finally said, "What happened?"

Jasher told her, "I went into the Overworld."

Philip asked, "What?"

Rapunzel and Talia told him at the same time, "The Spirit World."

Jasher continued, "I communed with a Dragon of Teysha. The Dragon explained my powers to me. I understand fully for the first time."

Rapunzel handed him the Bowie Knife. "Wow, that is incredible."

They barely had a chance to celebrate when suddenly, storm clouds began to form in the morning sky. With it, came no rain, but a harsh breeze that brought a chill to the air. The seven royals begin to rub their arms as goose bumps appeared.

Jasher asked, "What is going on?"

Talia looked up at the clouds. "This is a storm weaved by a spell, a dark magic spell. Someone is trying to intimidate us.

James sighed. "Of course, right after Jasher destroys the smoke factory."

Belle suddenly pointed to the horizon. "He did this!"

It was then that the Seven Royals saw him.

Talia asked, "What new devilry is this?"

Philip slowly drew his sword. "That must be Omri. They say that only the Ice Queen rivals him in power. We need to ready our weapons. He is indeed powerful. Many of my fellow knights fell from his scimitar."

Jasher's face suddenly shown red with anger. "Omri. He murdered my brother and sister."

By now, all of the slaves of Revenant had fled and only the seven Royal stood on the destroyed carcass of the once glorious city.

Chapter 45

Snow jumped off her horse and ran for the city of Revenant, crossing into the city limits passing dust and bones of Orcs. She was dressed in simple battle armor with a green cape and hood. She had her retractable spear and a bow with a quiver of arrows. She felt the unnatural wind and could see the Seven Royals near the castle and in the distance, she could see the great enemy. She was only a few feet away.

"Hang on, Jasher," she called out. "I'm coming!"

Across the newly formed battlefield, Omri looked down upon the children that stood before him. At first, he held a disbelief that they had destroyed the smoke factory. He knew by now all of the forces on Icester had died or been forced to retreat.

The disbelief began to subside, and now he stared at them with not just with anger, but with pure hatred. It was a hate so powerful, he could feel the satisfaction of killing them.

Now, here they were standing just down the hill.

The time was almost upon these princes and princesses to end this with their heads on pikes and paraded around the cities of Craih. That would give him great satisfaction.

They may have defeated his forces here at Revenant, but that did not matter. Omri would beat them, and what he thought as their fraud of a captain. They would die.

Omri raised his scimitar and shouted to no one in particular, "I shall take them, kill them! Their heads are mine!" He pointed to the one with the Blue Blade.

He got off the boar and stood his ground, then he gave a wicked smile. He reached for a bag that was tied to his belt. After he emptied out the contents on the ground.

Jasher watched as ten hills began to form at the same location as Omri.

"What is that?" Rapunzel asked as she raised her staff.

Belle replied, "I only see some sand hills."

Jasher looked at what was forming in front of them. It had everything you could want in a trap. There was forest on one side and the swamps they had come from on the other. There was no going forward, only backwards if they had to retreat.

He said, "Everyone, be ready!"

Omri smiled and ordered., "Sand Trolls forward!"

Jasher looked at the sand hills, suddenly, they started to move forward toward them.

Connor took out his sword. "What now?"

The six hills suddenly began to form into the shape of something.

Talia said, "Ooh, Sand Trolls! Maybe they're friendly."

The largest one roared and then fired a blast of lightning from its eyes, landing in front of them, causing them to jump backwards.

"Definitely not friendly," said Philip. He attempted to draw his sword but found it difficult.

Jasher grabbed his wrist, steadying it. "Keep calm and draw your sword."

Philip smiled as he steadied his sword in front of him.

He looked at Belle, "Take position in the tower. Give us some cover!"

Belle nodded and ran to a nearby tower, climbing up a broken staircase, she readied her bow and arrow.

Rapunzel stood there with a look of terror on her face.

One of the Sand Trolls looked at her and unleashed his blast, but Jasher pushed her out of the way and took the hit. However, instead of killing him, he absorbed it.

Rapunzel sighed with relief. "Thank you."

Jasher looked at her. "You are strong, my dear. You can do this."

"They are not pure born Sand Trolls," Talia called out, grabbing his attention. "I've studied them. They're held together by magic. That means they have a weakness."

Philip dodged as a Sand Troll tried to smash him, but he sliced its arm off. The creature cried in pain, but the arm just grew back. James did the same with the leg, but it too just grew back.

181

Belle started to give them cover fire with her bow and arrows by aiming at the Sand Troll's heads, but their heads just grew back.

Talia moved swiftly cutting at the Sand Trolls achilles tendons and while that gave them time to stab elsewhere, the Sand Trolls continued to heal.

Jasher used his Bowie knife to stab one in the heart, but it did nothing but aggravate the Sand Troll. It swung its arm and sent Jasher flying across the grass. He dropped his knife when he landed.

One troll tried to step on him and he drew the Blue Blade, stabbing the troll in the foot. The troll fell to the ground and collapsed, but quickly reformed.

Omri saw it and gasped. "It can't be.... It is the Blue Blade!"

Snow stood behind the tower and saw the battle that was raging. She had seen Sand Trolls like this and remembered where their weakness was located.

"I have to help them," she said, as she climbed up the tower. To her surprise, she found one of the Royals waiting for her.

Belle turned her bow to her. "Who are you?"

Snow White put down her hood. "No time. Aim for the nape of the neck. That is the Sand Troll's weakness." Snow pulled out three of her arrows. "They move fast. It'll be hard to target them."

Belle hesitated, but then did as she was told. She and Snow fired an arrow each, striking their targets.

The Sand Trolls cried out in pain and then they collapsed turning into sand.

"It's the nape of their neck!" Belle called out.

Talia was fighting with her two knives and using her Martial Arts skills to hold the men at bay, but these were not mindless Orcs, these were well trained men who also had fighting skills.

One of the attackers saw Rapunzel as she blasted an energy beam, killing one of the Sand Trolls and approached from behind, preparing to crush the little princess.

James turned around as one of them dissolved and saw the one charging at Rapunzel, he charged at it, leaping in the air, and striking it in the neck. It dissolved beneath him.

Rapunzel said, "I'm not good at this. Everyone keeps saving me."

Before James could respond, a Cave Troll formed behind him, but Rapunzel blasted it, not in the nape, but just enough to bring it down, allowing James to finish it.

He smiled and turned to her. "See Rapunzel. We save each other."

Rapunzel returned his smile, but then looked past him. Her face became horrified when she saw two Sand Trolls cornering Talia. "No," she shouted.

She started to run toward her friend. James tried to follow, but a Sand Troll stepped in front of him.

Chapter 46

Talia allowed two of the Sand Trolls to back against a wall. She smiled as she put her staff together and shouted, "Take this!"

She fired a blast of blue energy at their napes, allowing them to crumble.

"Ha, yes!"

Her celebration was interrupted when she heard what sounded like a spinning wheel. She spotted a door that she had not seen before. She walked through it and the noise got louder.

She could hear Rapunzel's voice calling out to her, begging her not to go in, but only the sound of the spinning wheel drew her.

She came to a room where she found a sewing wheel with a needle at the end of it. Everything inside of her told her not to touch it. A distant warning from her parents, the High Priest Tyroane's voice telling her to never touch one, but she reached out and pricked her finger.

Talia then understood when she saw Omri smiling in the darkness. The wall disappeared, and the open field returned.

Omri said, "Don't worry, I killed the fairy who cursed you after he told me what he did on the day of your dedication. To think, he was in love with your mother and cursed you in vengeance. It's a shame, you are still cursed, and you cannot seek vengeance."

Talia started to feel light-headed, but just before she collapsed, she said, "I never wanted revenge, just to go home."

Rapunzel caught Talia as she fell and began crying over her.

Omri raised his scimitar to strike her, as he came down, Jasher's sword caught it.

"You won't hurt anyone else!" Jasher said.

The Overlord laughed. "Oh, how I've waited for this." With his free hand, he struck the ground, sending Jasher backwards.

Omri raised his scimitar high in the air as he ran toward Jasher. Their blades sparked as it collided with the Blue Blade.

The Overlord taunted, "So, you're the mysterious one that has decided to imitate the heir to the Teysha throne! Well, I have news for you, it is mine! Midas gave it to me!"

"You mean after he stole it," he said.

Omri blocked another blow from Jasher. The evil overlord growled, "I know you are a fake. You would be much older than you are now. You're nothing more than a mascot." He backed up and motioned to the seven royals engaged in the fight. "Look around you, kid. You are losing this battle."

Jasher shouted, "I am no fake!" He raised his sword, but Omri kicked him with his long leg, sending him flying into a piece of rubble, and dropping the Blue Blade.

Philip held a Sand Troll's arm at bay just as an arrow went through its neck. It started to dissolve and crumble to the ground.

James and Connor walked up to him.

"That's the last of them," said Connor.

Philip looked around. "Where are the other?"

James said, "It appears that the battle scattered us."

Connor pointed behind them. "Look over there!"

They saw Jasher engaged in a sword fight Omri. In the same vicinity, they saw a collapsed Talia and Rapunzel funneling energy through her hair, in an attempt to wake her up. As she did so, it seemed her hair was getting longer and longer.

Philip asked, "We have to get over there."

Before they could run, three sand tentacles reached out from the ground grabbing them by their ankles.

James tried to pull away. "We have slain the Sand Trolls."

Connor replied as he struck the bizarre tentacle with his sword. "It's Omri! He's using sorcery to prevent us from helping them!"

Philip pulled all the harder saying under his breath. "Hang on! We're coming!"

Omri looked upon Jasher as he lay in the rubble. The overlord laughed.

"You are a fake! You are nothing but a cheap imitation of a warrior that is legendary throughout all of Craih! Wait until the Continental Army hears about this! Their newfound hope is nothing more than a boy who is not worthy to die by my blade!"

Jasher made an attempt to stand, but he only made it to his knees. He drew his Bowie knife. "Then what're you going to do, talk me to death?"

Omri put his scimitar back into its hilt. "No, boy, I'm going to make you suffer for imitating him!" He backed away and fired off a blast of lightning, but the magic energy just absorbed into Jasher's body.

"It can't be," said the Overlord. "You are him."

Jasher did not waste his distraction. With quick reflexes, he spun around with his sword, Omri barely had time to block, but the Dragon Prince was prepared. He spun around, kicking Omri in the left knee, as the dark warrior screamed in pain, Jasher struck the right knee causing his enemy to fall to the ground, kicking his sword away.

Omri tried to stand, but Jasher placed the edge of his sword to his throat. "Before I kill you," he said. "There's one thing I have to know."

Omri looked down and saw Rapunzel's staff next to him. He realized he needed to buy some time. "Ask me anything."

Jasher demanded, "Is it true? Did you kill Abigail and Aikin?"

Omri looked confused at first. "Kill them?" Then he let out a laugh. It was a deep, dark sinister laugh. It caused Rapunzel to shake with fear. She looked around for her staff and realized it was right beside the Overlord. "Jasher, you..."

"Kill them," interrupted Omri. "I did kill High Priest Tyroane. I did kill many others after that, but no Dragon Prince. I did not kill Aikin or Abigail."

Jasher was so surprised, he let his guard drop. "What? Where are they?"

Omri smiled, revealing his yellow teeth. "Fool, I do not know Abigail's present location, but as for Aikin, look into my eyes."

Jasher did. For the first time, he looked into his enemy's eyes and they had a familiarity about them. That was when he realized. "Aikin?"

Omri started laughing even more and he slowly put his fingers around the staff. "Yes. How do you think Fabius Thorne was able to cause the smoke to cover Craih so quickly? He did his part on Gorasyum and I completed the enchantment on Craih."

"Why," asked a confused Jasher.

"Because, brother," said Omri. "I hate you."

Rapunzel screamed, "Jasher, look out!"

James heard the scream as the tentacles fell back to the ground.

"We have to hurry!"

By now, Belle and Snow had joined them. Together, they ran to where the others stood.

Omri swung the staff so hard, it broke in half as it struck Jasher across the side. The Dragon Prince dropped his Blue Blade allowing Omri to grab him by the collar and pull him into a knee to the stomach.

Omri looked up and saw the others charging toward him. He knew he did not have the strength to beat all of them at this time, but he looked at the unconscious Talia, a shivering Rapunzel, and a stunned Jasher and knew he had to take this for now.

He spit at the others. "Not today!" He began chanting in some ancient language. Soon, a large circle begun to form around them.

Jasher said, "He's opening a rabbithole!" Jasher said, "We have to get to him before it opens fully!"

Belle said, "He's desperate. Only a fool would try this here."

Omri raised his hands and a portal opened in front of him. He threw Talia over his shoulder, grabbed Rapunzel and Jasher in each hand, dragging them into the rabbithole.

Then it closed.

Philip ran up, mere seconds later. "No," he whispered.

Connor swallowed hard. "We're too late."

Chapter 47

Midas walked out into the courtyard of the royal castle at Grandfire City. Like most everything in the capital of Teysha, it was circular. The rows of vines and shrubs continued on like a compass. As he passed through the garden, he touched the flowers and watched them turn to gold before his eyes. After a few moments of doing this, he placed his gloves back on and sighed.

Grandfire City was different than most of the cities across the nations of Craih. This one carried a certain kind of prestige, weight. It was a symbol that represented the Craih Kingdoms. The dark army knew this, that is why it was kept as fortified as it was to prevent the Continental Army from seizing it.

As Midas pondered this, he also wondered about everything that had transpired before him. He had watched Thorne and his Inner Circle scheme, plan, and carry out this war.

In all regards, Midas had everything he wanted. He had an adopted son, he had captured, killed, and conquered the enemies that he had envied. Yet, he still felt that he lacked something. All of the wealth, glory, and prestige was his, but he still felt empty on the inside.

He looked up to the window of the room where he was staying and could see the golden statue of his wife Aoelia. In a brief moment, Midas felt hatred overcome his heart. He clenched his gloves hands and his face contorted as he stared up at his wife's still statue. He had never felt this way about his beloved, but now that he had gone a ten-year war and still it had not brought him happiness. For some reason, he blamed her.

"This is your fault," he whispered.

"My Emperor," the voice belonged to Thorne.

Midas turned around and found Thorne walking towards him followed closely by The Wicker Man.

Thorne repeated, "My emperor, I suppose you heard of Revenant."

"No, what happened at Revenant?"

The Wicker Man looked up at Thorne with a sneer, as if angry that the emperor had given away something.

Thorne kept his cool. "Unfortunately, we have some bad news…"

"I want a full report."

Thorne opened his mouth, but before he could give an explanation, the wind started to stir, and the air became charged.

A purple vortex opened up in the courtyard, drawing attention of everyone in the castle. Many of the sorcerers, werewolves, gnomes, and trolls ran to see what the commotion was about.

Midas and Thorne walked up to the portal as Omri emerged carrying three bodies with him.

"What do we have here?" The viceroy asked.

Omri smiled and threw Jasher, Rapunzel, and Talia before him as the portal closed.

Talia was unconscious, seemingly in a coma. Jasher stayed on all fours but had a scowl on his face. Rapunzel huddled next to him and began to shiver.

Omri excitedly shouted, "Father, my lord, behold I have seized these three royals! And even better," he grabbed Jasher by the hair and lifted his head up. "I got us the Dragon Prince himself!"

Thorne smiled so broadly that Midas thought his face would crack. "I knew you could do it, my apprentice! Well done."

He looked around and said, "Where are the others?"

"The other four escaped," Omri said hesitantly. "But I did bring you a consolation prize." He lifted the blue blade in front of him. "This, the symbol of the Continental Army, the entire resistance, it is ours!"

Thorne reached for the sword, but Midas grabbed it with his gloved hand and started to examine the weapon.

"Fascinating," said the emperor. "I've never seen anything like this."

Fabius hid his annoyance at Midas for intercepting the blue blade and turned to face the three young people on the ground before him.

Jasher looked up at both Midas and Thorne. Though he had never seen them in person, he knew exactly who they were. He had dreamed of facing them, but not like this. Not forced on his knees before them, but with him standing over them with his sword raised high. A part of him wanted to hear them beg for their lives. He often wondered if he would give them the mercy that they so callously disregarded. Now, as he stared at them, he only fantasized about beheading them.

His fingers dug into the ground as he watched Omri take his Bowie knife and tie it to his belt.

Jasher brushed his onto Rapunzel's closest fingers and said, "It's going to be okay."

Thorne laughed when he heard this. "I assure you, Royals, it will not."

Jasher looked up at Fabius. His feelings went beyond the descriptions of anger and disdain, all he felt was rage. Inside Jasher was a white-hot hatred that filled his eyes with burning tears. He could feel the heat emanating from his skin through his broken armor.

Thorne could sense the storm of emotions coming from the Dragon Prince, so he said, "If you're hoping for a fairy tale ending where your parents are really alive, and you just need to find them, don't bother. As soon as we arrived, Midas turned them to gold and then had them melted down."

When the emperor heard his name, he looked up at his viceroy and then at Rapunzel, she was silently crying at hearing about their parents' fate. He could see the tears fall to the dirt beneath her and he realized that he could see small pieces of green growing in that very ground.

Then he looked at Jasher, he could see the anger seething from him, but for a brief moment, he saw the prince's eyes change. It was sorrow and... guilt. It was a look he knew well, for he had seen it in his own eyes in the mirror when he thought of his beloved wife.

Jasher's face turned back to rage and he yelled, "Murderer!" He mustered all his strength to lunge forward, but

Omri stepped on his calf to make him trip and fall to the ground.

Thorne laughed when he saw this, and every member of the dark army joined in.

"Behold your enemy!" The viceroy mocked him. "The great Dragon Prince of Teysha, Knight of Grandfire City, and the Captain of the Seven Royals!" The laughing grew louder.

Jasher realized that all of the humiliation he had felt as a child did not compare to this. To have your enemy mock you in such a manner, he was not prepared. Rapunzel's tears only increased and Jasher briefly stroked her hand.

When the laughter died down, he held out his hand to Midas. "My emperor, the sword if you please."

Midas hesitated and then handed it to Thorne.

Fabius held it, but to his surprise, he found it incredibly heavy. He had to fight the urge to drop it, but he could feel the metal draining the magical energy flowing out of him. He had to rely on his physical strength alone to lift it.

"I'm going to kill you."

Fabius' thoughts were interrupted by the voice of the Dragon Prince.

"I'm going to kill you," Jasher repeated.

Fabius pointed the sword's edge at Jasher's neck. "Shut up."

Rapunzel asked, "What're you going to do to us?"

Thorne smiled with his white teeth showing. "The sleeping beauty is powerful even in her sleep. Her mystical ability is still strong, so we will put her in a glass coffin as a monument to your failure. Rapunzel, my dear, you will be sent to the tower guarded by Blue Beard. Jasher, we have something special in mind for you."

A woman in blue stepped out from behind Thorne and Midas.

Jasher gasped when he saw her. "Abigail," he said.

The ice queen looked curiously at him. "I'm the Ice Queen. I will be handling you."

"Handling me?"

Thorne smiled. "Yes, before we execute you."

Jasher looked at his sister. "I don't know what they've done to you, but you will not allow me to be killed. I know you."

Thorne rolled his eyes. "Yes, how saccharine."

He waved over some guards. "Take the ladies to their accommodations and take Jasher to the presidential suite."

Jasher turned to Rapunzel, "Don't scream."

"But I'm scared."

"Don't scream."

Omri kicked him down as werewolves grabbed him by the shoulders, stripping off his armor and they dragged him along.

As Jasher looked around the courtyard that once belonged to his family. He could not help but feel a strong sense of loss as he went through the halls of the castle that rightfully belonged to him and his people.

As Midas watched the kids being dragged away, he asked, "Is this what we've come to? Are we harming children?"

Thorne turned to Midas and for a brief moment, the emperor saw something in his ally. It was something he immediately realized that he had chosen to ignore, because Thorne had flattered him and given him a throne.

He recognized it as a madness, but not in the typical sense. It was one that Midas realized Thorne would do whatever it took to accomplish his goal. Nothing would stand in his way, not even a moral code.

This was confirmed when Thorne gave him his answer. "I would kill a hundred children if they got in my way."

Chapter 48

Snow White stood with the other four Royals stood on the ruins of Revenant. They were stunned that Omri had just vanished with their allies. Now they stood helpless as their friends had been just been taken.

James suddenly let out an anger-filled roar. He grabbed a boulder and heaved it, causing to break when it collided with the ground.

"I was too late," muttered Snow.

"We have to go after them," shouted Prince Philip. "Omri took them and we have no idea what tortures they could be subjected to!"

Belle grabbed his shoulders and forced him to look her in the eyes. "Listen to me," she said. "We don't know where they went. We have to keep our heads."

Snow repeated, "I was too late."

James glared at her. "Who are you?"

Connor stepped in front of her. "This is Ezri Snow. She is an ally. I can vouch for her. She would feed my crew information on Thorne's naval movements. She's also a good friend of Jasher's."

James sighed. "I'm sorry. We need all the friends we can get."

Philip said, "Okay, okay," as he pushed Belle away. "So, what... what do we do? We can't just sit here in these ruins. Besides, they will send packs of werewolves soon."

Belle wiped her eyes. "They could be anywhere."

Suddenly, they heard a noise like a horn.

Snow opened her bag and said, "My magic mirror." She pulled out her small looking case and set it on the boulder.

Suddenly, they watched as Fabius Thorne's face appeared and she almost dropped it when it startled her.

"Hello, subjects of the Craih Empire," he said. "I have an announcement. The fake Dragon Prince Jasher has been captured. Though some of his friends remain at large, they will soon be in chains as well. As for the royal we have, he will be executed tomorrow morning in Grandfire City. Using my mirror magic, we will be showing the execution to the entirety of Craih. That is all."

The message was transported to all of Craih, from one village to another, they all mourned at hearing of the impending death of the beloved Dragon Prince.

Connor fell to his knees. "What do we do now?"

Snow pointed up the road. "We have to go! We have to save him!"

"Even if we somehow found horses, we could not make it to Grandfire City by sunrise tomorrow," Belle said.

James picked up another rock and heaved it, and then a little imp appeared in the general direction of the rock.

The imp moved out of the way just in time. He dusted himself off and said, "Boy, that was close. You've got a good arm." He dressed much like a jester, though as short and thin as a child with a long nose and sharp ears.

Connor stood up. "Who are you?"

Philip drew his sword. "Are you with the Sorcerer's Society?"

The imp laughed. "Ha! No! I'm Puck."

"Wait," said James. "You're the one who gave Midas his golden touch. Give us one good reason why we shouldn't take you out."

Puck rolled his eyes, snap his fingers, and James' sword dropped to the ground.

"I may not be all powerful," the imp said. "But without your only two mystics, you've got nothing."

Belle demanded, "What do you want?"

"To help you, of course," Puck replied with a grin.

Philip asked, "How can you possibly help us? Are you going to use your magic to disarm the dark army?"

Puck laughed. "No, I'm not that generous. Look here's the thing. Midas threw a hissy fit because he couldn't handle his wish. When I pointed this out, he tried to kill me with my own magic. Nice try, but you can't kill an imp with imp magic. He touched me, and I turned to gold, but I just turned into pure energy and escaped. He should've known. So stupid."

James sneered, "To the point."

"Right, right. So, I'm here to help you by sending you to Grandfire City. I owe that idiot Midas for trying to kill me. You being at the Dragon Prince's execution will be a perfect way to spoil his fun."

Belle said, "You're going to open a rabbithole?"

Puck laughed. "No that'll make way too much of a ruckus. I have a better idea." He snapped his fingers.

In an instant, Belle, James, Connor, Philip, and Snow found themselves in a forest full of blue leaves.

Belle asked, "Is this the Bluetree Forest?"

A voice called out, "Philip?"

Philip turned around and said, "Captain?"

Chapter 49

Jasher was suspended in his cell by vines created by the Wicker Man. They pinned him against the wall, drawn and quartered in an 'X' position.

"How does it feel, Dragon Prince," the scarecrow-like being said. "...knowing that you failed?"

Jasher looked up at him. "I'm not dead yet, but you'll wish you had killed me when you had the chance."

Fabius Thorne entered the cell, laughing as he did. "Oh, don't worry, Jasher. You will suffer death as your parents did, just in a different manner. I've gathered all the materials I need to cast a great mirroring spell. Everyone who has a mirror, a reflective metal, or a looking glass within Craih and on Gorasyum will watch as the great Dragon Prince is beheaded. Even if your friends somehow survive, the people will lose hope and will submit to me."

The Wicker Man grunted. "Ahem."

Thorne corrected himself. "I mean, they will submit to the Sorcerer's Society, of course."

Jasher glared up at him. "I will kill you. I swear it. You will die."

Thorne laughed at this. "How? I know about your cosmic energy. No moonlight will get in here. With the smoke factory still pumping, you cannot heal. I've given orders not to use magic on you, hence why I had the Wicker Man make wooden restraints. He can use magic on them, but it won't affect you. It's what I call a loophole."

Jasher said, "Do your worst. I fear neither pain nor death."

Thorne laughed. "But you fear your friend's death. If you try to escape, I will have the girl in the glass coffin murdered as she sleeps. The long-haired one will suffer even greater at the hands of Blue Beard."

"You will kill them anyways," Jasher replied. "The only reason they're even alive is because you want trophies. You're not some great leader, you're a thief. And every thief needs to have his accomplishments on display in the house he stole."

"You dare speak to me that way, Jasher? I know of you and your stories," the Grand Mage declared. "The people of Craih thought you would ride in here on a white horse, blue blade lifted in the air, slaying all of the dark army. Yet tomorrow, they will watch you die in humiliation. I will dress you in your father's armor and after your head rolls from your body, I will have Midas turn it to gold."

He released Jasher and headed for the cell-door, then he turned to Jasher. "I ask you as my colleague did, how does it feel to fail?"

Jasher started laughing. "Failed? You're the one who has failed."

Thorne was growing frustrated with the Prince's defiance. "Elaborate on that. I'm curious what delusion you hold," he said.

Jasher looked up. "What I said before is true. You are a common thief. You and your dark army claim that you are conquerors who subjugated a great society, but in fact, everything you have, you stole. You took advantage of a grieving emperor. You corrupted two of its children. You used a device that gave your soldiers an advantage and then marched on land that you did not till, sweat for, or bleed on.

"You took something that did not belong to you, Thorne, and even with all of your power, you could not defeat the defiance or the heart of all its freedom-loving people. You could not stop them, and you never will. You think it is some loyalty to the Seven Royals and our deaths will break them. Maybe the prophecy did give them a symbol, but the Continental Army of Craih will never surrender. I saw it in Revenant. They fought for freedom as soon as they could. What's even more sad is, you don't know why they fight."

Thorne had listened to this monologue with interest and now Jasher had just stopped. The Grand Mage waited patiently, but the prince said nothing. He clenched his fists and shouted, "If you're so smart, then tell me, oh wise one, why? Why do they fight?"

Jasher looked up with smirk. "Because this is their property and you're trespassing."

Thorne nodded to the Wicker Man, who lifted his hand. A green energy came out of it and the vines tightened around Jasher, who cried out in pain.

Thorne said, "We'll see when your head rolls off the chopping block. Once you're gone, I'll have no more use for Midas. He will die, and my dark army will reign supreme."

Thorne and the Wicker Man exited, walking through the dark hallways of the dungeon. They did not see Porlem hiding in the shadows.

The human soldiers shuttered as Blue Beard ate a barely cooked ham as he headed toward his tower.

He peeked inside a room that looked an old dining room. He saw the girl in the glass coffin, Princess Talia Rosebriar. She was one of the most beautiful girls he had ever seen. In her light violet dress, her alabaster staff to her side, and her hair made up in curls. Her metal staff lay beside her.

"No doubt Thorne got her all dressed up for this occasion," he thought.

Guarding it was the giant bull known as Daken. His coat was black with a red face and red underbelly. His eyes were solid yellow with his horns straight and pointed.

Blue Beard approached the glass coffin and stared at Talia. He licked his lips and said, "This pretty is more my age." He reached for the coffin's lock, but the bull snorted at him,

"Touch her and I will gore you," declared Daken. "The Grand Mage gave very specific orders to keep this girl safe. He wishes her to be a museum piece. He said if I guard her for one hundred years, he will reverse the spell I put on myself that turned me into this form."

Blue Beard took another bite of the ham, speaking through a full mouth, he said, "One hundred years, huh? You're powerful as a bull, why would you want to turn back into the wizard?"

Daken looked down, "Would you give up women for a more powerful animal form?"

Blue Beard nodded. "Good point." He chewed off the last of the ham and threw the bone away.

"That was tasty," he said. "Now, I'm going to get another blonde, long-haired treat."

Daken snarled at him. "You're disgusting, even for me."

Blue Beard smiled at that. He did not care what others thought of his behavior. He let his robe drag on the ground as he headed for the stairs.

Rapunzel could hear him coming up the stairs. She knew Blue Beard by reputation. She had heard what he did to maidens and she tried to contain herself, but she could not help but tremble when she heard his heavy footsteps.

"Princess! I'm coming," he called out.

Rapunzel wanted to shriek, scream, but she remembered what Jasher had told her.

The tower, though it was a prison, it was decorated like a little girl's room. The bricks were painted white, there was a pink vanity, pink bed, and a window. For a brief moment, she considered undoing her hair and trying to climb out, but she knew others were watching.

"Princess! Yoo-hoo! Are you there?"

The echo of the stairwell made his voice even scarier and she shook. She wanted to scream, scream with everything in her, but she grabbed a pillow on the bed and clutched onto it. Somehow, that gave her some bizarre strength. Tightening on the pillow helped her focus away from the fear and though it lingered, she could overcome.

He banged on the door. "Princess!" He bellowed. "Here I am!"

She said nothing and just continued to shake.

"Princess! I'm here! We're going to have a good first date!"

She stayed silent.

"Princess! Scream for me!"

Rapunzel then realized the truth. "He gets his power from fearful screams. Without them, he can't do anything."

"Do your worst," she shouted in defiance.

Silence from the other side. That was when she understood what Jasher had been trying to tell her.

Then she heard footsteps, but they were moving far away.

She sighed with relief. He had not encountered that before and it had confused him. She had bought herself one night, but deep down, she knew that would not work a second time. Tomorrow, he would charge into the room and would do all kinds of torturous things until he broke her.

Daken laughed as Blue Beard walked by.

Blue Beard pointed at him. "She... she's sick! Not even I would..." He paused, realizing how outrageous his lie sounded.

Daken snorted. "Don't give me that. She outsmarted you."

Blue Beard spit on the ground. "It doesn't matter. Tomorrow, when she sees the Dragon Prince slain, she will weaken, and she will be mine."

He stormed off into the darkened castle.

Chapter 50

Rapunzel had tears in her eyes as she leaned against the glass window. It was easy enough to open and she thought of escape, until she saw Midas' men building a giant chopping block platform in the courtyard below. They were also setting up stadium seating high above it where Thorne and his men could watch the execution. She began to cry harder, but then beyond the chopping block, she saw a small crowd gathering.

That was when she recognized a single cloak among many. It was a dark green cloak being ignored by many, but she saw the naval compass rose on it.

"Connor," she whispered. Rapunzel was surprised to see him there already She almost called out to him, but she knew that would be pointless. It would expose him, and another Royal would be captured.

She immediately turned to the pink vanity and began to tear it apart until she found an old cloth she could write on. She picked up some sort of black eye make-up and wrote a message on it.

She looked to the sky and spotted a blackbird. She called out to it with whispers of the animal tongue.

It flew down to her and bounced on the ledge. She looked around making sure no one was watching her. All of the guards in the streets and courtyards seemed preoccupied.

She whispered to the bird and it took the message in its claw before flying off.

"Creator, please help us." It was simple, but sincere prayer.

Connor watched with pain as the chopping block platform was being nailed together hurriedly by Midas' human men.

He sighed and turned away. There was no way he could get to the castle with all of the prowlers about.

Suddenly, a piece of cloth hit his head. He rubbed it and saw a blackbird flying off.

He looked down and realized the cloth had writing on it before picking it up.

It said,

HELP!

Talia and I are trapped in the East side. I'm in the tower and Talia is just below me.

They're going to kill Jasher! Hurry!

Connor looked up to the east tower. "Thank you, Rapunzel. I swore we will come for you."

He waved to the tower, not sure if Rapunzel could see it and then tossed the letter into a lantern to burn before vanishing into the night.

Chapter 51

Jasher could see some of the moonlight dipping through the sky, but through the filter of dark clouds, it mattered little. He could not access the Overworld, for he was too weak.

His cell door opened, and he saw his sister, veiled in that winter dress walk in. She was carrying a bowl with soup and a straw.

"Abigail," he said.

"I'm the Ice Queen," she corrected. "Why do you call me by that name?"

Jasher tried to reach for her, but the vines kept him pinned down.

"Listen, you are my sister. You really do not remember?"

The voice of an enemy answered him. "She remembers nothing, brother."

The form of Omri walked through the door. "I turned willingly to Fabius Thorne, but she would not yield, especially after our parents were executed, so I helped Fabius Thorne find a weakness and we turned her mind."

Jasher sneered, "You brainwashed her."

The Ice Queen stayed remarkably quiet, she merely looked between the two men.

Omri laughed. "She could not see the error of her family's ways. The two of us should have been rulers, not you. A weakling who got his power by chance. It was unfair. I should have ruled."

"What kind of a king betrays his own people?"

Omri laugh again at this. "Betrayed them? I helped them. There is no aristocracy. No nobility. Everyone is the same."

Jasher retorted, "Except for you and your cohorts. You've just made yourself the rich and made everyone else slaves."

"Well, aren't you the philosopher."

He turned to leave, but Jasher shouted, "Wait!"

Omri paused as his brother spoke, "Just tell me one thing, did you know about Mom and Dad?"

Omri spun around and with no irony said, "Yes. How do you think the dark army found them so quickly? I gave up their whereabouts. That was the price for my power and I would do it again."

"Dirty, rotten, TRAITOR," Jasher screamed as he tried again to pull against the vines, but they only tightened.

Omri laughed even louder as he walked out of the cell.

Ice Queen did nothing but held up the bowl to Jasher lips. He drank it down and said, "I promise you, I will save you."

She looked at him curiously but said nothing to the dragon prince. He seemed familiar to her, though she had not seen him before that day. Suddenly, he smiled at her, sending a fright through her. She exited without a word.

The Ice Queen passed through the East Wing of the castle and felt a stirring in her soul. There had always been a familiarity with Grandfire City and especially the castle, but now it seemed like it was a part of her. She saw a mirror in the hallway and looked deep into her face.

She then realized for the first time that she only had memories of the last nine years. When she tried to go further, it was hazy, as if a dream.

She made her way to the vault which was guarded by two trolls. She walked past them, and they did not even try to stop her. To them, she was the Ice Queen and they took orders from her.

The vault was empty except for a single display: The Blue Blade. She walked up to it as if it was calling her.

She reached for it, but then stopped herself.

"Jasher," she whispered. Then she touched it.

It started to glow and then a small circular blue wave shot from it, sending her flying against the wall. She cried out in pain as she collapsed to the floor.

All of a sudden, she knew. She knew who she was. She was not Ice Queen the Ice Queen. She was Abigail Kenan, the Dragon Princess. She saw her memories. A beautiful girl playing with Jasher, a teen learning mysticism, her parents being melted down right in front of her, and finally, her year of torture.

For a whole year, Aikin and Thorne brainwashed her with pain. She watched her brother slowly evolve from a man to the monster known as Omri. She remember when she broke and when she was crowned the Ice Queen.

When she saw everything, she screamed in agony. It was a deep painful wail that shook the Blue Blade on its display. Icy tears froze the ground below her as she laid on all fours.

Her scream did not carry through the castle, the vault trapped the sound, but it did attract the two trolls standing guard directly outside.

They rushed in. "My lady, are you alright?" The largest asked.

She looked up at them and then scowled. All her anger at what she lost. Her parents. Her people. Her independence. Her brother.

She stood up and yelled with rage and unleashed a cold from her hands like she never had before.

The trolls did not have a chance to react or even cry for help as their bodies froze in place.

They fell over and shattered.

Abigail heard a mock applause and stood up to find Omri standing at the entrance.

"Well, well, sis. Jasher did break you."

"Break me free, you murderer!"

She lifted her hands, but Omri lifted his and ignited a fireball. "Don't try it, sister."

Abigail kept her hands raised. "You don't get to call me 'sister' anymore!"

Omri said, "Oh please. Spare me."

"You tortured me when you should've killed me!"

Omri laughed. "We needed your power and we put it to good use. It's unnecessary now."

Abigail pointed at him. "I will break free and I will stop you. Jasher will be free."

Omri put out the fireball. "You know, this vault is powerful. It's not as strong as the Blue Blade, but it will take you days to use it to carve out of its thickness. Days of oxygen that you don't have."

Abigail suddenly felt a sense of panic.

"You'll be dead long after Jasher, but it's worth it," he said as he smiled.

Omri began to close the vault as Abigail fired a blast of ice, but it was sealed before she could stop it.

She heard Omri yell, "So long, sis," in a mocking tone.

Abigail grabbed the Blue Blade and began to strike the metal where she knew the lock was, and while it did crack, she soon realized it would take days to succeed.

She started to cry and slumped before the vault door. "Oh, Jasher, you did save me, but I cannot save you."

She did not notice the Blue Blade begin to absorb her magic.

Midas watched the sunrise from his window. The bedroom had once belonged to King Gideon and his beautiful. He had replaced their decorations with his own and he had perched his beautiful bride, the Queen Aeolia where she could see out the window.

He looked down and saw the chopping block that Thorne had ordered his men to build. The Inner Circle would preside over the death of a young man and the death of children.

He looked over and saw the long-haired Rapunzel in Blue Beard's tower.

He walked back and sat on the bed, looking at his golden wife said, "My bride! What have I done? They locked a young maiden in the tower of that mad man. Thorne has taken to bossing around my troops without my permission and here I sit."

"Aeolia," he said. "Why do I not feel happy?"

His door opened and Porlem walked in, but Midas was so entranced, he did not hear the eunuch enter.

The emperor got and stood next to her. "Why? I did all this to fill the void in my heart left when I lost my ability to touch things."

"My lord," said Porlem, but Midas still did not hear.

"Aeolia, why? Why did you jump into my arms? Now look at me! I'm overseeing the execution of a young man who has committed no crime. I'm allowing the imprisonment of a young girl in the tower of a monster. One cannot even wake up! I'm doing all of this. Why? Why?"

He became more enraged. "This is your fault!" Midas screamed at her. "Why didn't you stand back?"

Midas tore off his gloves and held up his hands in front of his wife's face. "You did this to me! This is you! You! You! You!"

"My Emperor, I must tell you about Thorne."

Midas turned around and grabbed Porlem. He planned to chastise him for interrupting him, but he realized he was not wearing his gloves.

Porlem's face twisted in horror as the golden metal began to overtake his body.

Midas screamed and jumped back. "No! No! Porlem! Not you!"

Porlem cried out one last warning, "Midas, Thorne is going to kill you!"

Then the faithful manservant turned completely to gold. He let go and backed away in horror at what he had done.

Porlem's golden body lost balance and fell forward, striking Queen Aeolia and together they fell to the ground, breaking to pieces.

Midas stood awestruck by what had just happened. It was like waking up for a dream. He cried out their names and ran to the pile of broken gold. He picked up the pieces and wept over them. They shattered to the point he could not recognize who was who.

When he realized they were gone, he stood up and saw himself in the mirror.

"I hate you!" He grabbed a pillow from his bed, watched it turn to gold and then threw it at the looking glass, shattering into pieces.

He saw the broken image of himself slowly sat down on the edge of the bed, careful not to touch anything as he continued weeping.

Midas looked on the ground and seeing his broken image, he came to a realization.

"There's no one left to blame, but myself."

Chapter 52

Jasher had been clothed in battle armor. A black metal chest plate that resembled a dragon's face. Black boots. Silver gauntlets with a golden dragon engraved on it. All of it recently oiled and shined.

Omri came in. "Don't you look dapper? All fit for battle, but about to die."

Jasher asked, "Why this, traitor? Why not strip me down and kill me?"

Omri shook his head. "The people see you as prince. They need to see you die as a prince. It will break their spirits."

Jasher just shook his head. "Where's Abigail? I thought she was my attendant?"

Omri chuckled. "Probably trying to get some air."

Abigail tried to freeze the cracks she had made with the Blue Blade to weaken the vault's metal door. While it did speed up the process, it would still be hours before she could penetrate the other side.

Her breathing was becoming more and more labored, but she pressed on, choosing to die trying to escape, then live the rest of her life in a mental prison.

Then, she heard a creak. She looked up expectantly as a rush of fresh air floated into the now unsealed room. She began to gasp for breath, trying to slow herself down to keep it out.

A figure squeezed between the safe door and she recognized it immediately as Midas, the man she had once called an emperor.

"What," she yelled at him. "Suffocation isn't good enough? You're going to give me mercy by turning me to gold and melting me down?"

Midas said nothing, but started toward her, causing her to scurry away, but she could not move fast enough, as she was still weak from the lack of oxygen.

He reached for her and she turned away, but then she realized he reached passed her and picked up the Blue Blade. It was then she realized he was gloved.

Midas lifted up the sword and removed it from its sheath. He took off his left glove and touched the sword with his pinky. It turned gold, but then the metal returned to normal before the sword briefly glowed blue.

Midas put his glove back on headed toward the safe door with the Blue Blade in tow.

Abigail tried to get up to run to it, but she was still weak from the night without oxygen. She knew would she would not survive another night. She struggled to stand as Midas left the room.

She braced herself for the sound of the seal clicking into place, but she heard nothing. Midas had not locked her in.

She tentatively headed for the door and squeezed out. What she saw in the hall stunned her. Orcs, vampires, sorcerers lined the hallways and all of them had been turned to gold. Several of them were members of the Inner Circle.

"Midas," she said. "He's betrayed them?"

Abigail picked herself up and tried to walk to help save Jasher, but she fell down still weak.

"Jasher," she cried out. "I'm coming! Just hold on a little longer."

Rapunzel watched as Jasher was led out by a group of armed guards and finally chained to the chopping block.

She said, "Oh Jasher, I want to help you!"

"Princess!" The voice came from the bottom of the stairway. It immediately sent shivers down her spine. "I'm coming! No more tricks this time!"

Rapunzel was frozen for a moment. She was not sure if she could last this time. She immediately started pushing the furniture against the door. She did not know if it would help, but she would have to try.

Belle, Philip, James, and Connor wore cloaks to hide their identities, trying to blend into the crowd that was developing around the chopping block. A giant Minotaur stood over Jasher with an axe.

The whole courtyard was surrounded by the dark armies' foul creatures and Midas' soldiers.

Philip said, "What should we do? There are too many of them. Even with back-up, it will be nigh impossible to take the castle without stronger numbers."

Belle replied, "We need a distraction."

Connor looked around. "What I wouldn't give to summon the Kraken."

Philip asked, "You've done that before?"

James looked up and caught a glimpse of Rapunzel's golden hair in the tower. "Look."

They all glanced up.

Connor said, "It looks easy enough to sneak to the base of the tower, but would good would that do us? We didn't bring any equipment to climb it."

James stroked his chin. "Is Snow in position?"

Belle opened a spyglass and saw Snow on the other side of the courtyard in a similar disguise.

"Yes. She's ready."

James said, "I've got an idea to help Rapunzel."

"Wait," whispered Belle, but James was already lost in the crowd.

"Don't worry, love. He's a big guy... as you've noticed," Connor said with mock jealousy.

Philip swallowed hard. "But what about Jasher? We've got to help him."

The Royals said nothing as they continued to watch as the dark army began to take positions on the stadium seating across from the chopping block.

Belle instinctively felt the edge of her bow. She had the desire to lob one poisoned arrow at one of them, any of them, for all the pain they caused. She and Connor had fought them at sea and here they were on land. It took every fiber in her body not to fire an arrow off, knowing that would ruin any hope they had of a rescue.

Philip kept his hand on the on the hilt of his sword. He felt the armor of the Blue Lacie knighthood from beneath his cloak. He believed in being honorable, even to those who were dishonorable, but the temptation to charge in and indiscriminately lob off his heads was stronger than he realized. But he stood by his moral code and would not give in. That was where he drew his strength.

Connor, though he deflected with humor, stood there unsure of his place with these warriors and mystics. He was a chef, buccaneer, a swashbuckler, but more importantly, a man of the sea. He felt grounded here and for a brief moment, he considered running. He looked back toward the entrance to the city. He could see the city gate even from here, but when he turned back and saw Jasher kneeling before the chopping block, he knew he could not run, and he would not.

James pushed all thoughts out of his head as he snuck to the edge of the tower. Connor had been right, with all of the dark army distracted by Jasher's potential doom, he was able to get past without being noticed and made to the foot of the tower.

At once, he realized, that not even with his great strength could he climb up to the top. Then he had an idea.

"Rapunzel, let down your hair!"

Chapter 53

"Princess! Here I come!"

Rapunzel was shaking as Blue Beard began pounding on the door. She could hear it crack and buckle from the pressure of his weight.

Then she heard it.

"Rapunzel, let down your hair!"

She looked out the window and then directly down where she saw James standing beneath waving her down.

"Princess, scream for me!"

Rapunzel swallowed hard, but in a moment of clarity, she began unfurling her massive ponytail as fast as she could, letting out her long strands go further and further down.

Then she heard the door jamb snap.

"Just a few more minutes!"

As soon as the hair was in reach, James bent his knees down and jumped as high as he could, grabbing the hair and immediately began to climb up as fast as his arms would allow him.

Blue Beard leaned his full body weight into the door, forcing all of the debris from the barricade through, sending it scattering throughout the room.

Rapunzel stood frozen by the window with her hair out of the window. Blue Beard could see from the movement that it was being tugged on.

He laughed at this. "Oh, how clever." Pulling out a small axe, he threw it at the window, hitting it in the frame, and cutting Rapunzel's hair down to her shoulders.

That was when Rapunzel screamed, "No!" She immediately covered her mouth and backed into the corner shivering. She realized what she had done and how she gave in. Now she was shivering for her dear life.

Blue Beard gave her a wicked smile and said, "Now we're talking." He began to slowly walk toward. He passed by the window and stood over her, leering down at her as she shook for her life.

Jasher was on his knees on the executioner's platform. He could not believe it had come to this. He watched as the crowd spectators stood around, gathering from all over Grandfire City. This courtyard should belong to them, but now they would watch as their Dragon Prince was beheaded.

The Orcs were installing magic mirrors above him, no doubt to help send his image across the kingdoms of Craih.

Jasher looked down at his reflection in the minotaur's shiny axe.

"This is your fault." he whispered to himself. "You did this. You should never have left your family's side. Now they are dead, and your friends are captured or scattered. You failed them. You did this."

The minotaur grumbled, "Quiet down there!"

Jasher swallowed hard, but he refused to let the Sorcerer's Society break him. They would take his life and he would die a disgrace prince, but he would not let them take his dignity.

He looked out over the crowd, he could see the despair on their faces and the prince who abandoned them long ago was about to die.

Then he saw something. It was just for a moment, but then, he saw an apple lifted in the air. He looked out and saw her. It was Princess Ezri, his Snow White. She wore a cloak, but he knew it was her.

She was in the crowd and was gazing upon him. She pointed to herself, then made a heart sign to him, and then pointed to him.

Jasher nodded. He mouthed to her, "I love you too."

She pointed to the side and he shifted his gaze where he saw three figures in similar cloaks. The one in the center pushed her cape aside and he saw her bow.

"Belle," Jasher whispered. He had no idea how she got there so quickly, but he did not care. He realized now that there was hope. That was all he needed.

Blue Beard licked his lips and that was when he felt a sharp point at his neck.

A boomy voice said, "Touch her and I'll kill you. This is your one chance to walk away."

Blue Beard turned around to see James standing there, the sword still at his neck. He recognized him from the description that Omri had giving the Inner Circle during his debriefing.

"Well, well, well," he said. "A prince climbing a tower to save the princess. Isn't that a bit cliché?"

He swung his arm so fast, that James barely felt the impact as his sword went flying out the window.

At once, Blue Beard jumped on him, he massive weight crushing the prince he tried to fight back as the brute's hands came down on toward his neck.

"You're mighty among men, Prince," said Blue Beard. "Unfortunately, you mistake might for right. That is a mistake!" He leaned in, putting more weight onto, who was now struggling to breath.

Rapunzel stood up, but she was still shivering uncontrollably. She did not know what to do. Anything she could attempt would be countered by Blue Beard's massive size, but she could not just stand there and watch the brute crush James.

She turned and saw the axe stuck in the window frame. It looked ordinary, except for the sharp point at the end.

Rapunzel grabbed the handle and pulled with all of her might, trying to get it out as she heard James gasping for breath. In a moment, she channeled all of the magic energy that came from her shortened hair and channeled it through her body, allowing it to give her just a moment's strength to rip the axe from the frame.

She set on the floor, hearing James' breathing more and more labored as Blue Beard continued to shift more of his weight onto the prince.

With all of her might, Rapunzel shoved the axe across the floor. It seemed to slide in slow motion as James scooped it up.

Blue Beard saw this and attempted to grab it, but James stabbed him in the heart with the handle's point. The brute gurgled and rolled over clutching his chest.

As James began to try to breath normally, Rapunzel ran to him and helped him stand.

The prince looked at the brute, who had started to cough up blood as he laid on the floor.

"Getting stabbed by your own weapon," said James. "Sounds a bit cliché."

Blue Beard tried to say something, but all that he managed to get out was a few gurgles before his eyes closed.

James picked up the axe and wiped off the blood. "Thank you." He placed it on his belt with a satisfied grin.

Rapunzel could not contain herself. She grabbed him and pulled him close, kissing him "Thank you." As he wrapped his arms around her, she realized that now, she felt safe. Because she felt safe, she felt strong. "It's like you said, James," she said. "We save each other.

James did not want to let go, but he knew there was little time, but before he could say anything, she said, "Now, let's save the others."

James walked to the window and saw a giant bull dragging the glass coffin that Talia rested in. Jasher was being forced to his knees on the chopping block as Fabius Thorne, The Wicker Man, and the other witches and wizards of the Inner Circle were gathering on the stadium adjacent from the executioner's platform.

James sneered as he saw Midas leave the castle and head toward the seating.

"Come on, Rapunzel," he said. "We have to get down there!"

Chapter 54

Fabius Thorne stood in the middle of the stadium seating. A pair of Orcs brought his magic mirror and sat it down.

The Wicker Man and Omri climbed aboard, but he saw a handful of his Inner Circle.

"Where is everyone?"

"I don't know, sir," Omri replied. "I've been out here overseeing Jasher. I'm sure they are watching from their rooms."

Thorne shrugged accepting this explanation.

He waved out to the commoners who had gathered to the square.

"Behold our kingdom," the Grand Mage declared. "They come to watch our victory."

The Wicker Man glanced around. "You're sure that his allies aren't here?"

Thorne shook his head. "They could have ridden all night and gotten past our outposts, they still could not make it in time. Even if they did, it would not matter."

Omri looked up at the sun. "Master, it is time."

Thorne lifted up his wand. "Here me, people across the land. This spell compels you to watch as you prince dies by our hand."

An energy came from his mirror and hit all the mirrors in the courtyard. When he saw his form, he knew his massive enchantment showed the image across Craih. In every mirror and looking glass, the citizens could see him and watch as Jasher died.

"People of Craih, behold your Dragon Prince," Thorne shouted. "It is not a double, a mascot, or a twin. It is him. The face of your decades-old prophecy. After today, he will die like the fraud he is and so will the resistance. Two of his friends are capture and the rest have abandoned you. Now he dies for nothing. Just like every member of the Continental Army."

He paused for dramatic effect. The mirror adjusted, showing Jasher chained at the feet of the minotaur.

"Executioner, raise your axe!" The minotaur did as he was told.

Thorne smiled. He had waited for this moment and nothing would stand in his way.

Belle reached her bow, Philip and Connor grabbed their swords as they began to push through the crowds.

Before they could get to the front, a giant troll stepped in front of them.

"Where are you three going?" He demanded.

Snow reached for her spear to throw it, but from her position, she could not get a good enough aim to kill the minotaur.

Each time she tried to aim, a bystander would get in the way as the crowd increased around her.

James and Rapunzel raced through the halls of the castle to get to the courtyard. To their surprised, they kept finding golden statues of what appeared to be Sorcerer Society members.

That did not stop them as they headed toward the courtyard, but even as they ran, they were not sure if they would get there in time.

The minotaur's axe was raised high in the air and he smiled just before the moment of truth.

Chapter 55

Thorne was just about to drop his hand when a voice called, "Wait!"

There was a gasp from the crowd as Midas came up to the platform.

Thorne turned around and saw the emperor standing there. He was so angry at the interruption that he did not notice he was wearing no gloves.

"My emperor, not to speak out of turn, but this is not a good time. We have an execution."

"I wish to say something to my enemy before his demise," Midas declared, "It is short and brief."

Thorne was annoyed, but he was ready to get a move on. "Very well."

Midas crossed the courtyard as millions all over Craih, including his own men standing beside the dark army, watched him.

Midas climbed up the steps and kneeled across from Jasher.

The Dragon Prince refused to look up at him.

Midas demanded, "Have you no courage? Look me in the eye!"

Jasher's face was consumed with anger as he looked at Midas.

Thorne's voice could be heard from across the courtyard. "My emperor, the people await an execution!"

Midas nodded and then looked at Jasher directly in the eye.

"This is not your fault."

Jasher was taken aback by this. "What?"

"I did this to you. Me. Me alone. There is no one to blame, but me, Midas. I took your lands. I enslaved your people. I killed your family."

The way he was saying it gave Jasher pause. The comments were not boastful, but they were in fact, remorseful.

"I know you can never forgive a bitter old man with a paper crown and a grass throne, but this is the least I can do."

Jasher looked down and saw the Blue Blade sitting right in front of him.

Midas swallowed hard. He held his bare hand in front of Jasher.

"This might hurt a little, Dragon Prince."

He placed his hand on Jasher's forehead and at first, it turned to gold, but then the magic began to absorb into the Dragon Prince. He had never felt so much energy circulate through his body. At once, his energy and strength came back to him as magic flowed into him.

At first, Thorne did not realize what was going on, but then he saw a glow coming from Jasher and he knew instantly what has happening.

He stood up and shouted, "Minotaur, stop him!"

Midas turned around touched the Minotaur's knee with his free hand, turning the large creature into gold, causing him to fall, breaking the barrier blocking the people from the courtyard.

Vampires and Orcs stormed the platform, but Midas head out his hand. "Come near me and I turned you to gold!" That caused them to back off.

Jasher flexed his body and began yelling as his hair turned blue and then gold. His irises disappeared, and the glow became more intense.

"Someone stop him!" Thorne shouted frantically.

The Wicker Man stretched out his hand. "Finally," he whispered as he fired a spear from his arm, striking Midas in the chest like an arrow.

The soldiers from Gorasyum gasped as they saw their monarch be struck down by the Sorcerer's Society.

The emperor looked at his wound. He backed away and fell to his knees. When he touched the wood, he realized that the wood was staying normal. Seeing this, he knew he was dying.

When Midas released him, Jasher stood and shattered his chains. He scooped up the Blue Blade and looked into the magic mirror across from him.

The mirror was sending him across Craih. He had one moment, and he had to make it count.

"Fight!" He yelled it out as he lifted his sword in the air.

Fabius Thorne grabbed a chair and used it to shatter his mirror and Jasher's image vanished, but it was too late.

The Continental Army heard the cry, as did the people. Men and women alike grabbed whatever weapon they could find and began to charge the dark armies.

The sorcerers and the other foul creatures became overwhelmed as Craih began to fight for their own. To make matters worse, those who bore the golden hand of Midas, sided with Craih. After seeing their emperor be murdered, they switched allegiances and began to attack orcs, trolls, and werewolves alike.

In Grandfire City, a riot broke out as human began to attack their enemies, determined to fight for their liberty. Captain Makeda and her Blue Lacie knights charged through on horses, throwing makeshift weapons to the citizens as they went to fight their oppressors.

Jasher looked down at Midas and though he was still filled with anger at him, but seeing the emperor now, he began to pity him.

Jasher reached for Midas to help him stand, but the emperor waved him away.

"No, Dragon Prince," he said. "My time is up. This," he coughed up blood. "This is my penance." Then he died, slowing turning into gold.

He heard Thorne scream, "Don't just stand there! Kill him!"

Creatures began to charge up the ramp again and Jasher raised his sword, and as the first Orc came, it was struck by an arrow and it fell over. Belle leaped on top, joined by Connor and Philip.

Jasher watched as James and Rapunzel emerged from the castle and began to charge the evil creatures before them.

Jasher said, "I knew you would come. Somehow, I knew."

Belle nodded. "We'll have time for that later as she let an arrow fly."

Connor leaped onto the ground and stood in front of several gnomes. "Right oh! Let's do this!"

Jasher looked at Philip and pointed to the bull. "Talia is in there. Get her!"

Philip nodded and jumped off making a run through the courtyard.

The platform shook, causing Jasher to trip and fall flat on his face. He rolled over to see Omri standing before him.

"I get to kill you myself. I killed our parents, sister, and now I fill you!"

"Traitor!"

"Not that again!"

Jasher reached for the Blue Blade, but Omri kicked it away.

"I don't think so," the dark prince yelled. He stood over Jasher and raised his scimitar, but that is Jasher saw the Bowie knife tied to his brother's belt.

The Dragon Prince reached forward and removed the knife, Omri tried to stop his swing downward, but Jasher used the giant's momentum against him and stabbed him in the heart with the knife.

Omri started to fade away. The wind blew the facade away and soon Aikin stood before Jasher, just as small and weak as he was before.

Aikin looked at the knife in his chest. "You, you killed your own brother?"

Jasher pulled the knife out. "Traitors deserve to die."

Aikin gasped his last breath and fell from the platform. Jasher looked down at his brother as he reached for Alilth. While he felt no remorse over what he had done, he did pity him for allowing bitterness to overcome him.

Jasher looked up and saw a strangely composed Thorne glaring at him from across the courtyard.

The Grand Mage turned around and entered the castle from a side door. He took one last look at Jasher, as if tempting him to follow.

Jasher bent his knees down and launched himself into the air. He used a great deal of energy that Midas had given to extend his power. As the battle raged on below him, this time he decided that he would not fly away but would fight.

He landed on the stadium seating and entered the same door that Thorne did.

Jasher yelled out, "I'm coming for you, Thorne! I'm coming for you!"

The response from deep within the darkness surprised him.

"Come and get me, Dragon Prince."

Chapter 56

Philip rushed toward the glass coffin as fast as his legs would carry him. Any foul creature that got in his way he struck down by his sword.

At last, he reached the edge of the platform and climbed up. Philip climbed up and looked upon Talia as she lay sleeping in the clear box.

He started to reach for it to open it, but then he was struck such great force that threw him to the ground.

Philip stood up as a bull jumped in front of him.

"I am Daken and I am the keeper of the sleeping beauty. I have no wish to kill you, but I will if you stop me from my only chance at returning to human form."

Philip said, "You fool! She's a mystic. If I can awaken her, she can break your curse."

Daken laughed. "My curse is so strong that even if I died, I would die as a bull. That I cannot stand."

Philip raised his sword. "I love her and if you get in my way, I will slay you."

The bull bent his head down, snorted, and said, "So be it."

He charged at Philip full speed and for a brief moment, and though the young prince dodged, the bull still managed to hit him with his side, knocking him down.

Philip picked himself up again and said to himself, "I cannot beat him in a head-on attack." Then he had an idea when saw a shield on the ground. "Maybe I can."

The bull was preparing to charge again, bending his horns down, scraping his hoof, snorting, and waving his tail.

Daken shouted, "This is your last warning!"

Philip scooped up the shield with his foot and grabbed it mid-air. "Bring it on!"

The bull charged faster than he had before. Philip lifted the shield, but instead of using it to protect himself, he threw it at the bull's legs, causing the bull to trip and slide on the ground.

Philip jumped out of the way as the bull crashed into the side of the castle wall, causing one of the courtyard mirrors to fall on him, crushing him. Daken let out one more gasp and then he collapsed, dead.

Philip briefly nodded to his fallen enemy, but then wasted no time in running to the glass coffin, breaking the lock with his sword, and throwing off the lid.

He saw her beautiful face and stroked it. "Talia," he whispered. "Please, it's time to wake up."

She lay motionless, with her chest barely rising and falling.

"Sleeping beauty," he said. "Please we need you." He paused. "I need you."

Philip leaned in and kissed her gently on the lips. "I truly love you."

Suddenly, he felt something wrap around his ankle. He looked down and saw a vine entangling him. Before he could cut it with a sword, he was lifted in the air, dropping his sword as he came face to face with a scarecrow.

"Wicker Man," he said.

The wooden sorcerer replied, "I know you, Sir Philip Hansel. You and your fellow knight killed the witch I used to capture children for my spells. How did she die?"

Philip sneered at him. "Not well."

The Wicker Man laughed. "So be it. She was just a tool after all."

Philip roared with anger and tried to grab the evil sorcerer, who just swung him back.

"I respect you, Prince. It's a shame I have to kill you."

Suddenly, a beam of blue energy blasted through the wooden arm, cutting it at the shoulder.

The Wicker Man screamed in pain as Philip fell to the ground. He shouted, "Who dares?"

He turned to see Talia standing there holding her two short swords. Blue energy was emitting from them. She stuck them together creating her staff.

"Touch him again and I'll kill you."

The Wicker Man started to laugh. "Brave of you, girl, but my power is second only to the Grand Mage himself. You don't stand a chance."

His arm grew back, and he lifted them toward her. "I'm three hundred years old. I've been studying the dark arts for all of that time. I don't even need a staff or wand for channeling. You really think you can overpower me?"

He fired a blast of green energy at her. She lifted her staff and fired out a blue energy. The two of them collided in the middle.

The Wicker Man laughed. "Interesting. Now how about I turn it up?" He slapped his arms together and formed a wooden cannon, increasing the power of the green energy, causing it to increase in size.

Talia said nothing, but just began to focus harder, channeling all of her mystic abilities in her staff. Her beam did not increase in size, nor did it change colors, however, it began to push the energy backwards.

"It can't be," said The Wicker Man. He tried to push harder, and while it slowed the blue energy, it just kept coming toward him.

Talia still nothing, but instead closed her eyes. The blue energy began to engulf her, creating a flame around her.

The Wicker Man started to shake. He could feel his canvas flesh begin to burn away, exposing the wood beneath it.

"No human can be this powerful," he said. He separated his hands and tried one last attempt to increase his energy, but it was pointless, the blue energy increased in speed.

Suddenly it collided with his body, engulfing him in blue flames. He cried out in pain and screamed for help as his wooden body was blown to pieces, scattering all over the city. One hand was flung into a nearby farm.

Talia collapsed as Philip ran to catch her. She smiled at him and patted him on the cheek.

"I know you'll always be there to catch me, Prince Charming."

James, Rapunzel, Belle, and Connor approached them. They all looked out as warrior and citizen fought for their freedom together as the dark army struggled to maintain control but seemed to be losing ground.

Talia looked around. "Wait, where's Jasher?"

Connor pointed to the door on the side of the castle. "He went after Thorne."

Talia stood up and said, "Then what are we waiting for! We have to help him!"

Snow struck down another Orc with her spear. She looked and saw the Royals head to the castle's side entrance. She started to follow, but then she heard a scream.

Snow turned to see a group of children pinned down by a werewolf. She pulled out one of her knives and threw it, hitting it in the chest.

It fell down, allowing the kids to scatter.

"He would want me to fight," she said. With that, she raised her spear and joined the battle.

Chapter 57

Jasher entered a large tower. He knew it well. Ages ago, it had been used for a lookout to warn when an invasion of Grandfire City had been eminent. Now, it was dark, dank, and reeked of smoke.

A voice said, "This is what you are looking for, yes?"

Jasher turned a corner into a large circular room. It was empty except for Fabius Thorne standing there. He had his signature black silk cloak wrapped around him, curly black hair flowing, his red eyes staring at the young prince.

Behind him was a cone-shaped device with gears, barbells, and a strange gray fire. Jasher followed the long device to the tip of the tower. He could see it pumping out a thick fog into the sky.

"The smoke machine," said Jasher.

Thorne nodded. "Identical to the one in Revenant, only bigger. I had it moved here from Gorasyum after the spell I used to spread it quickly wore off."

Jasher lifted the Blue Blade. "You were foolish to bring me here."

"Why? You would have found it anyway. Besides, what better way to die than standing just feet away from your victory?"

Jasher got into a defensive stance. "The people are fighting your forces. You can hear witches and orcs dying in the streets like the dogs they are."

Thorne let out a chuckle. "You merely caught my forces off guard. Without the sunlight, my armies will regroup and start to overwhelm Craih as we did a decade ago. Now here you are, and you will die."

Jasher grinned. "You forget, I'm immune to magic."

Suddenly, a brick launched up from the floor, hitting him in the chin.

Thorne laughed, louder this time. "Fool! You think you're the first warrior with an immunity to magic to challenge me? I know that you are only immune to direct attacks, but if I fill an object with magic, that can hurt you."

Jasher felt his chin and saw blood on his hand. He wiped it off and flung it to the ground.

"Face me like a man," he said. "Or do you fear me?"

Thorne rolled his eyes. He grabbed the center of his cloak and threw it off, revealing black armor done in a blade-like style.

"Fool," he said drawing his rapier. "I've walked Paraina for hundreds of years. You think I've only studied magic?"

Jasher lifted his sword. "Then bring it on, old man!"

Thorne placed a hand on his hip and lunged at the Dragon Prince, who blocked the stab.

The Grand Mage and Jasher clashed their blades together. No matter what the Dragon Prince tried, his enemy blocked every single blow, strike, and slice.

"Oh yes, mere practice," Thorne mocked. "Even with the power absorbed from Midas, you are finding that I'm more of a problem than you first supposed."

Jasher faked a swing to the right, which caused Thorne to attempt to pierce his neck, but the dragon prince used the momentum to slash toward the Grand Mage's face. Thorne spotted it in time and dodged, but not before Jasher barely sliced his cheek.

Thorne screamed and backed away, allowing Jasher to get into another defensive stance.

The Grand Mage felt his cheek and then look down at the blood.

"You dare," he whispered. "You dare!" The second time it was a scream.

Jasher heard a rumbling and turned to see bricks flying at him. He tried to dodge and while he avoided any major damage, one hit his sword hand. The blue blade was knocked from his grasp, sending it flying into the air and landing on the ground across the room.

Though Jasher drew his Bowie knife, he was not fast enough as Thorne stabbed him in the shoulder, forcing it all the way through and jamming it into the brick wall behind him, then pulling it out.

Jasher cried out in pain, using his cosmic power to stop the bleeding, but the rage-induced Thorne slapped him hard before he could make another move.

"You fool," he shouted. "No one has drawn my blood since I became the Grand Mage!"

Jasher snarled and spit in Thorne's face. This garnered another strike.

"You're still defiant? Isn't it clear to you? I've won!" Fabius motioned to the smoke factory. "You're done! I've beaten the prophecy! Midas may have betrayed me and the Sorcerer's Society, but it matters not! After I kill you, I will take my smoke machine to Icester where I will conquer it. I'm no longer interested in subjugation. My armies will raze Craih to the ground and sink it into the ocean. Not even the highest mountain peak will be remembered! Here, you will die alone, knowing you failed!"

Something sharp struck the backside of Thorne's armor. He turned around to see the Princess Belle standing at the entrance with her bow and arrow.

"He's not alone," she said, unleashing another arrow.

Thorne caught it in mid-air. Tossing it aside, he aimed his hand at her and grabbed her bow with is mind. She struggled to hang onto to it as it wrapped around her like a vine, before pinning her to the wall.

"You," he said as he approached her. "The beauty who lost her beast. Now she wanders, forsaking all forms of beauty and becoming this she-warrior. Pathetic."

"You're wrong," a sword struck his arm, but it did not pierce his armor.

He looked down to see Prince Connor.

"She beautiful, the most beautiful woman I know," the sea prince said.

Thorne looked at Belle, who was looking at Connor with both concern and passion.

The Grand Mage rolled his eyes at them and then swung his sword Connor, who blocked it. They remained locked in this position.

"You, the pirate..."

"Buccaneer."

"Whatever. You are the weakest of the Royals. A sea prince who has chosen the sea over land, tunics over armor, and cooking over study. Even as you are able to hold off my sword, I can feel you faltering."

He swung his rapier in a circle, sending the saber flying. Connor stood there defenseless and before he could say a word, Thorne swung his sword into his left eye.

Belle screamed, "No!"

Thorne lifted Connor in the air. "That's better! Now you look like a buccaneer." He laughed hysterically as he threw the sea prince across the room.

A burst of energy struck him, he turned to see Princess Rapunzel standing there.

"Look, the smallest, weakest princess. What're you going to do? Make me feel all warm and fuzzy on the inside?"

She pointed her hand at him but said nothing glowing with a pink energy.

Thorne took a step toward, but suddenly, a bat struck him in the face.

"What?" He looked around puzzled as an army of bats descended from the ceiling and a swarm of bats began to attack him.

He tried to swat them away, but there were too many. He could feel their claws scratching his armor. He finally bent down, building up his power from within, he fired off a blast of red energy that scattered the bats and sent Rapunzel flying backwards.

He started to breath heavily when a large object struck his side. To the Grand Mage's surprise, it actually hurt, but his armor did not break.

He turned to see Prince James lifting an axe to strike him, but Thorne lifted his sword in time. They collided, and their metal made sparks fly before they both backed away.

"Blue Beard's axe. Impressive," Fabius said. "Your might is..." But James elbowed him in the gut.

"You talk too much, Scum!"

He lifted his axe again, but Thorne created an energy field around his body. James' felt himself freeze into place just as he was about to strike him.

"As I was saying," Fabius said. "Your might is great, but your foolhardiness will be the death of you." He sent a burst of invisible energy at James, slamming him next to Belle.

"Stop, you fiend!" This voice he knew.

"Why, Prince Philip," he said turning to face him. "I know of you. You and your Blue Lacie knights have long eluded my dark armies. Most impressive."

Philip got into a defensive stance with his two-edged sword. "It pays to fight with honor."

"Does it though?"

Suddenly, vines cane from the ceiling, grabbing Philip and lifting in the air before tying him up.

"See? No honor, and I won."

The hair on the back of his neck stood up. He turned to see Talia standing there with her staff.

"Well, well, well. I felt The Wicker Man's energy perish not long ago. Was that you, dear?"

Talia started to glow with blue energy. She was not smiling, but instead she had an unnatural look of anger on her face.

"You, you killed my parents."

Thorne laughed. "Well, technically, Midas did, but Aikin and I melted them down."

Talia aimed her staff at him. "You don't deserve to live."

Thorne lifted his sword and it morphed into a wand. "What're you going to do about it?"

Talia's energy output increased. "I'm sending you to the abyss!"

She fired a blast of energy and Thorne fired a burst of green energy, to everyone's surprise, it canceled out Talia's beam.

Talia looked confused, but before she could do anything, vines came from the wall and wrapped her up in it, before pinning her to the wall.

Thorne said, "You may have been able to kill me. Your raw power is impressive, but that battle with The Wicker Man took too much out of you. Too bad, I thought you'd be a challenge."

He turned around and started walking to Jasher. "Now, you all will watch your friends die. Connor will be last since he can't see much these days."

He laughed at his own maniacal joke. "However, Jasher, you will die first. You've been a pebble in my shoe for far too long."

Jasher lifted his hand as Thorne walked toward him.

"What?" The Grand Mage mocked. "Trying to hit me with one of your cosmic blasts? I doubt you can summon anything in your state."

Jasher spit out blood. "There is one thing."

Thorne laughed at that. "And what would that be?"

Suddenly, a blade pierced through his chest, causing him to scream in agony. He looked down and saw the Blue Blade piercing through his armor.

"It can't be," he said. He screamed in pain again as it came all the way through and went into Jasher's hand.

Thorne looked at the wound in his chest. "I'm not healing."

Jasher lifted the Blue Blade. "That means you're dying. All the spells you have used to make yourself more powerful are fading."

Thorne punched the ground. "It can't end like this."

Jasher placed the tip of his blade to Thorne's neck. "I told you I would kill you."

Thorne looked at his hand and they soon began to turn to dust. Thorne fell over. He reached for his wand, but Jasher stepped on it, shattering the wood.

"Hundreds of years old, Grand Mage. Time has finally caught up with you. Now, you die alone."

Thorne looked down with despair as his face turned to dust, leaving nothing but an empty set of black armor.

Jasher started to fall, but he caught himself with the Blue Blade. Philip and Talia's vines broke. Rapunzel and James checked on one another. After Belle's bow turned to normal, she ran to Connor, who had torn off a piece of his sash and had wrapped the left side of his face with it.

"Hey gorgeous," he said. "You look good."

Belle touched his cheek. "Oh, my love..."

Connor suddenly kissed her. "Hey, I ain't dead yet."

James walked up and said, "You just took one in the face. Are you sure you're alright?"

Rapunzel whispered, "James."

Connor smiled. "I have a spare eye. I'll be fine."

Always the cheerful one, even after losing an eye."

Philip raised his sword. "Besides, we won."

Talia asked, "You mean, it's over?"

Jasher limped over. "No. We haven't won yet. We have to destroy the smoke factory. Otherwise, the dark army will rally and win like Thorne said. Without the sunlight, our armies will still fall."

"Then what're you waiting for?" Talia asked. "Blast it like you did at Revenant!"

Jasher leaned against the smoke tower. "I can't. My fight with Thorne took out all of my energy."

James looked at Talia, "Hit him with some mystical energy."

She shook her head. "I'm drained too."

Rapunzel said nothing, but just nodded in agreement.

Jasher said nothing but started to bang against the machine with the Blue Blade, while it started to make cracks, it was causing virtually no damage. He started striking it more frantically and he eventually let his injured arm drop, striking it one-handed.

Talia pleaded, "Jasher, stop!"

"No!" Jasher kept hitting the smoke factory. "If we don't do this now, the armies will try to retake the castle! In our weakened state, we couldn't possibly take them!"

Talia tried to run to him, but Philip grabbed her. The others watched in silence, all hanging their heads, not knowing what to do.

Finally, Jasher dropped the Blue Blade and slumped to his knees, breathing heavily. His hands to fist, angry at his weakness and embarrassed by his failure. They had defeated their enemies and now on the edge of victory, they were grasping at defeat.

"We have to, we have to do this," he whispered.

"No. I'll do it," the voice came from the entrance of the tower.

They all looked on in surprise as Abigail walked into the room. She approached Jasher and helped him stand.

"Abigail, sister, is it you?"

She smiled. "Yes. You saved me, brother. Now, now I'll save you."

"What're you talking about?"

She walked up to the smoke factory. "I did terrible things as the ice queen. I can't even begin to tell you, but maybe, just maybe, I can start on a new path."

Abigail placed her hands on the smoke factory and ice began to come forth from her palms. It began to spread rapidly, covering it from top to bottom until it was one big iceberg. Suddenly, the smoke stopped coming from the top.

Abigail backed up, clapped her hands together, and the ice began to crack. The Seven Royals watched as the cracks traveled up the smoke factory, causing the tower to shake.

James shouted, "We have to get out of here!" He swept up Rapunzel in his arms and ran out the door, with the others not far behind.

They followed the tunnel as they heard the rock buckling behind them.

Jasher was limping at the back, but he marched behind them. He collapsed but caught himself with his sword again.

Belle turned around and reached out her hand. "Come on, Captain. You're not going to miss this."

He smiled and took her hand as she helped him to feet.

Chapter 58

Snow stabbed a witch with her spear before she could cast another spell. As the witch fell, Snow could see that the battle was turning against their favor. More and more of the dark armor were starting to take over.

Then she heard it. There was a loud crack. It was a noise she had never heard before and it was so loud, that the fighting paused.

Everyone in the courtyard, as well as in Grandfire City, looked up at the castle. They saw the smoking tower began to crack, all along the sides, and up to the cone-shaped top.

Snow looked as the Seven Royals emerged from the doorway at the front of the castle, seeing Jasher with a bleeding wound in his shoulder, she ran to him as fast as she could.

She embraced him and whispered, "Jasher, are you okay?"

"I am now," he said. He tapped her shoulder and pointed up.

The smoke ceased from the tower and suddenly, it fell. As it crumbled to the ground, everyone in Grandfire City, watched it fall to the ground. It happened in slow motion, as if time was moving at a snail's pace.

It finally hit the ground.

Though fighting had been happening almost seconds ago, there was nothing but silence now.

Then it happened.

A ray of sunshine broke through the smoke.

In the Giving Forest, Maris was hard at work cleaning the tables in her village tavern. She was distracting herself from the fact that her mirror had stopped showing what was going on in Teysha. She worried desperately for her adopted brother and wiping the tables was the only thing distracting her.

Suddenly, her daughter burst into the door.

"Mommy, Mommy, come and see!"

Maris ignored her daughter.

"Mommy!"

"What is it, Naurice?"

Her daughter squealed, "It's the sun!"

Maris threw down her rag and ran outside.

Sunshine was breaking through the clouds.

"You did it, Brave Woodsmen. I knew you could."

The headmistress at the all-girls academy smiled as she watched the smoke dissipate from her window.

"She did it. That crazy girl did it," she said.

Aboard the *Fiery Wing*, the crew begin to take off their hats as the sun began to shine on the sea once again.

Captain Hull yelled, "Ha-Za!" And the crew joined in. "Ha-Za! Ha-Za!" They began to throw their hats in the air in celebration.

The Purple Fairy was sitting in front of her mirror crying wondering what happened to Rapunzel. Then she noticed something, a light hurt her eyes.

She jumped up excitedly. The Purple Fairy flew above the trees and watched as the sun pierced into the forest.

"You did, young one," she said. "You did it."

Jengo and Zuri watched from their island as the enormous cloud began to disappear.

She said, "He did it."

Jengo nodded. "Yes, and I'm proud we were part of it."

Captain Makeda was the first to notice when she saw the sun reflecting on her sword. Then she looked at the vampire in front of her.

He was staring at his hands intently as he began to turn into dust. As the others watched, the vampires all began to turn into dust. Then a troll in the corner yelled out in pain as it turned into stone. The Orcs all screamed as their bodies began to boil and melt.

She said, "The sun. I can't believe it. They did it."

Jasher was being held up by Snow as they saw the sun's light get brighter and brighter.

He had forgotten what it was like, even the few days on this journey, he had forgotten the look of a sun filling the sky with its light.

Rapunzel climbed down from James' arms. "It's so clear," she said.

Philip raised his sword. "We did it! We did it!"

James said nothing, but folded his arms, giving a rare smile.

Talia just shouted, "Weeeee!"

Connor shouted, "It's over! Yes!" Even with his one eye, he could see as the sun came through. He turned to Belle and said, "My love, marry me! If you'll have a man with half his sight."

Belle grabbed him and pulled him into a deep kiss. The others backed away as they had never seen her give so much affection.

She released him and said, "I'll take you as you are."

"But I'm no beast."

She stroked his hair and winked at him. "I'm in love with a buccaneer."

A sound like a mighty roar broke through the sky.

"What was that?" Abigail asked back away in fear.

Jasher replied, "The sky isn't toxic to them anymore. They are coming."

Snow asked, "Who?"

She did not have to wait long for an answer.

The Dragons descended from the mountains, emerging from the Overworld and flying down upon Craih.

They were the size of elephants, with scales that shined of various colors, red, blue, green, brown, purple, black, and so many more. They had long, scaly necks and large yellow eyes. Their wings were wide and their tails long and pointed. While they looked similar, each had something unique about them, whether it was their fangs or the spikes along their back. They were strong, powerful, and majestic.

Their fire descended onto every base, tower, or castle that had once belonged to the Sorcerer's Society.

Their fire spread onto the battlefields, where any member of the dark army not weakened by the sun was still fighting.

The people of Craih cheered them on as their patron guardians helped them in battle. Their fire spread even to the ocean, where they sank the ships of the dark navy so fast. They even flew to Gorasyum where they melted down the castle of Midas, where only evil dwelt.

The Dragon known as Shade landed in the courtyard of Grandfire City. Everyone began to back away, except for Jasher who approached the mighty fire drake.

"You saved us," said Jasher. "Thank you."

Shade shook his head. "No, you did this, young prince. You and your friends saved your people. We only helped in this moment."

"You have my eternal gratitude."

Shade bowed his head and opened his wings.

"Wait," shouted the prince. "You just got here!"

Shade turned around. "Yes, now the kingdoms of Craih are safe once again."

"You can't just leave!"

"We're not leaving Craih. We'll be keeping an eye out for anymore danger."

Jasher smiled. "You're watching over us?"

The dragon began lifting himself into the air. "Oh Jasher, we're always watching."

Snow walked up to Jasher and clasped onto his hand.

"Jasher, there's something you need to know about my mother. She betrayed you and I..."

Jasher interrupted her. "Snow, I love you. I want you to be by my side. The two of us together. This proves it. I said I would return to you, but you came and found me. That's all I need."

Snow threw down her spear and embraced him. They shared their second kiss as the other Royals watched.

Chapter 59

Cold. That is how this autumn feels.

It has been one year since the Smoke End and the sun continues to shine. So much has happened during that time.

The other Royals chose to decline their crowns, becoming instead Lords and Ladies of the land, serving on a council. Following that, the people voted to make me King of Craih, with Grandfire City as its capital.

I was humbled and honored to follow in the footsteps of my fathers to become the Dragon King.

A knock on the door to the library interrupted his thoughts. He returned his quill pen to its place.

"Come in," said Jasher.

His wife, Queen Ezri Snow Kenan, walked into the room. She was wearing a black dress with white, lacy trim. A simple gold tiara with a snowflake in the center rested on her head. Her white eyes beamed at him.

"Jasher, my love, I need your help in the den," she told him.

He stood up, wearing his father's armor and wearing a thin crown with the emblem of the dragon at the front.

"Are you still decorating the castle," he asked her as he followed her down the hallways.

Snow laughed. "Hey, can you blame me? I'm restoring it to your family's glory."

Jasher took her hand. "You're doing a good job. It's looking like a castle instead of a lair."

"Wait, didn't you finish the ballroom after our honeymoon?"

Snow winked at him. "Be careful bringing that up."

Jasher blushed as she opened the door.

"After you," she said.

Jasher was surprised to find the ballroom dark as he stepped inside. Suddenly, the lights came on causing his vision to go white for a moment, then he heard the yell, "Surprise!"

240

As his vision adjusted, he could see his friends, the rest of the Seven Royals, along with his sister Abigail, dressed in her uniform as the Governor of Gorasyum. No longer was the emblem a golden hand, but a golden dragon since Craih had annexed it.

"Happy birthday!" The men and Belle were dressed in their finest armor, with Rapunzel in a magenta dress and Talia in a blue dress.

Snow placed a hand on his shoulders and shoved him inside as they started gathering around him, shaking his hand.

"The new high priest sends his regards. He wanted to be here, but I have a feeling he's still reeling from the quadruple wedding he performed," Abigail said.

Jasher shook his head. "No, this is the perfect crowd. Who thought of this?"

Belle replied, "Who else? Talia."

Philip answered, "Yes, my wife got all in Grandfire City with absolute secrecy."

Talia said, "Oh Heavens, you know that you helped too, Belle."

James motioned to his bride. "Wait till you see the cake Rapunzel made."

Rapunzel said, "Connor taught me well."

Connor motioned to his patched eye. "Yes, well, it's been a bit harder to get the recipes down. Better to pass on my skills and keep learning how to see the world through one side of my face."

Jasher said, "But how? Why did you do this?"

"You know why," said Snow. "Your eighteenth birthday was a disaster. You were asleep for your next ten birthdays and then you spent your next birthday recovering from your icy nap."

Jasher said, "This is all very nice. Thank you everyone!"

Philip replied, "Wait till you see your present."

Abigail rolled in a cart where a large, flat item sat covered in a massive drape. She motioned to it and said, "We made it especially for you."

Jasher walked up slowly to it, before grabbing the drape and pulling it.

Tears came to the Dragon Prince's eyes as he looked upon the painting. It was one of him, Abigail, and their parents. It was absent someone else, someone else long forgotten, but it was his family, exactly as he remembered it. His father in his white robes. His mother in hers. He in his armor, with his blue blade in its hilt. Abigail in dress matching her mothers.

He wiped his eyes. "Thank you. Thank you, my friends."

The friends all gathered together in a circle, each putting their arms around each other's shoulders.

Jasher smiled. "We'll always hold each other up."

Belle replied, "Always."

"Oh Heavens," Talia yelled out. "Yes. This is what we do."

"Agreed," said James.

Rapunzel replied, "We save each other."

"Because we are stronger together." Philip chimed in.

Connor nodded. "Together!"

Jasher said, "Yes, together! We are the Seven Royals!"

They all yelled in unison, "Together!"

Snow and Abigail stood side by side staring at them with smiles on their faces. Though the moon began to shine in the windows, Jasher did not try to hide, for even as the only scar left, the scar over his eye, shined, he stood there with his friends and each one of them felt a bond that could never be broken.

EPILOGUE

A farmer outside of Grandfire City looked up at the stars and the moon, saying, "I remember a time where that beautiful sight was cloaked."

He turned his attention to the scarecrow in front of him in the cornfield. He was very proud of himself. He used a black shirt, red trousers, and had dyed the potato sack he used for the skin white to give it a ghoulish look.

He was especially proud of the face. It was eerily round, with sharp wooden teeth, green eyes, and a straw hat.

The farmer said, "It looks like a ghost if I ever seen one."

He stepped on something and looked down. To his surprise, it looked like a hand. He picked it up and examined it.

"Looks like wicker," he said.

He looked back at his scarecrow and realized that while he had put black, pointed shoes on it, he had only tied a scythe to its right arm. It did not have hands at all.

The farmer shrugged and placed the wicker hand into the right side where the scythe rested.

"Well, a one-handed scarecrow is scarier, I reckon."

He walked back into the cornstalks, heading back to his house.

The hand began glowing a green color, then wrapped around the scythe. A surge of green energy began to flow into the scarecrow, filling it. A left hand grew from the wood and then the face started to form bizarrely, until a seemingly real face appeared.

Then the Wicker Man smiled.

CPSIA information can be obtained
at www.ICGtesting.com
Printed in the USA
LVHW030952040219
606286LV00002B/174/P